MOON CROSSED

(SKY BROOKS WORLD: ETHAN BOOK 1)

EMERSON KNIGHT
MCKENZIE HUNTER

McKenzie Hunter

Moon Crossed

© 2017, McKenzie Hunter & Emerson Knight

McKenzieHunter@McKenzieHunter.com

ISBN: 978-1-946457-98-1

ACKNOWLEDGMENTS

This book would never have reached your hands without the support of some wonderful people who have my humble thanks for their feedback and encouragement. First and foremost, I must thank McKenzie Hunter for allowing me to play in her world. Without John P. Logsdon, Shayne Silvers, Orlando Sanchez, and Benjamin Zackheim, I would never have met McKenzie. Those guys are great people and fantastic authors.

I would like to offer a special thanks to Gloria Knowles, C. Hindle, Stacy McCright, and to my beta readers who provided a steady drip of feedback that gave me the confidence I needed to move forward knowing if I messed up, they would point me in the right direction.

Lastly, my thanks to you, the reader. Without you, I wouldn't be able to do what I most love to do, write.

CHAPTER 1

*B*etween the corn and soybean fields outside of Chicago, I drove the Range Rover slowly up the quarter-mile dirt driveway, the headlights extinguished, bringing the vehicle to a stop at the edge of an ornate garden of abstract iron statues. A dozen yards away, the main house was dark while lights blazed inside the neighboring steel-walled workshop. A lone black Ford pickup truck was parked in the nearby garage.

"He's alone," Winter said beside me, her long black hair framing her delicate round face. The Midwest Pack was one of the largest packs in the country, with a variety of were-animals among its members, but Winter was among the rarest—a venomous were-snake. She was even more dangerous in human form, which explained her youthful rise to the pack Beta's right hand—my right hand. Winter had not been born to our pack. As a child, she'd had the misfortune of falling under the control of a conservative pack, one that viewed her animal as an abomination. Upon hearing the desperate pleas of Winter's family, Sebastian, the Alpha of the Midwest Pack, had flown to Egypt to rescue her. After single-handedly destroying the controlling pack, Sebastian

1

had brought Winter to us. He and I had taken her under our wing at a young age. She had never failed either of us.

Before disembarking from the SUV, I took my time surveying the scene, just to be sure. Winter followed as we approached the workshop, wary of any surprises. She glided across the unkempt grass yard, her movements smooth, rhythmic, and sinuous like the animal she shared her body with. I took a position beside the door, just out of sight, before she knocked. She was forced to knock again, louder, before I heard the grumbling inside. Then the door opened.

"Winter," Jeffrey said, surprised and pleased and sounding slightly confused. I could hear his heart rate accelerate. "Board game night is next week." He glanced at her empty, sun-kissed hands. "You just stopping by to say hello?" He chuckled nervously, a halting sound like a sputtering engine.

Winter remained stoic. "This is a professional visit."

"Cool." I heard his breath tighten as he threw a glance back into his workshop. "I'm kinda busy right now. If you come back tomorrow, we can—"

I eased myself out of the shadows to stand beside Winter, catching the barrel-chested blacksmith by surprise as I loomed over him. While his upper body was wider than mine, thick with lean muscle derived from hard labor, Jeffrey lacked the overall power of the sculpted frame I'd constructed over a lifetime of meticulous, structured work-outs. If it came to a fight, he might prove a handful, but his gaze was anxious as he met mine, pupils dilating as his heart rate accelerated from attraction to fear. Judging by the shrub of short, thick curls that bloomed from his head and face, Jeffrey had a powerful aversion to grooming. He looked from Winter to me, and then back to Winter.

No comfort there. I smirked and watched the already ample sweat bead on Jeffrey's forehead.

"This is Ethan," Winter said flatly, brushing past Jeffrey without a second glance. He willingly turned aside, and I followed her into the blacksmith's workshop, a large open space with a burning forge at the center and an anvil waiting nearby. Two other machines were close at hand, along with a rectangular trench filled with water. My eyes darted quickly to the rear exit—a plain metal door secured by a single sliding bolt—and a pair of windows easily broken should an unexpected escape become necessary. I liked to know where my prey might run, if it should come to a hunt. The smell of hot metal hung in the air, lightly stinging my lungs with each breath.

"You're the pack's Beta," Jeffrey stammered, taking a protective stance next to his forge. "What can I do for you? I'm pretty busy, but if you need a sword, I'd be happy to work you into the schedule. A friend of Winter's is a friend of—"

"She speaks highly of your work," I said, absorbing the intense heat that radiated from the forge as I observed the various pieces of wrought iron hanging on the walls. A three-tiered workbench stood next to the forge, the surfaces covered in tools of various shapes and sizes, many of which would serve as impromptu but deadly weapons. As my hand passed over the workbench, I noticed a tremor in Jeffrey's jawline that hardened as I moved my hand over a piece of burlap. "I'm sure your backlog is extensive," I said, turning from the workbench—to the blacksmith's palpable relief.

"Not a problem." Jeffrey's eyes flicked toward Winter, searching for an explanation. "Happy to do a favor for you people." He laughed nervously, an obnoxious sound that grated on my nerves. "I mean the pack. You guys and your peeps. We're friends, right?" he asked Winter and then turned to me. "Right?"

Pathetic.

"Just call me tomorrow and we'll set something up. At the moment, I've got a lot of work to do, so I should probably get to it." He gestured awkwardly toward the entrance, positioning his body between me and the workbench, but I ignored the unsubtle suggestion.

"I require something special."

The blacksmith gratefully shifted into work mode, nodding aggressively as he crossed his arms over his chest and stroked his beard. "Okay. Like enchantments? I have some witches I work with. Very professional. All highly experienced, but expensive. I can give you a deal for the work, but any enchantments will be at the full rate."

I stopped to examine one of several racks that held the fruit of his recent labor. A pair of longswords waiting for hilts hung next to a thin, elegant spear with a hardwood shaft and ivory grip. I lifted the spear gently, testing the balance in my hand—perfect. The blade was sharpened to a razor's edge, with a fine, deadly point. "The Zulu Iklwa," I said, admiring the craftsmanship.

Jeffrey's eyes brightened at the recognition, surprised. "The weapon that brought the colonial British Army to its knees in Africa," he said, taking a deep breath as he gestured to the spear, happy for the distraction. "A simple design, but effective in close quarters and ranged combat."

"Exquisite."

"The ivory is a nice touch," Winter said as if she had somewhere else to be. She strolled deeper into the rectangular workshop to run her hand over one of the other machines. Jeffrey winced at the intrusion. He half gestured, starting forward to protect his precious equipment, but stopped short, preferring instead to maintain his anxious guard of the workbench. I answered his nervousness with a fraudulent smile. The more nervous the blacksmith became, the more he revealed.

"You must have wealthy customers," I said.

He shifted, shaking his head apologetically. "I never discuss my clients."

A metal clang startled him. He turned back to Winter,

4

who stood over a pronged iron tool that she had dropped to the floor. "Oops," she said with an innocent pout while making no move to retrieve the tool. Jeffrey scowled. Unable to restrain himself, he strode to pick it up and returned it to its place on the wall. Deciding against scolding Winter, he turned to find me once more hovering over the workbench. His heart rate accelerated drastically as I gently lifted the piece of burlap to reveal a silver ingot next to an orange medicine bottle with an eyedropper lid. Next to the ingot was a sand-cast mold of an arrowhead. I turned to Jeffrey for an explanation.

"Oh, boy," he said, trying to catch his breath. "I can explain. H-how did you know?"

"I can appreciate that you maintain client privilege, Jeffrey. But you do like to talk about your work."

"It's a weakness," Winter admitted, pressing a reluctant Jeffrey toward me.

The blacksmith began tugging at his beard, eyes darting between Winter and me. "I just handle the jobs I'm given. I don't ask what my creations are used for. I never asked Winter what she does with my swords."

"You know," she said, cocking her head sideways while giving Jeffrey a reproving frown.

"Not all my customers are from your world," he pleaded with that nervous chuckle. "You'd be surprised how much of my work is for humans."

"Your client is human, then," I said.

He tensed, his eyes beginning to dart about as he stammered. "Most of them are nerd types who like to play fantasy games on the weekend. You know, Renaissance Fairs, Comic Cons. The rest are just collectors."

"I hear silver arrows are all the rage." Winter's sarcasm passed entirely undetected as he gestured to her, nodding zealously. "Exactly. It's a fad. Entirely decorative, I'm sure. I mean, silver is expensive, right? Who would shoot arrows with silver heads? That's ..." He caught my baleful glare and stopped short, his words trailing off. "Seriously, I don't know what these are for. I just work the metal. I don't take sides. Everybody knows that. Right?"

I lifted the medicine bottle from the table, read the label, and then showed it to him. His anxious sincerity collapsed into crestfallen dread. "If I tell you, she'll kill me."

She.

After gently placing the bottle onto the table, I calmly entrenched my fists into the collar of his flannel shirt and then lifted his muscular frame onto his toes as I hauled his panicked eyes to my teeth. "Tell me everything."

Jeffrey glanced at Winter for help. Her pupils elongated into long, vertical slits as the snake in her rose threateningly to the surface. "Oh, shit," he whispered.

"Talk fast," I growled.

He did. "It's a neurotoxin for coating the arrowheads."

"Devious, but not a complicated job," Winter said. Her hazel eyes returned to normal. "Why come to you?"

"She wants the arrowheads to be brittle, to break apart into at least a dozen pieces *after* the head pierces the flesh. That takes some sophisticated temperature control, very precise calculations. I just took the job for the challenge."

"And the money," I said, tightening my grip.

Jeffrey swallowed, unable to avert his gaze from mine though he desperately wanted to. "A blacksmith's got to eat."

"You said your customer is a human. A woman. Give me her name."

"I'm not ... ugh ..."

"No point in holding back now, Jeffrey," Winter said with a shrug. "You've spilled too much already."

"Chris. H-her name is Chris. That's all I know. Sincerely."

My body ached at the name, caught by an unwelcome rush of longing. Chris had left me months ago. After months of arguing to the point of nearly killing each other, her actual departure had been a quiet, somber affair, leaving just a diffusing, light floral scent as a doomed reminder. It couldn't be Chris. She was long gone, but this was exactly her sort of deviousness. If she were hunting wolves ... Jeffrey read the worst in my hesitation.

"I'll q-quit the job. Shit. I'll tell her it c-can't be done," he stammered. "The arrowheads were too brittle. The poison fell in the forge. I can sell it. No problem."

"No." I pushed him back, releasing his shirt. "You're going to complete the job."

"Seriously?" he asked warily.

"With a slight modification."

"Okay."

"If you betray me, I will kill you."

"Shit."

We left the blacksmith a short time later, confident that he understood both the instructions and the stakes. Winter followed me out of the workshop, leaving Jeffrey with his forge. I welcomed the cool night breeze on my skin as we strode toward the Range Rover. "Board game night?" I scoffed.

"You said to keep an eye on him."

The blacksmith's reputation for quality work was well documented, but I didn't trust anyone with pack business without an initial risk assessment. Trust was essential. And if I found out a few of his secrets along the way, so much the better. To that end, Winter had spent the last few—obviously miserable—weeks ingratiating herself into the blacksmith's world.

After a moment's hesitation, she asked, "Did you know Chris was going to do something like this?"

My frown deepened. "When Jeffrey's done, make sure he moves out of the area. Out of Illinois."

"He's skilled."

"He has no sense of loyalty. And he talks too much. Not

worth the risk." I unlocked the doors of the Range Rover as we approached.

"What are you going to do about—"

"Don't ask," I snapped. I was climbing into the driver's seat when my phone rang. "Go ahead."

My brother spoke in a breathy rush. "She's in danger."

"When?" I asked, starting the SUV with the touch of a button.

"Now. Demetrius has sent his vampires to capture her. We can't let them—"

"I'll take care of it." I snapped the phone shut, set it into the cup holder between the seats, and sped down the long driveway to the main road. We were at least fifteen minutes away from the target's home on the outskirts of Chicago. "Demetrius is making a move on the target. Who's on watch?"

"Steven," Winter said, drawing out her own cell phone. "Why do we care about this lone wolf, again?"

I felt my jaw clench as I weighed the cost and benefits of sending Steven alone into a fight he might lose to save a girl of indeterminate value. Despite his youth, Steven's ability to kill vampires was well established, but I had no idea how many vampires, or which ones, he might face. I had almost no intelligence at all. I trusted Josh, but he didn't always think things through. Maybe this girl's fate was tied to the pack, as my brother believed, but he had yet to offer any proof—just a hunch. I didn't like making life-or-death decisions based on someone else's hunch.

"No heroics. If he's outmatched, Steven is to wait for us. Follow if they take the girl, but I'll not risk a pack member for this target. Not yet."

"You'll get no argument from me," Winter said as she tapped her phone.

I pushed the Range Rover as hard as I felt the local police could reasonably ignore. Their inattentiveness was bought and paid for, but there were limits to the established order. Cars on the road honked angrily as the Ranger Rover sped past them, changing lanes as it weaved between traffic. I kept an eye out for trouble, hoping to avoid the kind of token stop —the appearance of justice for the locals—that we were sometimes obliged to endure. I simply had no time for such nonsense. As we entered the suburbs, Winter placed her sheathed katana across her thighs. Her hazel eyes were calm, alert. She was ready to leap into the fight.

Ten minutes later, we found Steven waiting in the trees beside the target's house, pacing like a feral animal mad with a lust for the kill. Unable to contain his animal, Steven changed the moment he saw the Ranger Rover swerve into the driveway and brake to a hard stop. His long, slim frame dropped to all fours, copper-colored wavy hair disappearing almost instantly among a sprout of dark brown fur as his body transformed into a large coyote that shook off its drape of human clothes. In his eagerness for the fight, he was now useless as a scout. How many vamps were we dealing with? Enough that Steven didn't feel he could take them on alone, though I'd no doubt he would have if not for my order.

As I leapt from the Range Rover, Winter did the same, taking a cursory measure of the neighborhood before she revealed her drawn katana. Steven was clawing at the closed front door of the two-flat, biting at the old-style handle, when I brushed him aside and kicked in the door with the flat of my boot, entering the dwelling behind a spray of wooden shrapnel that caught two vampires, just a foot from the door, by surprise. Steven leapt onto one, sinking his canines into the throat as he took the scrambling vampire to the hardwood floor. Somewhere, a woman screamed as I deflected a blow from the other vampire, countering with a quick-fire double punch to the chest.

A quick glance to assess the situation revealed another three vampires in the living room of the house, a woman with short, bleached-blond hair and Asian brother-sister twins. The target struggled violently in the grip of the male vampire, her arms pinned behind her back, while the target's mother hung limply in the arms of his twin. Blood dripped from the gaping wound in the mother's now pale neck. Outraged at the disruption of her meal, the vampire hissed at me, baring blood-drenched fangs. At a command from the blond vampire, the other female released the mother, who fell to the floor with the thud of a dead weight. The two female vamps tried to encircle Winter while the male twin tried to pull the target into the kitchen—no doubt to carry her out the back door—but the target continued her desperate struggle, bracing her legs on either side of the doorway. Her screams filled the house with fear, horror, and rage.

I recognized each of the vampires. Demetrius had sent some of his best, but they were unprepared for our arrival. The element of surprise was on our side—not that it was needed. Returning to my immediate threat, I broke my vampire's knee, and then elbow, before twisting my arm around the neck and breaking it with a sharp, powerful twist. Arterial spray drenched me as Steven tore out his vampire's throat beside me. Winter took out the female twin with a quick flurry of short, elegant swings of her katana, slicing off one arm, and then the other, before slicing her blade across the side of the vampire's neck, causing another spray of blood that drenched my shirt.

The blond vampire roared indignant rage, as if we'd spoiled a birthday party. Not wanting anything to do with Winter's katana, she charged me—her last mistake. As the vampire leapt at my chest, I dived low, sweeping her legs into my embrace and slamming the back of her head onto the floor. Before she could rise, I was on her chest, roaring my own rage as I snapped her neck with both hands. A growl from Steven caught my attention as the last vampire, the male twin, released the target. He was young, and was giving his sister's dismembered body a panicked look that suggested he was experiencing the limits of his immortality for the first time. In a gesture of surrender, he slowly raised his hands above his head while sidling cautiously along the wall, signaling a circuitous path toward the front door from which it seemed he hoped that he would be allowed to escape.

Meanwhile, the target seemed oblivious to the fight we waged for her life, stepping gingerly among the fallen bodies and pools of blood toward her mother's limp form.

I joined my growl with Steven's, encouraging the vampire to sidle farther away from the target. He was halfway to the front door when Winter barred the way, her katana held at the ready. Seeing his fate was set, the vampire charged her in a bid to break free. In a single motion I caught his arm, swung him about, and snapped his neck. The moment the body hit the floor, Winter severed the head. She had efficiently severed all of the heads, I noticed, a necessary brutality to guarantee the corpses could not be resurrected.

Once I was assured that Winter and Steven—still in his animal form—were unhurt, a different sort of anger replaced the void of my bloodlust. We had killed five vampires. Were there others that had escaped? Had a sentry been stationed outside, now racing back to the Seethe with word of the pack's intervention? If word reached Demetrius, the leader of the Seethe, our pack could find itself at war over a girl of indeterminate value to the pack. She had come to our attention through my brother, Josh, who served as the pack's warlock. So far, the only explanation for our observation was that Demetrius had plans for the target. That alone made her worthy of our attention, but I needed more to put the pack at risk. I didn't like having my hand forced.

A soft, ragged plea drew me from my anger. "Come on. You can't leave now. Come back."

I followed Steven's gaze to find the target on her knees,

desperately administering CPR to her mother's corpse, the deceased's expression frozen in a liminal state of shock and fear.

"Come on," the target—Skylar—pleaded repeatedly, rhythmically pumping the corpse's chest with both palms. She stopped to administer a rescue breath, and then returned to pumping, her mahogany hair bouncing with each effort. I watched, entranced by the rawness of the moment. A rib cracked beneath Skylar's palms, eliciting a tearful curse from the girl, but still she refused to give up. She was soft and small and naïve to the world that surrounded her, but driven by a singular, defiant will. And there was something about her I couldn't place—something familiar. Minutes passed while I watched the futile effort, entranced by Skylar's tenacity, before she finally gave up. Her hair dangled over the mother's chest as she lowered her head in failure.

Reminded of our presence by the clatter of Steven's claws on the hardwood floor, Skylar jumped to her feet, ready for flight, her green eyes wild with fear. I gestured, intending to calm her, when the change came suddenly, painfully. I could see the agony in her expression as she transformed into a gray wolf and shook off her clothes with a growl. At my approach, she splayed her front paws in readiness to leap to the attack or to flee. Staring into those wild, pale gray eyes, I saw only the wolf there. Though I was aware that Skylar did not share her life with her wolf, I was surprised and disgusted to find just how disconnected she was.

Winter positioned herself in a fighting stance between the wolf and the broken front door.

I held up my hand to her. "No." Slowly, so as to not exacerbate the wolf's alarm, I shed my suit jacket, button-down shirt, and pants, welcoming the sudden, cool comfort as my body elongated. By the time I landed on all fours, the change into my wolf was complete. The sight of my wolf, nearly twice her size, deepened Skylar's panic. She began to pace, showing her uncertainty. Taking measured steps, I approached her cautiously, my head slightly lowered. Though she bared her teeth, she nervously allowed me to nuzzle her fur. Having gained her reluctant acceptance, I turned and plodded toward the door, growling at Winter to move aside. Skylar anxiously skirted the others, but she followed me out the door. I nudged her gently in the direction of the retreat, and then took the lead, careful to maintain a pace she could follow.

CHAPTER 2

*D*elivering Skylar's wolf to the safety of the retreat proved an agonizing affair. Her reluctance to cross roads, her anxiety at the proximity of humans, and the easy distraction of potential prey told me even more about the girl's relationship with her wolf, which was almost nonexistent. More than once I was obliged to offer her encouragement or redirect her attention toward the objective. By the time we came within sight of the retreat, the sun was beginning to rise. There wasn't much of a chance I could convince a wild wolf to trot into the house, climb a flight of stairs, and hop into a bed, but it was worth a try. As expected, Skylar shied away from the house, trotting and pacing rather than following. Before she chose to run, I gave up and walked her a short way into the woods to a secluded patch of flat, dry grass. Beneath the low-hanging branches, surrounded almost entirely by thick shrubs, I finally coaxed her to lie down and rest. I lay beside her, resting my snout on my forepaws and watching her intently. My stomach growled, but I didn't dare leave Skylar while I hunted. I could force the change into her human form at any time, but I didn't want a frightened girl on my hands. Like most were-animals, I was fully conscious in my animal form, but the disconnected, like Skylar, would experience their animal as a barely remembered dream, if they remembered anything at all. When Skylar did eventually wake up in her human form, she was going to panic. She would need someone to hold her hand and explain her new reality. Despite my empathy for her loss, Skylar had taken enough of my day already. By now Winter and Steven had informed Sebastian that we had engaged Demetrius's vampires. Had an unseen scout escaped, Demetrius would know as well. At this moment, pack and Seethe might be at war.

For what? I wondered, watching the wolf's eyes reluctantly close. I hoped that Josh hadn't made a serious misjudgment by placing the girl under the pack's protection before he had deciphered her actual value. Many times my brother had proven his worth to the pack, but if he were wrong now ...

The slightest sounds caused Skylar's eyes to flick open, her snout to snap up, her body tensing for potential flight. The efforts to soothe her anxious nerves and coax her to sleep were maddening. Eventually her heart rate slowed along with her breath, heralding a loss of consciousness. Resting my snout on her shoulder, I forced the change, which came easily, leaving a naked Skylar curled in the grass in a desperate sleep, pain frozen onto her face. She was fit, though not exactly athletic. Her mahogany hair flowed in thick curly waves that framed her oval face. I admired her deep-set cheekbones, supple lips, and olive-toned skin. Repressing an unexpected urge, I gingerly scooped her sleeping form into my arms and carried her toward the retreat. Sebastian opened the door at my approach, took one look at Skylar, and then silently directed me to bring her inside, where I found Winter and Steven waiting.

Skylar began to stir, her agitated body squirming. Glancing down at her, I noticed several long scars on her forearm—forlorn cuts repeated too often to heal properly.

"Doctor," Sebastian snapped in a baritone voice, observing Skylar with his arms crossed.

Dr. Baker arrived wearing a red surgical smock and gloves, a loaded syringe at the ready. His expression of perpetual concern complimented the spreading gray in his silver hair. My grip tightened around Skylar, securing her warm body to my chest as he expertly administered the tranquilizer. Her reaction was immediate, her body slumping into a relaxed bundle as she was obliged to go into a deep sleep.

"I prepared a room upstairs," Steven said with a hushed tone. "End of the hall."

Turning slightly for clearance, I carried Skylar up the flight of stairs to the guest room and gently lay her onto the bed. Joan arrived as I turned to leave, making a clucking sound as she gently drew the paisley-patterned duvet from beneath Skylar to cover her. Indifferent to the senseless rebuke, I returned to Sebastian and Winter at the bottom of the stairs. The pack Alpha was a massive, powerful figure— the only pack member more powerful than myself. We didn't always see eye to eye, but we had an arrangement.

"We left a mess behind," I said, answering Sebastian's expectant look.

"The mother was the only human victim," Winter added. "We brought the body with us, but we'll need to follow up on the vamp corpses. For now, they're inside the house, secured from prying eyes."

"Josh will return in five days," Sebastian said, turning to me. "Can it wait?"

I nodded. My brother's magic had proven an efficient means to clean what would be considered a crime scene by the outside world, removing anything from bodies to blood to fingerprints with minimal effort. "We'll keep an eye on the house until then. Remove the daily mail. There is no other family to be concerned of."

"Any clues to her value?" Sebastian asked.

"Demetrius sent some of his best for her. And wants her alive."

"You're certain?"

"The vampires could have easily killed Skylar upon our arrival. Instead they tried to carry her to the Seethe. The mother was killed out of hand."

Sebastian nodded thoughtfully. "Dr. Baker's sedative will last about one hour. Question her when she wakes, Ethan. Find out what she knows."

"Whatever Skylar means to Demetrius, she's clueless. The house was completely defenseless. Either she or the mother must have invited the vampires inside."

"Learn what you can." Sebastian glanced between me and Winter. "Were you followed?"

I gestured with an aggravated sigh toward our sleeping guest. "She was difficult, but we didn't encounter any more of Demetrius's Seethe." I turned to Winter.

"All tracks were accounted for, but one," she answered. "I can't be positive it belonged to a vampire."

"We have to assume so," I said. "Demetrius will answer."

"We will take precautions," Sebastian said, turning to leave when Winter interrupted.

"When searching the house, we found a cage and a store of sedatives."

My scowl matched her obvious contempt. Sebastian was no less disgusted. My wolf was the soul to my flesh. To hide from it by locking myself into a prison and sedating myself into oblivion was a horrific thought, akin to the cruelest torture. No doubt Skylar lived in the ignorant fallacy of a gothic horror movie, every month counting her dread as the nights ticked closer to the inevitable full moon. Her irrational terror dominated her existence. Such an existence was worse than nothing. My thoughts returned to the scars on her arms.

In my room, I found the clothes I had shed at Skylar's house folded on my bed. I tossed those into the hamper, fetched clean trousers and shirt, and then made my way to the kitchen to prepare a steak, searing the outside while leaving the inside raw and bloody. I was mostly finished when I heard stirring upstairs, as if Skylar were rifling the guest room.

For a moment I considered sending Joan upstairs. The were-jaguar possessed a more nuanced social skill set then the typical were, myself included. While I had neither time nor patience for social niceties, Joan had a way of making others comfortable and talkative, a skill set she'd transferred to her adopted son, Steven. But Joan wasn't a pack member. Joan was the visiting Beta of the Southern Pack, and I wasn't about to relinquish my responsibilities to a guest.

Pushing my unfinished plate aside with a growl, I went upstairs. At my approach, the guest room door creaked open, revealing a pair of green eyes widening in panic at the sight of me. The door began to close but then suddenly flung open as Skylar, naked but for the white blanket wrapped around her body and clutched to her chest, burst from the room. "Skylar!" I shouted, only just catching the edge of the blanket as she flew past me toward the stairs. Irritated, I yanked hard, jerking her backward to crash to the floor and slide backward until she slammed with a thud against the wall. Believing her stunned, I reached for her ankle to drag her back to the bedroom, but got a sharp kick to the chest instead. Skylar had caught me by surprise. The kick was precise and strong. It occurred to me that I had misjudged our guest when she pivoted on her backside and kicked me again. She stayed there with her legs cocked, willing and apparently able to fight from her back, which was more than I had given her credit for. But this was not a training session. Skylar was an unwelcome guest making a nuisance of herself, and I was done playing around.

18

"I'm not going to hurt you," I growled, but she didn't seem to believe me.

Skylar was strong, a gift from her wolf, but she wasn't used to others of her kind. Her surprise at my speed and strength was apparent as I bundled her legs in my arms and scooped her upright, compressing her against my chest in a tight bear hug. Her fingernails scratched, but it was her teeth sinking into my shoulder, gnawing at my flesh through my shirt, that pissed me off the most.

"Stop fighting," I snapped, but she persisted, seemingly oblivious to my command. I kicked open the guest room door and threw her onto the floor, earning a seemingly endless scream for my trouble. Awed by the childishness of her tantrum, I watched as her face turned beet red, and then purple. Still she screamed as if her life depended upon it. She was on the verge of passing out when I leaned down, my face inches from hers. "Shut up!" I bellowed. When that failed, I clasped her wrists, combining them over her head into a single grasp so that I was free to cover her mouth with my other hand, pinching her nose shut at the same time. Still, she screamed. "Stop it!" I shouted. "If I wanted to hurt you, I would have. And you've given me more than enough reasons to do so." I glared into her eyes, demanding obedience, but it was the lack of oxygen that finally shut her up. Her screams still ringing in my ears, I released my grip from her mouth, cautiously at first, until I was reasonably confident the screaming would not reoccur.

Panting as she caught her breath, Skylar glared up at me with a look meant to kill. Glowering down at her, I noticed for the first time the orange quarter ring in a corner of her right pupil—a terait, the physiological tell that betrayed the unquenched bloodlust of a vampire. *Impossible*, I thought, taken aback. Skylar was a wolf. I'd seen her—helped her—change. "What—what *are* you?" I demanded. My eyes danced over every detail of her body, recording evidence that might eventually help explain the impossible. The idea disgusted me. If true, Skylar was an abomination best removed from the world. The sooner the better.

"What are you?" I demanded again, squeezing her arms until she flinched.

"Ethan, get off of her," Joan snapped from behind me. I turned to find her in the doorway, her red hair pulled back into a ponytail and her round face set in a firm expression of command. I accepted Joan as a guest of the pack, but there was only one Beta here. Before I could put her in her place, her expression softened, aided by the sprinkling of freckles about her nose and cheeks. "Ethan," she said, pale brown eyes casting a gentle gleam as she pleaded for my cooperation.

Rising, I stepped back to the door, my gaze firmly fixed on Skylar. The abomination. By all rights, she should die. Now. At my hands. A vampire werewolf would be a danger to us all, but such an abomination wasn't possible. Werewolves were not susceptible to the vampire disease, and vampires could not succumb to lycanthropy. Yet Skylar sat staring from the floor, terrified and furious, the faint orange glow in her right pupil defiantly screaming at me. Could Joan not see it?

"Give me a moment," Joan requested warmly, startling me from my reverie. "Please."

We needed to know as much as possible about Skylar, the sooner the better. I was prepared to force my demands, but perhaps it would be better to give Joan her chance before I did any permanent damage. Good cop came before bad cop. We were beyond simply helping this girl now. Regardless of any empathy I had previously felt for Skylar, she would now need to explain her existence. I gave her a baleful glare, glanced a warning to Joan, and then left her to the interrogation.

On my way down the stairs, it occurred to me that Skylar's mother had probably not invited the vampires into her home. Most likely, they needed no invitation. Sebastian and Winter were in his office. "She has a terait," I announced after closing the door. Winter stiffened, while Sebastian sat upright in his desk chair.

"Are you certain?" he asked.

I nodded, my expression grim.

"Then we know why Demetrius wants the girl," Winter said flatly. "We should kill her. I'll do it, happily."

Sebastian brushed her offer aside, drawing his fingers into the shape of a pyramid as he leaned back, deep in thought. We waited, respectfully still, until he spoke again. "Ethan, did Josh know about the terait?"

"No. Josh wouldn't withhold information from the pack." I hoped.

"We need to know exactly what Skylar is."

"Why not kill her and be done?" Winter asked.

Sebastian remained pensive. "If she is a vampire, the threat goes beyond her. We need to know how she was made. Is Demetrius responsible? Has he turned others of our kind? What is her precise value to him? For now, Skylar is safe with us. If she is a danger, she will die, but for now we will give Josh time to solve this puzzle. Until we know more, Skylar has the protection of the pack."

"Skylar is stubborn and combative," I said, my jaw stiffening. "She sees herself as a prisoner. I doubt she will be coaxed into sharing, even if she knows what she is."

"Give Joan a chance. Skylar can see herself as a prisoner or a guest, I don't care. Either way, she does not leave the grounds."

Emerging from Sebastian's office, I discovered that Steven and much of the rest of the pack had gathered in the communal area, spread out among the two claret-colored sofas, one on either end of the room, and the array of muted, geometric-patterned accent chairs that filled the space in between. They were muttering among themselves as if in private conversation, but I knew Skylar had become the main attraction. I couldn't blame them. Before I could say anything, we heard the creak of the door upstairs, followed by footsteps approaching the stairwell. The others scattered about their business as Joan descended, Skylar following behind her looking ashen. Their pace was slow and grim, as if part of a funeral procession. My eyes flicked toward Dr. Baker's medical bay, where the body of Skylar's mother was stored.

Driven by morbid curiosity, I followed from a discreet distance as Joan led Skylar into and through the living room, crossing over the ornate wool rug at the center flanked by durable tan sofas. I watched as Skylar took in the room with a muted curiosity, her eyes scanning the rust and cream walls, along with the wildlife photography that masked a number of dents and holes that had been patched over the years. The decor masked the bloodstains just as well. Over time, nearly every room in the retreat had seen its share of blood.

The slump of Skylar's shoulders deepened with each step as Joan led them through a pair of white double doors into the newest part of the house, a massive expansion that had been built to Dr. Baker's exact specifications. He was a talented physician. The pack's willingness to spend such a fortune on his needs demonstrated our respect and gratitude for his service. Down another hall, they turned left into the sterile white hospital with the high-gloss, easy-to-clean tile floor. Skylar paid grim attention to the padlocks on two of the recovery rooms. She was probably making notes, drawing a map in her mind in case she needed to escape. *So she has a strong survival instinct, despite her obvious grief.* I held back a little farther behind, not wanting to be noticed. Finally, they made a right turn, and Joan opened the double doors that led to the chilly morgue, releasing the smells of disinfectant, sulfur, and death into the hall.

I waited until the doors closed behind them before observing through the glass portals. The morgue was a large open room divided by curtains that shielded nine beds—seemingly a luxury, yet there had been times when bodies had been stacked on the floor. Pack life was expressed in long periods of relatively peaceful prosperity marred by occasional violence that at times occurred on a grand scale. Though the pack experienced its losses, the morgue served primarily to process the corpses of our enemies and those who simply got in the way. There was an incinerator as well, in a nearby room, for final disposal once Dr. Baker had satisfied his medical curiosity. An examining table stood at one end of the room, a table with a microscope and testing supplies at the other. Medical cabinets were dispersed throughout the room.

With a delicate gesture, Joan drew back a thin white curtain to reveal the pale body of Skylar's mother lying supine on an examining table. At the sight of the bloating corpse, I expected another outpouring of hysterical emotion, but Skylar remained surprisingly dignified. Only a mild shudder in her shoulders betrayed her grief. A puzzle, this girl, seemingly strong and weak in almost the same breath. I couldn't vouch for her fate, which might by necessity bring her to an early demise, but it was hard to deny her pain. She hadn't lived the life of a wolf, fraught with the constant threat of violence and death. Instead she'd lived like a human, unaccustomed to the frequent tragedy of gruesome loss that stalked our kind.

Dr. Baker emerged in his smock and gloves from behind another curtain to observe Joan and Skylar, clearly surprised by their presence. Our gazes met before he addressed her, his voice muffled by the door. "Skylar," he said with the gently firm tone that belonged to medical professionals.

For a moment, Skylar didn't respond. Eventually, she

slowly turned, took in Dr. Baker, and then demanded icily, "Who are you?"

"I'm Dr. Jeremy Baker," he said, casting an empathetic glance at her mother's corpse. "You are welcome to call me Jeremy."

Skylar returned her gaze to her mother, ignoring him completely.

"I wish there had been something I could have done for her," Dr. Baker explained, "but she was gone before she got to me. We couldn't even consider changing her." At Skylar's indifference, he ran his fingers through his thinning silver hair. After a moment, he gave her a reassuring pat on the shoulder, and then gestured for Joan to follow him out of the morgue. As they emerged through the double doors, Joan noticed my presence for the first time and stopped to join me. Dr. Baker offered us a pleading look, an entreaty to follow, to give the girl time and space to grieve alone. I ignored him, not just out of curiosity but out of a keen awareness that Skylar might be clever enough to try and escape. Dr. Baker left begrudgingly. Joan remained a step removed from the portal, her arms crossed in discomfort as I returned to watching Skylar in the morgue.

She remained standing at the table, staring down at her mother. After a long, uncomfortable silence, she crumpled into the small space next to the table and cried. Having seen enough, I left Joan waiting by the door.

CHAPTER 3

A few hours later, I paced in my room, unable to relax, my thoughts a bramble of unanswered questions. It was difficult not to feel sympathy for Skylar, but perhaps that was what made her dangerous. By all appearances she seemed the innocent wolf, forced to endure a belated and cruelly abrupt introduction to our world, but there were signs of cunning. Was she as helpless as she seemed, or was her grief just a magnificent performance? En route to the morgue, she'd managed, despite her intense grief, to make a very keen observation of her surroundings, perhaps with an eye to escape. And she was more than just a wolf. According to the terait in her right eye, she was a vampire as well, and vampires were cunning, soulless deceivers. If Skylar's helplessness were just an act ... I left the room abruptly, in time to pass Joan on her way to meet Sebastian. Steven was in the game room, distracting himself with the Xbox.

At the top of the stairs, I found Winter lurking in the hall. "What are you doing?" I demanded.

"Just hanging around." She gestured with a sideways nod toward the closed door of Skylar's room, her expression pregnant with distrust.

I strode to the end of the hall and opened the door. Instead of answers, I found the curtains lightly dancing in the breeze at the edges of the open window. A quick check in the bathroom confirmed that Skylar was gone. Through the window, I peered out into the dwindling light of sunset, fruitlessly scanning the ground below for a sign of Skylar's passing. Her scent was on the breeze, but the wind shifted deceptively. She couldn't have made it far. Given her discomfort with her wolf, she likely was traveling on foot.

Clenching my fists in anger, I turned to find Winter alert in the doorway. "Find her," I said. Without hesitation, Winter ran and leapt through the window. I hurried down the stairs, snapping at Steven and a few others to follow. Outside, I peeled off the others, sending them in several directions. "I want her alive, if possible, but she does not leave the grounds. Steven—" I gestured for him to follow as I trailed Winter's scent.

With every step my anger deepened. Steven walked alertly beside me, his nose in the air, ready for anything. After a few minutes I heard a faint snap nearby, followed by another. Not the crisp snap of a twig, but the hard snap of bone. Turning toward the sound, I led Steven up a shallow hill. At the rise I saw Winter with her back to us fifty yards ahead, crouched as if holding something. Cresting the rise I saw Winter was facing a panicked-looking Skylar held in the clutches of a vampire with distinctive, spiked black hair— Chase, one of Demetrius's most dangerous minions. After a quick glance around to be certain we weren't walking into an ambush, I gestured to Steven to spread out and take a different approach.

Chase noticed my approach, his expression more irritated than concerned. After all, he had Skylar by the throat. My jaw clenched at the sight of blood seeping from a wound in her shoulder, but I kept that anger to myself. Any display of emotion could only encourage Chase. Winter, I realized, had an impressive bargaining chip of her own, crouched over the limp figure of the vampire Gabriella, her limbs useless and broken in several places. Winter negotiated with a knife held to Gabriella's throat.

"How long have you been together?" Winter asked. "Forty, fifty years? She knows all the weird things you like. From what I hear, they are quite sick, yet she still loves you. How long do you think it will be before you find someone like her again? How empty was your life before her? Own those memories, because, if you don't let Skylar go, you will return to that life of loneliness."

"Let Skylar go, Chase," I commanded as I reached Winter's side, "and we will let you go unscathed to nurse Gabriella's wounds. You know Winter's just looking for a reason. Don't give her one."

Frustration rose to a boil in the vampire's expression before he reluctantly pushed Skylar aside and dashed to his mate's rescue. At my gesture, Winter rose, taking a cautious step back as Chase scooped Gabriella's broken body into his arms. His fangs bared, he hissed a promise of revenge at Winter before hurriedly carrying his mate's body to safety. We were watching them leave when the other vampire attacked. Where he came from, I couldn't say, but he had kept himself downwind. He was nearly upon Winter when Steven struck unexpectedly from the flank. Knocking the vampire to the ground, Steven stunned it with a vicious beating before drawing a stake from his back pocket and stabbing the vampire in the heart.

The air filled with the foul stench of necrotic tissue as the vampire's body decayed in rapid order, first melting and then hardening into a mummified state. Skylar gasped in horror at the sight, only turning away when Steven drew a knife from his belt and efficiently removed the head from the corpse. No doubt Skylar saw the decapitation as a confirmation of our violent nature, but removal of the head was a necessity. Even in a mummified state, a whole vampire could be revived with blood. I nodded my approval to Steven as he cleaned his knife on the vampire's shirt, and then I turned to Skylar, who seemed to have remembered her mortality. Tears streaked down her cheeks as she felt the growing bruises on her neck and then dipped her finger in the blood that seeped from the wound in her shoulder. Panic seemed about to overwhelm her, but this time I offered no sympathy. I could hear her heart beating the rhythm of panic.

My sharp tone seemed to snap her from her hysteria. "Is anything broken?"

"I'm fine," she stammered, attempting to gather herself.

"Good." I still didn't care. "Follow me and try to keep up." Winter guarded our left flank while I led the way back to the retreat, setting a pace that proved too much for Skylar. At my signal, Steven hung back, as much to encourage as to protect her. En route to safety, we remained alert for another attack, but the odds were unlikely. Chase and Gabriella weren't the bait. They were the trap.

On our approach, Sebastian emerged from the retreat in a rage, purposefully striding directly toward Skylar with his massive fists clenched. *He's made up his mind.* I expected an abrupt act of violence that would end the lone wolf's life and the pack's problem in a single, merciful gesture. As the pack Alpha, Sebastian was well within his rights to take her life. Skylar recoiled at his approach, and at the last moment Sebastian stopped short. He glared at her for a long, tense moment, and then walked away. I understood exactly how he felt.

At my gesture, Steven ushered a bewildered Skylar into the retreat behind Winter. Dr. Baker was anxiously waiting just inside with his medical bag. "Anyone injured?"

"Not really," Winter answered, gesturing carelessly behind her toward Skylar. "You may need to check the problem. Chase used her shoulder as an appetizer. He really hates me now," she added with a self-satisfied smirk as I began to pace. Against all norms, the vampires had violated the retreat grounds in order to attack Skylar. Because of her absurdly foolish flight, the pack had been put at risk. If any harm had come to Winter, or Steven, or any of the others ... I fumed, struggling to tamp down my rising anger. Given Skylar's stubborn nature, exploding at her might be counterproductive. I needed to be calm if I was going to try and talk some sense into her.

Winter continued as I paced in the background. "He's probably plotting his revenge as we speak—undoubtedly something long, torturous, and bloody. I suspect if I tried to die too quickly, he would revive me just to prolong the torture. I win," she announced to the gathering pack. "I am clearly the one Chase hates the most in this pack."

What was Skylar thinking?

"It's not a competition," Dr. Baker said reprovingly, "and definitely not one you should be involved in. Winter, what did you do?"

Winter casually examined the fingernails of one hand as she said, "I broke Gabby's arms in eight places."

"That was rather unnecessary."

Does Skylar ever think at all?

"I had no other options," Winter answered with mock innocence, which Dr. Baker rejected out of hand. He cocked one eyebrow in judgment, and Winter gave up with a heavy sigh. "Okay, fine, they bug me! They are too weird even for vampires! *Ugh*, every time I see them I just want to break something on them. She dyed her hair this ridiculous burnt orange; she looks like a bruised carrot. He looks like a Goth Abercrombie & Fitch model."

"Chase is an ass," Steven added, drawing the doctor's attention to the wound in Skylar's shoulder.

Only a matter of time before Skylar gets one of us killed.

"May I?" Dr. Baker asked, approaching. A nod from

Skylar and he drew the torn shirt open at the wound, enough to expose the extent of the damage. I continued pacing, but the anger was quickly building into a rage. *A bite wound*, I realized, glancing at Skylar's shoulder. Judging by the way the doctor probed the wound with his fingers, the damage was minimal.

Dr. Baker eventually drew a sharp hiss from Skylar. "It's just a puncture wound," he declared, withdrawing his fingers. "You'll heal just fine."

"It hurts like hell," Skylar muttered, a gutless whimper.

Finally, my temper boiled over. I pushed past Dr. Baker to get into Skylar's face. "What the hell was that? Weren't you supposed to stay in the damn house?" Skylar stared up at me, refusing to answer out of shock or fear or both, but I held my ground, towering over her as I fought the urge to throw her into a wall. I watched as shock gave way to determination, resistance building in her expression, in her posture. She tried to push me away, but I slapped her arm aside.

"Ethan," Joan said, her tone soft, cautious.

I ignored her. "Why would you run when you knew the vampires were after you, especially at dusk? You cannot be this stupid."

"Ethan," Joan repeated, her tone firming. I growled at her, tired of her interference. "She chose to leave," Joan said. "It is an option I feel she should have been given in the first place. She's been through a great deal today. I don't think yelling at her like an uncivilized brute is going to make Skylar feel safe in a home in which we are asking her to be our guest."

I glanced from Joan to Skylar, wondering just how Joan could be so naïve. Skylar was now a greater threat than ever to the pack's security. Not only was it obvious we couldn't trust her, but Skylar didn't trust the pack. No doubt she would run again, and Demetrius would be waiting to use her for whatever nefarious scheme he'd devised. If I'd had my way in that moment, Skylar would have been restrained and locked in a cell. Finding myself unexpectedly backing away, I followed my instinct and stormed into the next room. Marko barely escaped from a sofa before I threw it one-handed into a wall, followed closely by two unsuspecting chairs. Stopping to gather myself, I heard Joan in the next room, explaining as if to a child, "Skylar, I am extending an invitation for you to stay here as the Midwest Pack's guest and allow us to help you. Will you accept?"

What was the point of pretending Skylar was our guest when we had already made it apparent that she wasn't? Receiving, I assumed, a nonverbal answer, Joan added, her tone more conciliatory, "You may join us for dinner if you would like."

"I'm not hungry."

Ungrateful. I snarled.

"I'll have Steven bring you something."

After Skylar had gone upstairs to her room, Joan appeared in the doorway. "Steven—"

"No," I snapped. "I'll go to her."

"If we want Skylar to accept our help, we need her to understand what's at stake."

"I'll make her understand," I snapped. "We don't need her cooperation. We need her obedience."

"She's frightened of you."

"Good." I knew Joan was right, but I couldn't shed the overwhelming desire to shake some sense into Skylar. "Maybe she's not frightened enough."

"Ethan," Joan said carefully. "Some people can't be cowed by threats of violence. The more she fears you, the more she resists. She is more stubborn than you think."

I slapped another chair into the wreck of the sofa.

Joan continued, unmoved by the violence. "Skylar responds well to Steven. Perhaps she'll respond more to the carrot than the stick."

I sighed, squeezing my fists repeatedly to release the

tension, and then gestured sharply for Steven to follow his mother's instruction.

The time I spent in the retreat's gym transformed into a marathon of weights and cardio concluding with three rounds of sparring that sent Dakota, the were-bear, to the medical bay clutching a broken rib. After a shower, I went to bed exhausted and sore, yet sleep was the last thing on my mind. While I had left my rage in the gym, the puzzle that was Skylar dogged my thoughts.

Frustrated, I got up to don a shirt and pants. Deciding against another session in the gym, I roamed the halls of the retreat, taking comfort in the secure silence of the night, until I heard the faint sounds of bare feet plodding about, followed by the gentle jiggle of a locked door handle. My jaw clenched as I followed the noise to discover Skylar at a table in the library, hunched over a tome that she was reading by the glow of her phone.

"This is a private library," I said, flicking on the overhead light. Skylar jumped to her feet in a moment of fear as I snatched up several books from the table, returning them to shelves.

"The door was unlocked," she said pointedly.

"This is a private library," I repeated.

"Then it should have been locked."

I turned to chastise her, finding her inexplicably willful while wearing an entirely purple ensemble of fluffy fleece, looking like an exotic animal from a children's story. *Are you twelve?* She stiffened at the attention, simultaneously self-conscious and defiant, daring me to judge her. I held her gaze for a moment, listening to the excited beat of her heart and the shortness of her breath that indicated more than just defiance and fear. A slow smirk twisted the corners of my mouth. "It's private just to you."

"Perhaps the next time you have guests, they should be informed of what's public and private domain."

"*Guests* don't snoop. What are you doing up?"

"I couldn't sleep."

"There's a television in the room."

Skylar shrugged. "There wasn't anything on."

"There are two hundred channels. Surely you could have found something to hold your interest."

Her nose lifted slightly as she said, "I prefer books over television."

"Then I will get you a *Cosmo* in the morning."

"I prefer novels," she snapped. "Since I don't have my laptop or e-reader, I thought there would be something interesting in here."

"Fine. I'll bring you a couple of romance or YA novels off the best-seller list."

"I like legal thrillers."

My frustration finally broke against her willfulness. I chuckled, surprising myself. "Fine, Skylar, I will get you the books. You look tired." My gaze flicked toward the library door, a not-so-subtle gesture. "Maybe you should see if sleep will come now."

"You're right," she said with a mischievous smile as she swept up a book from the table, clutched it to her chest, and started for the door. Not one to be fooled, I intercepted her, barring the way. She innocently batted her eyelashes as I snatched the book from her grasp. On my way to the shelf, I noticed the title on the spine, *VAMPIRES*, and smiled. *This time, you have bitten off more than you can chew.* I returned the book to her with a gracious gesture. "It'll be good night reading for you." She accepted it with a newfound wariness.

Laying my palm over the small of her back, I gently guided her out of the library, locked the door, and then escorted her back to her room. "Good night, Skylar." I started, and then turned back just as she stepped inside still wearing that bewildered look as if I finally had gotten the advantage over her and she wasn't sure how. "The next time you decide to sneak around the house, you should be a little quieter. You sound like a herd of stampeding elephants when you walk."

She uttered an abrupt laugh that she quickly muted just before closing the door.

I returned to my bed, embraced with the warm satisfaction that once Skylar opened that book, she would find no sleep tonight, or for many nights to come.

CHAPTER 4

The next morning I awoke at dawn, thinking of Chris. Whatever she had planned, it was only a matter of time before she made a move. I went about my daily business until a reasonable hour, and then made a few phone calls, planting seeds that might eventually bear fruit.

Over the next three days, pack life at the retreat quietly returned to normal due in large part to Skylar's stubborn insistence on hiding in the guest room. There were no more attempts to escape, at least, and no further signs of vampires on the property. It seemed Demetrius had learned his lesson the first time, though we were well prepared for another attack. Soon Josh would return with answers, and Skylar's fate would be decided.

As Joan had observed, Skylar responded best to Steven, no doubt due to his youth and the boyish charm he used to great effect. Though I suspected his empathy for her was genuine, there was no doubt he would conduct himself in the pack's best interest. Should Skylar's actions prove too dangerous to tolerate, Steven was more than capable of killing her in a merciful manner.

Steven had killed his first vampire at the age of nine. His

sister, who had raised him after their parents died in a car wreck, caught the unfortunate attention of an obsessive vampire. For weeks, the vampire visited her in the night, erasing her memory of the assault and using his saliva to heal the bite wounds that by morning appeared as mysterious bruises on her neck—obvious signs of a vampire bite, but neither Steven nor his sister were were-animals. They knew nothing of our world. As the attacks continued, the sister grew paranoid, unable to shake the sense that she was being stalked. After a few weeks of this torture, Steven walked in on the feeding and attacked the vampire with a child's wooden baseball bat. In the ensuing fight, the bat was broken, and so was Steven. The vampire, believing the boy was dead, returned his attention to the sister. Despite Steven's horrible wounds, he managed to rise and drive the broken bat through the vampire's back, piercing the heart.

Joan, who had been tracking the vampire, discovered the scene. Steven was found near death, lying with his arms wrapped around his sister's corpse. Only the powerful healing abilities of a were-animal could save him, but he was too young and too weak for a wolf. Joan could have changed Steven into a jaguar, but jaguars were largely solitary animals. She wanted Steven to live and thrive with the Southern Pack, so he was changed by a coyote. He was raised by Joan until he eventually transferred to the Midwest Pack, where he'd proven himself to be a tremendous asset.

On the third evening, Joan finally coaxed Skylar out for dinner. Judging from Sebastian's demeanor, he didn't appreciate the effort, and neither did I. Skylar was welcome at our table, but I preferred she come of her own volition. At the sight of our anxious guest, most of the pack simply stared, surprised. Winter greeted Skylar with her forked serpent tongue darting from her mouth. The sight sent an obvious shiver through Skylar, but a low growl from Sebastian tempered Winter's satisfaction, though she couldn't help the corners of her mouth twisting into the hint of a smile as she cut into her steak. Presumably to break the tension, Steven rose to pull out a chair for Skylar, who gracefully accepted. He pulled a neighboring chair for Joan.

"Thank you for joining us." Sebastian greeted Skylar with measured politeness as he cut a bloody piece from his steak.

"Thank you for inviting me," Skylar answered primly, fixing Sebastian with a curiously appreciative gaze. A true Alpha, he was physically imposing and powerful—a match even for me. His prominent cheekbones and strong jawline gave him a passively stern expression, which he used to great effect. Tracing her gaze, Skylar seemed especially taken by Sebastian's full lips, his brown eyes, or perhaps his espresso-brown skin. So transfixed was her gaze that she seemed not to notice my attention, a slight I found surprisingly irritating. For his part, Sebastian remained indifferent.

As Skylar was served, the once robust conversation was replaced by the ghostly clinking and scraping of cutlery and the clunking of wineglasses on the table. Despite her trepidation, Skylar managed at least to conduct herself throughout with a tense grace, resisting the curious stares of the others along with Winter's outright hostility. Eventually, Sebastian broke the silence. "We are going for a run after dinner," he announced with an expectant glance toward Skylar.

It was understood that this would be a run for the wolves and their relatives, an opportunity for Skylar to benefit from bonding with her own kind, as well as with her inner wolf. Lone wolves were dubious creatures, and Skylar had been alone for too long, though not necessarily by choice, as it seemed she'd never had a proper introduction to her animal nature. I relished the opportunity to run with my kind, which had its own rules and dynamics that were unique from those of other species of were-animals.

The meal ended a few minutes later when Sebastian rose from the table and strode toward the front door. I followed, drawing the others in my wake. Once outside, Sebastian disrobed to change into a massive wolf with auburn highlights on dark brown fur. The others changed as well. There were nine of us total, including five wolves, a dingo, a jackal, and a second coyote in addition to Steven. Waiting for Sebastian to begin the run, the others chased one another, nipping at noses and heels, and jumping on backs, growling and snarling in play. I shed my clothes to join them, but decided to check on Skylar, who I knew would struggle with the transformation.

I found Joan by Skylar's side. As a jaguar, there was no place for her in this run. She belonged inside with Winter and the others, but Joan was busy calming Skylar, gesturing as she explained what was happening. Better Joan than me. I watched as Skylar took in the scene with wide eyes. She had seen wolves, I realized, but was getting an introduction into the broader world of were-species. Judging by the fear in her eyes, she was perhaps seeing for the first time that were-animals were more than monsters. She seemed especially fascinated by the bleached pale fur and deep jasper eyes of Hannah, a rare albino dingo, as well as the lean, ancient look of Bryce, a jackal.

At my approach, Joan instructed Skylar, "Go play with your family," then returned to the house, leaving Skylar scrambling to avert her eyes from the fullness of my nudity while simultaneously gawking—the sort of attention I frequently attracted from women, to the point I rarely bothered to notice without intent. I never understood the human embarrassment over the naked form, something Skylar would best shed immediately. It was time to run, and I had no patience for her insecurities. I did, however, take a moment to enjoy her curiously satisfying struggle.

"Change," I instructed her. To my bemusement, she closed her eyes, progressively squeezing them tighter and tighter until her forehead wrinkled. "It'll be easier," I said, explaining the obvious, "if your clothes didn't restrict you. It usually hurts when you have to tear through them." I gestured to my own nakedness as an example.

She seemed to shrink as she glanced toward the others.

I sighed. "You can go to the side of the house to change."

She scurried around the corner. I waited, watching the others chase and tackle one another. After nearly a minute, I strode to the other side of the house to find her naked, her face even more tense than before with the effort to change. Alarmed by my arrival, she covered her breasts with an arm and her groin with a hand. Chill bumps stood up on her pale skin as she shivered.

"Problem?" I reached out to assist her change, but she shied away, surprising me. She didn't remember that I'd helped her wolf change once before, I realized, but my patience was at its end. *Enough of this drama.* I fell forward as I instantly changed into my wolf, showing her how effortless and painless the process would be if she stopped resisting. Needing her trust, I trotted slowly toward her, preferring not to frighten her. As I gently nuzzled her face, some of the tension melted from her body. Her fingers gently stroked my fur, tentatively at first, but growing in confidence. Once she was calm enough, I lowered my snout to her shoulder and forced the change. As her body elongated, gray fur rising from her skin, her initial panic transformed into surprise and delight just before the transformation was complete. In wolf form, she shook out her fur and smiled.

Eager for the run, I reared back and howled to the others, who called back in harmonious answer. For each of their voices, I instinctively determined direction and distance, but there was only one voice I needed to track. Sebastian. He was nearby, with the others close at hand. Even in times of leisure, discipline mattered. I led Skylar's wolf to the others, calling out to them once more to announce my presence.

Excited by the howl, Skylar appeared tempted to join, but held her tongue.

Sebastian began the run and I followed, with Skylar close behind until Steven playfully knocked her to the ground and licked her face. She tried to push him aside, but he pressed his playful attack, licking her face until she finally voiced her displeasure with a growl. Steven retreated a step, and then pounced on the grass between them, feinting another attack, before running off in search of other game. Skylar raced after him, quickly peeling off to chase Hannah and Bryce. I watched with a growing satisfaction as Skylar played. Sebastian noticed as well, looking on with quiet approval. If she could learn to control her stubbornness and trust her wolf, there was hope for her.

A howl from Bryce brought the pack's attention to a deer darting through the woods. I took off in eager pursuit, Sebastian quickly surpassing me to take the lead while the others ran along the deer's flanks. Skylar dropped off a bit, preferring the chase to the hunt, but I ignored her. Well ahead of the rest, Sebastian and I raced each other, charging through the spray of dirt and grass kicked up by the deer's heels. I was the one who brought it down, but Sebastian commanded the choicest portion for himself. While the pack ate, Skylar paced the edge of the scene, resisting her natural desire to join the meal.

Eventually, we returned to the run until, two hours later, Sebastian signaled a return to the house. As we approached, I transformed in stride to my human form, as did the others— all but Skylar, who seemed taken aback by the ease of our transformation. I considered the possibility that, having enjoyed herself for perhaps the first time, she might be reluctant to relinquish her wolf form. Her increasing agitation as the others changed, however, demonstrated a different challenge. Sebastian and I exchanged a silent understanding;

Skylar expected someone to help her transition, but this was a skill she needed to learn on her own.

She lay down onto the ground and closed her eyes. I waited, watching, expecting her to change, until I realized she was falling asleep. Shaking my head, I strode forward, touched her head, and uttered the guttural command that triggered the change. As I watched her slow transformation, the wind shifted, delivering the familiar scent of copper. Turning back toward the house, I saw Steven and Bryce on alert, their expressions tense and focused on impending violence. A trail of blood on the grass between them led into the house. I hurried inside to find Winter leaning exhausted against the kitchen island. Sebastian and Joan, looking calm but intent, were at Winter's side.

"What happened?" I asked, joining them.

"Vamps on the property," Winter said.

"How many?" Sebastian asked.

"Three less than they started with. Two more escaped, so five total. Maybe more," she added, doubtful.

Joan tensed, her normally brown eyes now chestnut encircled by a yellow feline ring as her animal rose close to the surface. "They are getting quite bold," she said in a tone that promised retribution.

Sebastian growled. "Demetrius is quite determined to obtain Skylar."

"This is her fault," Winter spat, her gaze transfixed behind me. Following her gaze, I found Skylar fully dressed in the doorway, taken aback by the accusation. The pupils of Winter's hazel eyes transformed into long vertical slits, the snake in her drawn by anger. Winter's body tensed, as if preparing to strike, but then she left the room before I needed to intercede. Sebastian followed, as did I, leaving Joan to comfort Skylar.

The conversation continued in Sebastian's office behind a closed door.

"We should just kill her," Winter said, pacing, her pupils still slits.

"We don't know yet why Demetrius wants her," Sebastian said from his desk, fingers angling into a pyramid at his chest.

"*If* he wants her."

"Explain," Sebastian said.

"What if Demetrius's efforts are just to convince us to take the girl in, make her one of us so that she can betray us at a crucial juncture?"

That was possible, though the more time I spent with Skylar, the harder it was to imagine her capable of such a delicate subterfuge. She could barely take care of herself. But then helplessness was exactly the impression a spy or saboteur would wish to create. I didn't like the idea, but it merited some consideration.

Winter continued. "Whatever Demetrius has planned, it ends when Skylar's dead."

"Not necessarily," I said. "What's Demetrius's plan B, his plan C? Whatever his plan A, we know it requires Skylar. Remove her from the board and we're entirely in the dark."

"I see in the dark just fine."

I looked to Sebastian, who considered calmly before speaking. "Until Josh's return, we proceed as planned. Ethan, keep Skylar under surveillance. During the day, she's free to roam the grounds with accompaniment, but I want her inside well before dusk. She is safe within the retreat."

"If she stays inside," Winter said as she left in a huff.

I met Sebastian's hard gaze with a nod, and then left him alone.

Josh might very well return with the answers to all our questions about Skylar, but Winter wasn't wrong—we couldn't afford to wait. If I was going to decipher Demetrius's plan, I needed to know exactly what I was dealing with. Determined to use my imposing presence as a bludgeon, I strode up to Skylar's room and burst through the door, expecting to launch directly into my interrogation. Instead I found an empty room. I glanced at the open window, but the sound of the shower running in the bathroom told me what I needed to know. Crossing to the open door, I peered inside to find Skylar in the shower, unaware of my presence. Distracted, I observed through the smoky glass shower door as she rinsed the curls of her mahogany hair, turning to display her olive-toned figure. When the shower door opened unexpectedly, I surprised myself by pulling back into the bedroom. After a moment, she emerged with a towel wrapped around her shapely figure. I expected to be seen, or for my presence to be felt. I was prepared to use her fright as the crux of my interrogation, but she didn't seem to notice as she dropped onto the bed, leaned back supine, and closed her eyes. Her attempts at slow, deep breaths were ragged and shallow. She shifted to find comfort, but the tension in her expression betrayed her anxiety. If she was a plant, she disguised it inexplicably well. In a quiet moment alone, she should be thrilled, engrossed with the pleasure of a successful mission unfolding on the path to victory. Yet the encounter with Chase and Gabriella had truly frightened her.

Or Skylar was far more cunning than I gave her credit for.

Dissatisfied with her efforts, she sat up. Her eyes still closed, she crossed her legs and settled herself, forcibly slowing her breaths.

"You never learned to control your wolf," I said, startling her. She grasped instinctively at her towel as she shifted back on the bed, glaring at me, indignant and horrified, as if she'd been violated. I glared back, watching for the slightest hint of deception. "You let it control you." I began to pace, watching and waiting for some sort of response but she only stared back, transfixed. I'd come here for answers, but I let the silence settle. Most people talked into an uncomfortable void, but not Skylar. She was far too stubborn. Eventually I stopped pacing, leaning on the dresser as I gave her an expectant look. Her eyes shifted toward the door, and then returned to me, narrowing to green slits.

"What, have you not gained control of your hearing, either?" I demanded.

"My hearing is just fine," she said stiffly, averting her gaze. "I've always been afraid of that part of me. It's a miserable inconvenience that I have to deal with each month during full moons and I chose not to deal with it any more than I had to."

I strode to the edge of the bed and leaned toward Skylar until our eyes were inches apart. Despite being startled, she held her ground, staring back. The orange glow of the terait was undeniable. I had hoped somehow that it had been an illusion, but there it was, daring me to explain Skylar's very existence. I sniffed at the skin of her neck and then returned to pacing. "You don't smell like a were-animal," I snapped, "and the vampires enter your home without an invitation as though you were one of theirs. Why is that?"

She visibly struggled with the answer, opting instead for silent resistance, scowling back at me.

"I don't like it," I said.

"You are welcome to go dislike it somewhere else."

"Not before I have answers. What exactly are you?"

"What?"

"What. Are. You?" I growled.

"What answer do you need to make it easier for you to leave?"

"If I staked you, would you start reversion?"

"I am not sure. As a general social rule, people don't go around staking people. It's really frowned upon in mainstream society. But I suspect that it would be the same as

44

with you—pain and lots of blood. Sometimes I cry when I get hurt. So maybe I would cry a little, too."

Is that what you want? her look said. I laughed. Despite Skylar's obvious fear, it seemed my efforts to intimidate only fueled her defiance, adding to her mystery. I shook my head. "Something about you is wrong. Off. I don't like it and I need to know what it is."

"If you need answers, I am not the right source." I noticed her fingers fidgeting with a silver charm bracelet on her wrist.

"You don't have an aversion to silver," I said, surprised. Skylar blew out an exasperated breath, her eyes flicking unsubtly once more toward the door, but I ignored her. "You're not a true were-animal."

"Yet every full moon I turn into a wolf."

I strode toward her, leaning in once more to reexamine her terait. "What are you?"

"You tell me," she snapped. "It seems that everyone knows as much or maybe even more about me than I do. You are the one with the source who seems to have all the answers. We've played 'getting to know you' long enough. And I can assure you I am quite tired of it. It is time for you to leave." She rose from the bed, strode to the door, and held it open, watching me expectantly.

A smirk crossed my lips as I made a casual show of sitting on the edge of the bed. At my defiance, she opened the door wider and cocked an eyebrow. Our silent battle of wills transformed into a game of chicken that became increasingly frustrating. Once again I found myself stymied by the unmovable wall of Skylar's willfulness. Tired of wasting time, I rose to pace the room as I stoked my anger.

"Our information is limited on what you are," I said. "You lived your life ignoring the animal within. What else dwells in you that you chose to ignore? You don't expect me to believe you have been foolish enough to live this pseudo-human life with that woman you called mother, oblivious to all things."

Skylar winced. Her fists tightened into tiny balls as she leaned forward. "That woman," she spat, striding toward me, "that I called mother was my mother by every definition of the word, despite the fact that she did not give birth to me. I am so sorry to disappoint you, but yes, I lived my life with no desire to know anything more about my origin other than the fact I am a werewolf. All I knew was both my parents were dead. I only wanted to live as a human or as human as this wretched wolf would allow me. I wanted nothing more than to do human things and ignore anything that made me anything but." She made an effort to calm herself. "Until I came here, I had only experienced my wolf during loss of emotional control. Every full moon, I was sedated and slept through it, locked in a cage. This is something I chose to do. And this is the way I chose to live. If your job is to know, wouldn't your time be better spent trying to find out why the vampires have this newfound interest in me, instead of grilling me with questions I can't possibly answer? The sooner we know their intentions, the faster I can get out of this house. I believe that would make us both happy."

When I didn't answer, Skylar said, "Should *I* leave?" It was an odd question, since we were standing in her room. Obviously she understood the absurdity, because she made no effort to leave, only glaring until I finally gave up, shook my head, and left. The door slammed shut behind me. A thin smile crossed my lips as I strode toward the stairs—until I realized I had left the room with as few answers as I had entered with. Something broke inside the room, accompanied by a muffled curse. Stepping quietly, I returned to the door and faintly heard Skylar's voice count backward from one hundred, interrupted by spontaneous grunts and growls from her wolf.

I cursed myself. I had let my emotions get the best of me

and pushed Skylar too hard. My intensity was my strength, but at times it could be detrimental. Nothing good would come of Skylar, driven by rage and fear, changing spontaneously. I didn't need an angry wolf on my hands. "You need to control yourself," I said through the door, careful to soften my tone. "You shouldn't change again today. It will fatigue you too much."

Silence.

I slowly opened the door to find Skylar sitting on the bed, her expression a tense storm of frustration and fury. I had pushed her to the brink of an emotional breakdown. This was my doing. A pack draws its emotional baseline from its leaders. I was reminded that brute force was not the sole requirement of leadership. If I was ever to become an Alpha, I needed to embrace a broader skill set. More than his strength, it was Sebastian's self-control that made him the most powerful Alpha in the country.

Skylar averted her gaze as I eased myself onto the edge of the bed, resting my forearms on my knees as I clasped my hands. I gathered myself, brushing my emotions aside to bring myself to as near a sense of serene calm as I was able. Once I'd established that, I shifted slightly on the bed, surreptitiously bringing my arm into gentle contact with Skylar's. She flinched, but did not withdraw, which made my influence simpler as I consciously directed my calm to her. Through her arm, I felt the tension melt from her body as she leaned into me. Surprisingly, my own serenity deepened at the increased contact, as if the connection between us had unexpectedly become symbiotic. After a moment, I gently removed myself from the bed and left.

CHAPTER 5

I was on the patio, reading the latest issue of *Car and Driver* magazine, when Sebastian called me into his office. "Skylar needs to run an errand in Chicago," he announced, to my surprise. "I want you to escort her."

I couldn't understand why Sebastian would willingly allow Skylar to leave the grounds of the retreat. "I can bring her whatever she needs."

Sebastian's brow tightened in frustration. "As I explained to her."

"It's too dangerous."

"If I don't allow it, Skylar will likely sneak out a window in the night and walk there," he said, exasperated. "It'll be a daylight trip. Give her an hour or two, nothing more. Consider it damage control," he added, cutting off my retort. His voice was flat, determined. He was making a mistake, but once he'd made up his mind there was no room for debate.

Joan played a role in this. I caught her scent in the room.

"I'll take Skylar first thing tomorrow morning," I acquiesced. It was my role to obey the Alpha's order, but I didn't have to like it.

48

"She'll meet you in the driveway momentarily. Damage control, Ethan. Let's get this nonsense over with."

I left, fuming on my way to the garage to fetch the SUV. I tried to wrap my head around how Joan had convinced Sebastian to let Skylar off of the property, let alone to travel to Chicago. True, the vampires were only a threat between dusk and dawn, but Demetrius had the garden at his disposal —a group of human wannabes that inexplicably gave themselves as servants to the vampires. Primarily, the garden functioned as a source of food and entertainment for the Seethe, but it was not unusual for them to serve their masters in other ways during the daylight. More fools than warriors, the human servants were not normally a threat to the pack, but in the crowded city there would be plenty of opportunities for them to attempt to earn their master's gratitude. The smarter among them would find other more capable hands in the city willing to do the dirty work. The only element on our side for this journey was surprise—Demetrius would never expect Sebastian to do something as senseless as expose Skylar to the plethora of risks involved in taking her to the city.

I brought the black SUV to the front of the house and waited outside the vehicle. And waited. I glanced at the time on my phone to see the morning was already giving way to noon when Skylar finally emerged from the house with a bag over her shoulder, looking as pleased to see me as I was to play her chauffeur. I opened the door for her, as courtesy required, but said nothing as I drove the SUV onto the narrow, dirt road that wound through three miles of dense woods before reaching the limits of our property. The main road was a one-lane affair, but paved and rarely used, making the journey much quicker. I thoroughly ignored the speed limit, eager to get this foolishness over as quickly as possible, but I was also watchful for an ambush.

Thankfully, the silence between us continued as we drove

into Chicago, where my hopes for a quick journey were dashed by crowded streets and gridlock, testing my patience to the limit. "Where do you need to go?" I asked.

"Just park near 96th."

"Where do you need to go?" I demanded.

"Just park near 96th," Skylar insisted as if correcting a child.

I answered with a baleful glare, firmly aware that she was goading me. The slow pace of traffic, creeping from one light to the next, did nothing to ease my mood. We were sitting ducks, with potential danger coming from any direction, from any vehicle or pedestrian. While I remained vigilant, Skylar gawked obliviously at the city as if she had been absent for months rather than days. After some aggravation, I found street parking within a block of 96th. As we emerged from the SUV, she walked directly toward a nearby coffee shop, Marissa's.

"Are you serious?" I scoffed. "There's coffee at the house."

Skylar ignored me entirely, a satisfied smile on her lips as she entered the shop.

Inside, the rich smell of coffee barely masked the musty odor of used books that filled tall shelves in each corner of the shop. An eclectic variety of sofas, lounge chairs, ottomans, and the occasional dining table were scattered about the vast open space, surrounding a large, double wood-burning fireplace at the center. The entire decor left an ad hoc impression of a thrift store. Thankfully, the shop was not crowded. Sight lines were simple. I directed Skylar to a floral loveseat in the back corner and left her with explicit instructions not to wander while I fetched her order.

I used the time waiting at the counter to scan the patrons. Young professionals, mostly. A few tourists. Despite a number of feminine glances in my direction—particularly the two young women giggling like schoolgirls by the door—our pres-

ence seemed to go unremarked, but I didn't like the vulnerabil-
ity. Still, being inside the shop was better than aimlessly
wandering the streets of Chicago. Surely Skylar insisted on this
trip for a greater reason than to sit in a coffee shop. Surprisingly,
she remained where I left her, surfing the Internet on her laptop.

I returned to the loveseat with her chai latte and a blue-
berry muffin, which she scoffed at.

"I didn't want a muffin."

I shrugged. "The barista gave it to me."

"I think she wants you to have her muffin." Skylar
grinned as she pushed the pastry toward me.

I glanced at the waitress, who was staring intently. She
smiled, cheeks flushing from my attention. "What is she,
sixteen?" I asked before sipping my latte. "Drink your tea so
we can leave."

Skylar sipped her tea at a deliberately frustrating pace.
Not wishing to reward her goading, I kept my irritation to
myself, instead focusing my attention on the comings and
goings of the patrons while she dawdled on the Internet. A
frustrating hour later, she finished her tea and closed her
laptop. I gathered myself to leave, plotting the best route out
of the city, when Skylar, wearing a thinly disguised smile,
handed me her cup and asked for a refill. I blinked at the cup
before reluctantly accepting it. Given that dragging her by
the hair out of the cafe and back to the SUV wasn't an
option, I fetched the tea as requested. The next twenty-five
minutes and thirty-two seconds were agonizing as she
simply sat there staring off into space, sipping her tea
without a care in the world. I began tapping the table
absently until I noticed Skylar's lips thin as she gave me a
sideways glance. I tapped louder, matching the rhythm of her
heart. After a moment of pretending not to notice, she
turned to me with an annoyed expression.

"You need to hurry up," I said. "This is boring me."

"Well, that's something you should take up with Sebastian. I'm not bored and that is why I wanted to come alone."

"That wasn't going to happen."

"Then it seems like you need to just grin and bear it," she said in a cloying voice.

I glared down at her, intending to put her in her place, yet the look she gave me could've peeled paint from a Bentley. My glare transformed into an ironic smile. "Most people tend to want to stay on my good side. It would be good that you learn from their example."

Skylar chose not to answer, but her demeanor became less confident. She drank faster. After another few minutes to finish her tea—presumably to save face—we left Marissa's, emerging into the crowded streets during the lunch hour rush. Too many bodies for one wolf to monitor. If I wasn't worried about the time, I would've pushed Skylar into another coffee shop until the crowd thinned. "Where?" I asked. She pointed down the block and I pulled her through the crowd, pushing and shoving and snarling at anyone in my way or who pressed too close. She apologized on my behalf with a quick "hello" or "pardon us." Pretty soon people were going out of their way to steer clear of me. I wasn't concerned about their comfort. My job was to keep Skylar alive and well. None of these people mattered. Most were mundane fools, living dull lives by someone else's clock.

"Would you like to put a leash on me?" Skylar snapped after I pulled her close to stop her incessant wandering.

"Don't tempt me."

She twisted, yanking her hand free.

"Where are we going?" I demanded. Frowning, Skylar pointed to a shop down the street, and then to another, and then to another. Before I could respond, she ducked into a candle store, where the intense blend of numerous fragrances and perfumes would numb my olfactory senses for hours. I was considering throwing her over my shoulder and hauling her back to the SUV when she slipped out to the sidewalk. I followed her outside just in time to see her disappear into an arts and craft store where she meandered with a look of complete disinterest. Perhaps this entire adventure was just a form of revenge. Once outside, I confronted her. "You haven't bought anything. I thought you needed to get something."

"No, I said I needed to go to the city. I am going to check out some shops."

I sighed, exasperated. "As long as we're done by four."

"Cinderella had to be in the house by the time the clock struck twelve," Skylar corrected me.

"Cinderella wasn't being hunted by vampires that wake at dusk."

In the moment I took to notice a reputable steakhouse across the street, she'd changed direction, striding into the crowd with a newfound sense of purpose—perhaps to lose me. I caught up with her quickly, gripping her elbow and pulling her close. "Let's go there," I said, guiding her toward the steakhouse.

"Are you ever not hungry?"

I smiled. "A hungry wolf is a mean wolf."

"Then you must have a tapeworm."

The hostess behind the podium brightened when she saw me—to Skylar's obvious contempt. The woman was reasonably attractive with a curvy figure, blond hair, and too much lip gloss emphasizing a toothsome smile. She batted her extended eyelashes at me, drawing attention to the mascara above her large jasper eyes. Not my type, but I wasn't above offering some flattering attention if it made her day and got me what I wanted. And if flirting irritated Skylar, so much the better.

At my request, the hostess led us to a quiet booth in the back of the restaurant that afforded me a sightline to the entrance and the kitchen. I didn't like surprises during my meal. I didn't appreciate surprises in general.

"Thank you," Skylar said dismissively as we slid into the booth.

"Don't I know you from somewhere?" the hostess asked me, grinning.

Skylar rolled her eyes and sighed loudly as she unbound her napkin and placed it on her lap.

"You do seem familiar." I smiled back.

I allowed the guessing game to go on for a couple of minutes, long enough to give Skylar a taste of her own medicine, before bringing it to a close. "Perhaps I've seen you at the gym."

The hostess brightened. "On West Fullerton?"

"Yes. West Fullerton."

"I knew it. Perhaps we'll see each other again." She winked and strolled rather suggestively to her podium.

"I'm sorry," Skylar snapped, "would you like me to leave so you can continue this inane flirting?"

"No, I'm done, but thank you for the offer. I wish you could be this considerate most of the time. It would make being around you much easier."

The waitress arrived to take our order.

"About the trout," Skylar started. "Is that skin on or off?"

"On."

"Hm." Skylar glanced pensively at the menu. "I'll have the grilled chicken, mashed potatoes—on a separate plate—and a Caesar salad, no anchovies. Wait, yes to anchovies, but only half the usual, and on the side. With the dressing."

I thought I would starve to death while awaiting my turn. "Two New York strip steaks, blood-rare, and a loaded baked potato." Once the waitress had left, I scolded Skylar. "What's with you, chicken and salad?"

"What do you mean?"

"You ordered chicken and salad, like a typical woman."

"I am a typical woman," she said defensively.

"No. You are not. You are a werewolf."

"What would you have me do? Ask them to point me to the nearest pasture where I can find a grazing cow that I can attack and devour for lunch while you watch?"

"You can order real meat and have it prepared in a manner that's most appealing to your animal."

"I'm forced to be a wolf one night a month. I am a woman for the rest of the time."

"The wolf is always there. The fact that you can hear the woman at the next table questioning her husband about his so-called business trip without trying to eavesdrop demonstrates that you are not just some woman. Or the fact that if necessary, you could take down most of the people in this room, even with your limited fighting skills, demonstrates that you're not just some woman. It's your wolf that makes those things possible. You may sit here and pretend to be just a typical pretty woman but you're a wolf all the time. You may have chosen the human part of you, but that won't stifle the wolf or make it go away, even if it is only allowed to take physical form during full moons." Skylar stared back at me, briefly defiant, and then lowered her gaze toward the back of her hand on the table. "And that's your wolf, as well. You may not be part of our pack but your wolf understands pack structure and knows its place. Once you truly accept the wolf, then you will see the beauty in it. Instead of running, learn to appreciate the enhanced abilities, strength, and senses."

She shifted in her seat, her demeanor softening. She fidgeted with her napkin before asking, "When did you first change?"

"Eight."

"How did you deal with changing so young?"

"There wasn't anything to deal with. My father was a wolf and I couldn't wait until my wolf matured to change. I had the strength, speed, and senses early on, but it was the actual physical transformation that took so long."

Skylar seemed surprised. Understandable, considering she had grown up without guidance or direction. As frustrating as I found her attitude toward her wolf, I had to wonder if I would have followed a similar path without the guidance of my father.

"How do you change so fast?"

I shrugged. "You do anything often enough, it becomes easy. Become one with your better half and when you call, it will answer freely."

Skylar's eyes widened in surprise, but she accepted my statement quietly. She had much to learn. At least now she was listening. The next few minutes passed in silence as she processed what I'd told her. Periodically her gaze met mine. I couldn't help but notice the terait. She remained oblivious to it, both in appearance and in nature.

Eventually, she caught me staring. "What are you looking at?"

I smiled. "You have nice eyes."

Pink blossomed in her cheeks before Skylar looked away.

Shortly thereafter, the food arrived. Once the waitress had departed, I speared Skylar's chicken with my knife, swapping it for one of my steaks. She accepted the change without complaint. I watched as she ate, my attention focused on the terait. After a few bites of blood-rare steak, the orange glow of bloodlust faded. She caught me staring once more, answering me with a curious look.

"It's rare I can bring a woman such pleasure with just food," I said, smirking, and then set about consuming my own meal, leaving the chicken untouched. As soon as we'd taken our last bite of food, I checked the time, cursing myself for losing track. Dusk was close. Too close. I placed more than enough cash on the table and rushed Skylar out the door.

Already the sun was disappearing behind the tall buildings of the city, casting long shadows across the streets. It was the end of the workday and we were stuck with heavy foot traffic, heavier than we had encountered all day. Foolish, on my part—wasting time on a nice meal. The longer we stayed in the city, the greater the risk, and now we wouldn't reach the retreat before dusk. I held Skylar close, guiding her through the crowd. Thankfully, she chose to cooperate, though she seemed distracted by the sounds and smells of the crowd that threatened to overwhelm the heightened senses of her wolf. Then there was the mazelike cloud of odiferous perfumes and cologne, and the endless chatter of one-sided schizophrenic conversations with cell phones. There were the clicks, scrapes, and shuffles of heels, loafers, and tennis shoes on the pavement. Even with my experience, the distractions could be overwhelming. Watching Skylar struggle with her senses reminded me how young she was to her true nature.

"This way," I said, encouraging her to focus.

Intending to take a shortcut, I steered her into an alley that reeked of garbage-filled bins—even more distraction. She was scrunching her nose at the smell when I caught the familiar scent of vampire. I ducked into a neighboring doorway, pulling her with me, but she jerked free, perhaps reflexively. Before I could retrieve her, I saw a look of acknowledgment in her eyes, indicating the stranger's approach. Not a vampire—it was not yet dusk—but the man reeked of them. One of Demetrius's garden, for certain. As the scent grew stronger, Skylar's look became confused. She greeted the stranger with a placid smile just as the man strode in front of my hiding place. As he tried to draw something from his jacket pocket, I stepped behind him, grasped his head with both hands, and snapped his neck. Skylar gasped, watching horrified as the man uttered a faint, strangled cry, and then collapsed.

"What the hell did you do?" she demanded, her voice cracking. Tears welled in her eyes.

We weren't out of danger. I glanced at both ends of the alley, and then gestured for her to follow me back to the street. "We must—" She ran toward the street, driven by a combination of fear and panic. "Skylar, wait!" I gave a muted shout, and then raced after her, my shoes pounding on the pavement. "Skylar!"

A tall, thin man appeared at the end of the alley just before she collided into him and fell back onto the pavement.

"I'm sorry," Skylar muttered, confused, as she picked herself up. The stranger yanked her up by the hair. With a loud, pained grunt, she instinctively shifted her body, flipping the stranger over her hip and onto his back, breaking his grip in the process. She turned to flee out of the alley when the stranger swept out an arm and grasped her ankle, bringing her to the pavement. I was just a few yards away when I saw the stranger draw a Taser from his pocket. He struggled to make solid contact as Skylar fought from her back.

Two more strides and I snatched the Taser from the man's grasp, hurling it against a brick wall. As the man turned, I wrapped my massive hands around his thin neck, lifted him from the ground, and drove him into the wall. Enraged, I held him there, his feet dangling inches from the concrete alley floor as I squeezed the life out of him. I stared into his bulging eyes, watching his face turn from red to purple as his hands pulled and pushed and scraped uselessly at my grip.

I heard the click of a pulled trigger just before the bullet struck my chest, spinning me sideways. The pop of the gunfire followed, echoing in the alley as I dropped to the pavement, the sudden shock of pain leaving me breathless.

"It's going to be okay." I heard Skylar's anxious voice, her lips close to my ear.

Forcing my eyes open, I saw the man who had shot me standing a few feet away, aiming his pistol for another shot. I tried to warn Skylar, but there wasn't enough air in my lungs. Seeing the danger, she picked up the Taser from near my feet and threw it at the gunman, striking him in the face. The man's gun arm dropped as he stumbled back. Before he could recover, Skylar leapt onto him, driving him to the ground. There was a brief struggle, the man initially fending off her blows, but Skylar was on his chest, her knees wedged under his armpits. Inevitably, she landed a solid blow to the man's temple, stunning him. His body went limp.

Don't stop. Don't give him a chance to get back up. I expected Skylar to give up too quickly, to recklessly leave the danger behind her as she came to my aid or ran. But she didn't. Lost in her wolf's rage, her blows rained down on the defenseless stranger. I heard skin tear and thin facial bones crunch. I heard the wet sound of a bloody mess as Skylar, grunting and growling, beat the gunman to death.

I approved.

Her rage spent, she stood up, her gaze shifting from her bloody knuckles to the irreparable damage they had done. I knew the thrill that coursed through her veins, challenging her notions of right and wrong that didn't apply to our world.

"Skylar," I said, my breath returning.

Her head snapped around, and I saw the wolf in her eyes before they returned to normal.

"It's okay," I whispered as she helped me up. I leaned into her, working against the pain in my chest to give her a sense of calm. Once we reached the street, I had no choice but to stand on my own. A bleeding, bent-over man shuffling to his car would attract the wrong attention, so I bore the pain, walking awkwardly with Skylar behind me until I reached the SUV.

By the time I climbed into the passenger seat, I already

had my cell phone in my hand, dialing Dr. Baker. Sweat dripped down my forehead as I handed Skylar the keys to the SUV. The line connected. "I've been shot."

"Silver?" Dr. Baker asked without hesitation.

I winced from the pain. "Of course it was silver. I wouldn't call you if it weren't."

"How far away are you?"

"In the city." I glanced out the window as Skylar pushed the SUV into traffic. "On our way out now." With my other hand, I tore open my dark blue Henley shirt from the buttons. The wound was necrotic from the silver. In addition to being poisonous, silver inhibited the healing process.

"Should I come there?"

"Skylar's driving," I said with a grimace. Even with my extraordinary toleration for pain, the wound was excruciating. "I should get there before there's too much damage." I ended the call, letting the phone drop to the floor. Each moment was now a battle for consciousness. A glance outside the window revealed the SUV slowing, approaching what appeared to be endless gridlock. "Skylar," I said through gritted teeth, trying to point out an alternate route, but she saw it, turning the SUV onto a backstreet. The change kept the vehicle in motion, but not fast enough to shorten our travel time, and my chances for survival diminished with each breath. I considered fishing my phone from the floor to call Dr. Baker to meet us when Skylar offered, "I think I can take the bullet out."

She didn't sound entirely confident. Neither was I, but I wasn't going to finish the trip alive with a silver bullet in my chest. I nodded. After a moment, she pulled into an unused parking lot that belonged to a closed insurance company. She disappeared around the back of the SUV. I didn't bother to turn when the trunk opened, instead using all my concentration to fight the pain. She reappeared after a moment with the emergency kit and a toolbox.

Skylar gingerly probed the wound with shaky fingers. "I can feel the bullet," she said, hopeful. "It's close to the surface." After sorting through the kit and the toolbox, she raised a box cutter to the wound and hesitated. At my encouragement, her lips tightened into a thin line of resolve before she pressed the blade into my dying flesh. I can't say how I maintained consciousness through the pain as she cut a path through my flesh to the bullet. The blade slipped more than once in her nervous grip, but she maintained her resolve. Her nervousness eased when she finally set the box cutter onto the floor and fetched a pair of pliers from the toolbox. I felt the tugging of the bullet from the grip of my flesh as Skylar extracted the it from the wound. The removal of silver from my body provided instant relief. I laid my head back into the seat, panting as she cleaned the wound with alcohol and then bandaged it.

I laid back against the seat, catching my breath as I watched her merge the SUV back into traffic. "Why did you run from me?"

"Scared," she said softly. "I was scared. I thought you had killed someone without cause."

"You think I am capable of that?" Judging by her expression, she did. I wondered what else Skylar thought me capable of.

"I didn't know what to think," she finally said. "Who were they?"

"They were part of the vampires' garden—humans who serve the Seethe in various ways but mostly as a food supply. Some do it in hopes of being changed and others to satisfy their own perverted needs. Those who do it in hope of being changed become slaves, willing to do anything to please their Master, including abducting you." I shifted, raising myself enough to look out the window. Traffic had returned to normal as we were leaving the city. "You don't trust us."

"I've never had to trust anyone other than my mother,"

she said, a deep sadness in her gaze. "I don't think I know how to."

I remained silent for the rest of the journey, replaying the events in the alley while my body began the accelerated healing process common to all were-animals, in the absence of silver. Skylar was like a child in a dangerous world, but she had courage. She had strength. Once the silver bullet had incapacitated me, she could have run, leaving me to my fate. Instead, she probably saved my life. She remained silent as well. More than once, she appeared about to talk, but thought better of it. Eventually, she parked the SUV in the driveway of the retreat and came around to open the passenger door for me. She held out her hands to help me as I swung my legs over the edge of the seat. I hesitated there, taking a moment to feel a few strands of her mahogany hair between my fingertips. Her lips parted as she gave me a curious expression. "You need to trust us," I said gently. I understood her reluctance, but it was her distrust that put us all at risk. "At the very least, learn to fake it."

Before she could answer, I eased myself into her arms, allowing her to assist me to the house. Dr. Baker opened the door, his face etched with concern until she handed him the bullet the way a cat presents a mouse, and then guided me into the house.

"Well done," Dr. Baker said behind us. "Ethan, how's the shoulder?"

"Still here."

"Meet me in my office. I still would like to look at it."

I nodded, easing myself from Skylar's embrace. Sebastian emerged from his office, observing my bandaged wound with a half-smile. "It's been a long time since you've felt the tinge of silver on your flesh."

"It's a pain one never forgets. I don't need a reminder of it anytime soon."

"Skylar, I see that your day trip was quite eventful,"

Sebastian said contemptuously. "You now see that the vampires don't have to take a stroll in the daylight to get to you. There won't be any more trips for you until this is over. So don't ask again."

He should've never allowed the trip in the first place.

Skylar's jaw twitched. "Being attacked every time I go out of the house really makes for a bad day. And because of the ever-so-sweet way you asked," she said cloyingly, "I think I can comply with that."

Sebastian's eyes narrowed as he watched her disappear up the stairs. "Josh has returned," he informed me, and then gestured toward his office.

CHAPTER 6

*J*osh was waiting inside Sebastian's office, wearing a slight smirk, tattered jeans, and a small hoop earring in each ear. I was pretty sure there was a new tattoo among the others peeking out from every part of his black graphic t-shirt. His caramel-colored hair was a contrived mess that went along with his deliberate five-o'clock shadow. "Ethan," Josh said cheerfully, not bothering to rise. I acknowledged my brother silently, waiting for his report.

Sebastian closed the office door, and then eased into the seat at his desk. "Go ahead, Josh."

"It starts with a dream, or rather, a nightmare."

I bit back my frustration. Josh was prone to dramatics. Despite the urgency of the situation, this was going to be no exception.

My brother continued. "They were given to me by a fae."

That was unusual. "Explain," I said.

"I received them as they were relayed to her, in bits and pieces, confusing and incomplete, but when Demetrius revealed himself at the heart of the mystery, I knew this was a matter of great importance. 'A lone wolf will stir the vampires and damage the pack,' she said, and then pointed me in Skylar's direction."

"Why would the fae care one way or the other about the pack?" Sebastian asked. Were-animals were not well regarded by the fae, who had little appreciation for the magic that allowed vampires and were-animals to exist. The distrust was mutual.

"I think she cared more about her nightmares."

I scowled. "You could've shared all of this in the first place."

"I had to be sure. I've spent the last few days seeking confirmation. Try as I might to pry the news from those familiar with the Seethe, all I've found is silence, which is unusual of itself. Everybody gossips, just not now, apparently."

"What's the next step, Josh?" Sebastian asked.

Josh's jaw twitched, his abundant confidence waning. "I am going to journey for Skylar."

"Magic," I grunted. "You said using magic was dangerous. You said without knowing what Demetrius has in mind or who he is working with, using magic might draw more attention than gain answers, might put Skylar and the pack at greater risk."

Josh gave me a hard look from beneath his eyebrows. "At this point, we don't have a lot of choices."

"Josh," Sebastian said, "have you performed this magic before?"

"I could try, but there's no telling what we may find. Better I work with someone experienced."

"Who?" I demanded.

"Thomas," Josh said defiantly, leaning back in his chair, his legs splayed out. "A lone warlock living in isolation on Sapelo Island in Georgia."

"You've had dealings with this warlock?"

"I only know Thomas by reputation."

I gave him a look that made clear my dislike for this idea. "There has to be another way."

"There are other options, but you won't find them acceptable."

"Try me."

"Caleb, for one."

I scoffed. "Trust a rogue vampire?"

Josh turned to Sebastian. "There are risks, but the only other choice is to wait for Demetrius to reveal his plans. I am more powerful than Thomas, though I doubt he knows that. If necessary, I'll be happy to show him. In fact, I'll probably have to to get his cooperation. He's a level two warlock," Josh added, addressing my doubtful expression. "I'm a level one." The way witches and warlocks measured themselves, there were five levels in all. As a level one, Josh was among the most powerful, but that didn't make him invincible.

"Thomas has agreed to help us?"

Josh shifted in his seat, just enough for me to notice. "He's a difficult man to reach."

Reckless. "You think Thomas will appreciate you showing up at his doorstep asking for a favor?"

"If I had a better option, I'd offer it."

"Was a debt incurred with the fae?" Sebastian asked.

"No. I did as much a favor for her by accepting her burden as she did for me by sharing."

Sebastian considered for a long moment, tapping his fingertips together. "Ethan, have Joan check with the Southern Pack. Find out what they know about this warlock. If they have no concerns to add, then have Joan make the arrangements for your arrival. Take Steven with you."

I didn't relish putting ourselves into the graces of the Southern Pack. I trusted Joan, the pack's Beta, but I wasn't on the best of terms with all of the pack members. Owen, in particular, was a dubious character. I had shamed him, and I had no doubt he would take any opportunity to return the favor. "I'll take care of it."

Josh smiled, satisfied by his small victory. "Now," he sighed, "it's time I meet this Skylar. This will all go much smoother if I earn her trust first."

"Ethan," Sebastian said, "arrange the introduction as soon as possible."

"I'll bring her to the library in the morning."

Josh grinned. "Perfect."

Three hours later, I found Skylar prowling in the halls. "Are you lost?" I asked, surprising her.

"Ethan. No, just looking around." Her eyes darted about. She was a terrible liar.

I leaned against the wall, studying her. "What were you looking for, Skylar?"

"You," she stammered. "I was looking for you. I hadn't seen you since earlier and I wanted to make sure you were alright."

More lies. "I'm fine. You did well today. It is greatly appreciated." I didn't give compliments lightly, but she'd earned one. Her pleased smile became anxious as I stepped into her space, placing a palm onto her sternum and gently but firmly driving her back against the wall. I held her there, taking in her scent as I lightly brushed my nose along her jawline until my lips rested against her ear. I inhaled her scent, the sweet redolence of Rose de Mai and orange blossom. "You've lived so long in your human world that you have not developed the skills to successfully lie to a were-animal," I whispered. "Do you hear it—your heart rate? It's beating too fast, and your breathing's changed. It's irregular."

"Perhaps my heart is beating fast and my breathing is irregular because a scary werewolf has me cornered in a dark hallway."

I moved closer, my chest pressing into hers. "I really hate to be lied to. Tell me, what were you looking for?"

Skylar tried to slip away, but I pressed even harder, pinning her. Her body stiffened against mine, but a faint tremble of fear betrayed her faux resolve. I smiled at her false bravado.

Her tongue brushed lightly over her parted lips. "I want to talk to Josh," she admitted.

I listened to her heart until I was confident she was finally telling the truth. "No. Not today."

"Yes," she said defiantly, despite her obvious fear. "Today, and preferably now if you can make that happen."

This time I allowed her to slip out from under me, but I caught her arm, gave it a quick, hard squeeze so that she understood I was allowing her to escape. "No."

"If he's here, why do I have to wait until tomorrow? Why can't we just get this over with tonight?"

"Because," I said, stifling a satisfied grin at her growing frustration.

Skylar guffawed. "This is bullsh—"

"Skylar, you will speak to Josh when it is time. Throwing a tantrum isn't going to change things. Go to sleep."

She answered with a hate-filled glare. I scowled back at her. Did she need a stronger reminder of her place? "Go to the room or—" Frustrated, I held my tongue, not wanting to escalate the situation further. Her ignorance of pack hierarchy was no excuse for her childish defiance, but she had proved herself today. She had been resilient, decisive, and loyal. And she had killed. Her first kill. I sighed, calming myself. "Okay. You can speak with him tomorrow morning. Good night." Drawing on every ounce of self-control available to me, I turned and walked away.

In the morning, I led Josh through the library to the door of the study, where Skylar and Joan were waiting on the other side. "While I appreciate your confidence in your ability to charm women," I told my brother, not bothering to mask my sarcasm, "winning Skylar's trust has been ..." I grimaced, choosing my words carefully. "She is stubborn beyond all reason."

Josh answered with a boyish grin. "After dealing with you, I'm sure she hates us."

Scowling, I pointedly opened the door and entered first. The study was a unique room within the retreat, specifically designed to provide tranquility to anyone in need. Like all were-animals, pack members tended toward emotional reactions, often accompanied by violent outbursts. Over time, blood had been spilled in every room in the retreat but this one. The furnishings here were comfortable and light in color—two overstuffed, soft gray sofas placed on either side of the room. On the walls hung framed nature scenes—the sun setting, birds flying through a clear sky, a deer drinking from a river surrounded by mountains. Sunlight peeked into the room between light gray and silver panel curtains.

The room was not chosen by chance for this introduction. Skylar was on her guard with the pack. Even Steven had not entirely earned her trust. We needed Skylar to trust Josh. To that end, he strolled into the room behind me, thumbs hooked into the pockets of his jeans and a slight smirk on his face.

Skylar was already in the room, standing between the couches. To my irritation, her eyes lit up as she saw Josh, her expression vacillating between surprise, confusion, and raw attraction. She glanced between my brother and me, as if assessing whether we, with our divergent styles, could actually be brothers. At times, I wondered myself.

"The woman of my dreams," Josh said smoothly as he approached Skylar with his arms casually outstretched. Not surprisingly, she reacted shyly, attempting to back away, but

Josh persisted in invading her personal space. "May I?" he asked. Before she could reply, he placed his palms over her cheeks, gazing deeply into her eyes as he gently brushed his fingertips along her temples to her jaw. He grinned at her, amused. "So you're the little lady who's been causing the big uproar."

"Are you getting anything?" I asked, urging my brother to get to the point. Earning Skylar's confidence didn't require such a grotesque display.

Josh rolled his eyes at me, sighed, and shook his head slowly. "How many times do I have to tell you that I don't get visions from touch? They come to me in my dreams. I was just taking this opportunity to play with the beauty from my dreams." He turned back to Skylar, who took a few cautious steps away from him.

"I've had enough of this," I muttered, turning to leave the room when the door slammed shut in front of me.

"Stay," Josh demanded in a taunting voice, glancing over his shoulder at me.

"Oh look"—I gestured toward the door—"cute magic tricks. I didn't realize the circus was in town."

"I probably can make a clown appear. Would you like that?"

My brother could be even more willful than Skylar. At the moment, he was putting on quite a display. "Well, if that's the best you can do, I think I will have to pass. Perhaps Skylar will find your performance amusing." I left, slamming the door behind me. A few minutes later, I was passing through the entertainment room when I glanced outside the windows to the front of the retreat. Skylar appeared in Josh's arms in the driveway—blinking into existence, and then disappearing just as suddenly. I shook my head and continued on to the gym.

· · ·

The next morning, I heard from Joan. The Southern Pack was aware of Thomas, though they had no dealings with the warlock, who mostly kept to himself. As she provided no reason to cancel the journey, I accepted Joan's travel arrangements. Her choice of boarding was less than desirable on a personal level, but practical. Owen's property was secluded, unlikely to be watched by anyone observing the pack, and close to the island. We took the short plane flight to Savannah and picked up a rental car for the remainder of the journey. Steven rode next to me in the passenger seat, while Skylar and Josh sat next to each other in the back.

"There's no one following us," Josh said after glancing over his shoulder a number of times. "Ethan, slow down before you get us all killed."

I scowled at Josh through the rearview mirror, a warning he discarded with a dismissive gesture.

A few minutes later I felt the SUV conspicuously slowing, despite my steady pressure on the gas pedal. I pressed down and felt the SUV try and fail to accelerate. "Josh."

He responded from a daze. "Hmm? Oh, sorry. I was distracted by the terrain whizzing by."

Josh gestured, and I felt the SUV come back into my control. Fifteen minutes later, the SUV slowed again.

"Josh!" I snapped.

He smirked at me through the mirror. "The goal is to get there in one piece, Ethan."

"All of us, or just you?"

Josh turned to Skylar. "My brother likes to control everything. Ethan"—he gestured to his messy, spiked hair—"do I have a hair out of place?"

I squeezed the steering wheel with white knuckles. "If you're uncomfortable with my driving, I can leave you at the side of the road."

"Somehow, I think Thomas will respond better to me."

Through tremendous effort, I managed to hold my

tongue and we finished the rest of the eighty-mile journey in relative silence, eventually arriving at a white ranch-style house surrounded by a wraparound porch. As I parked, Owen emerged from the house, sauntering toward the SUV to greet us. By design, he appeared to be the quintessential Southern gentleman, but looks were deceiving. To me, he was a slender fuck, with the lifeless eyes of a shark and mud-colored hair. I took great pleasure in watching his congenial smile waver as I emerged from the SUV. Hesitating, his body became rigid, but he quickly recovered, mustering a plastic smile as he continued toward us.

"Ethan," he greeted me in a neutral voice.

"Owen," I answered coolly.

He opened the car door for Skylar, greeting her as she emerged. "Welcome, Skylar. I'm Owen, the pack's host." Judging by Skylar's smile, she bought his charm instantly, perhaps lulled by his Southern drawl. He offered her a limp handshake, and then took her bag for her. After exchanging brief handshakes with Josh and Steven, Owen directed us to his home.

I fell behind, familiarizing myself with the property, noting likely approaches and retreats. Once inside, I made a blatant sweep of the house, not bothering with permission, courtesy, or explanation as I opened doors and checked windows in every room, much to Owen's chagrin. The back of the ranch, as seen through large bay windows, revealed acres and acres of unused land except for a lone peach tree on the far side of a small vegetable garden. I completed my sweep of the rest of the house, and then found Owen with the others in the living room.

"Skylar, you are welcome to stay here as long as required, but I didn't realize there were going to be so many companions." Owen's gaze turned to me, losing all hint of warmth. "Perhaps you can wolf it tonight."

I chuckled. "I don't think that would be a good idea. I

hear you have some very motivated hunters here. But thanks for the suggestion."

Owen's lips pressed together into a thin line. "It's going to be crowded. There are a couple hotels about sixty-five miles away. I wouldn't be offended if you decided to stay elsewhere."

"We'll make do," Josh interrupted before I could answer. "The accommodations here will be just fine. Thank you for offering your home so that we can stay close to our destination."

Owen accepted the pleasantry with a wan smile. "I am going to sleep in my office. Skylar, you will take my room, and there are two spare rooms. You guys sort out who gets the floor," he said, leading us to our accommodations.

"I wouldn't want to inconvenience you," I said. "Skylar will take one of the spare rooms. I will sleep on the sofa."

"I will have no such thing. That's not the way a Southerner treats his guest, especially a beautiful woman such as Skylar."

He left myself, Josh, and Steven in the spare rooms before leading Skylar to the master bedroom. I left my bag in the largest of the two spare rooms. "Of course," Josh grumbled before Steven led him to the smaller room. Ignoring them, I strode along the hall to the master bedroom, where I found Owen and Skylar staring at a hanging portrait of a lion as it emerged from tall, thick grass. Unlike the other rooms, which were painted a neutral khaki, Owen's room was colored in deep greens and light browns, no doubt to simulate the feeling of being in a savannah where the lion could openly roam.

"You're an artist?" Skylar asked, impressed.

"An artist at heart and an accountant by trade," Owen said with false humility. Josh joined me in the doorway, drawing Owen's attention. "Is there something you need?" he asked me in an icy tone.

"Interesting picture," I said. "You seem to have a lot of free time since you transferred from our pack."

"You'll be surprised how much you can accomplish when you're not dealing with political BS and trivial pack responsibilities."

"Yes, it can be burdensome being the strongest pack in the country. It's not a responsibility that just anyone can handle." I withheld my satisfied smile as Owen approached me, fingers squeezing into fists. I relished the challenge, but Josh intervened, slipping between us.

"It's been a long day for all of us," Josh said. "We have a ferry to catch tomorrow, and Ethan, you have a pretty long drive yourself. We should get some shut-eye. Now."

Owen calmed himself with relative ease, no doubt grateful for the intervention. That was him in a nutshell, always posturing but rarely sincere. He cared more about appearances than substance, which is what made him a weak Beta before I defeated him and took his place as the Beta of the Midwest Pack. I took his woman, as well. Instead of fighting to the death, as I would have chosen in his place, he tucked tail and fled to the Southern Pack here in Georgia.

I gave him a smug, knowing look before backing out of the room. "Skylar, I'm right next door if you need anything."

"Okay," she answered, confused.

Owen snorted. "She's just as safe here as she would be in the retreat home in Illinois."

"I just wanted her to know I was close. After all, that is my job as the Beta," I said, and then left. Josh followed me, no doubt to keep me from turning back.

The next morning I dropped Skylar, Josh, and Steven off at the ferry. "You're not coming?" Skylar asked, perplexed, as I remained in the driver's seat, the engine running.

I looked to Josh, letting him know his ass was on the line if any harm came to her.

"He's got something less important to do," my brother said dismissively, turning his back on me as he strode toward the ferry that was making a final call for passengers.

For a moment, I considered joining them. If something went wrong with Thomas and I wasn't there ... but Josh was best equipped to deal with a warlock. He was powerful, a fact I would never directly admit to my brother—he had enough ego as it was. As the oldest, I should have inherited our mother's magical talent, but the same magic that made me a werewolf prevented me from being a witch. I was made of magic, but I couldn't wield it. So my mother's abilities passed to Josh. He relished the power—sometimes too much.

Once I saw the ferry disembark, I put the SUV into gear and made the long drive south to Jekyll Island, wondering how McClintock would react to my presence. After some careful probing, Joan had confirmed the old hunter's presence. She had also recommended I stay clear of Jekyll Island as long as McClintock was there. But if anyone knew what Chris was up to, it was her old ... hunter partner, the one she had briefly taken up with after her mentor, Ryan, had died. Getting McClintock to tell me without using violence was going to be the hard part.

Once on the island, I drove to the most secluded corner, where the road was barely more than a trail flanked by live oak trees draped with Spanish moss. Had it not been for my GPS, I would've missed the turnoff, which was expertly camouflaged with dead brush. McClintock didn't want visitors. No surprise there. After clearing the debris, I honked the horn—three long bursts—to announce myself, and then waited. It didn't pay to surprise people who lived removed from society. McClintock had more reason than most to be anxious, and he was much deadlier. After a few minutes, I slowly drove the uneven dirt road that lead to a dilapidated, rustic bungalow with a crumbling roof. Dust and debris littered the roofed veranda that wrapped around the front and one side of the bungalow. An old wooden chair sat crooked with a broken leg. The front door was ajar, hinges creaking as the door swayed in the breeze. Perhaps Joan's intelligence was wrong. McClintock had any number of safe houses. Even if he was in Georgia, I would likely never find him.

I emerged from the SUV, cautiously checking my flanks for an ambush. The bungalow was dark and quiet, without signs of recent activity. As I neared the porch, I was met by the familiar scent of dead meat wafting on the breeze from inside. Instantly alert, I charged into the doorway, only to pull up short at the wrong end of a double barrel shotgun. On the other end of the barrels was a young woman with steady chocolate eyes, a dark complexion, and black hair tightly bound in a tactical bun. She wore a SWAT-style bulletproof vest and black cargo pants.

"The slightest move," she said, finger wrapped around the trigger. Her eyes and hands were steady. I would not be her first kill.

"Ethan." McClintock emerged from a side room wearing a plain green tee, black cargo pants, and the smug expression of a hunter who had finally caught his prey. McClintock's face was lean but aging, with a prominent scar that cut from the bridge of his nose across one shallow cheek—that was new. The long hair I remembered was more gray than black, and trimmed to a military cut. "If you came for violence," he said, "you are woefully unprepared."

"Tell the girl to put the shotgun down," I growled, "before she gets hurt."

"The *girl's* name is Tonya," McClintock admonished me, "and the shotgun stays just where it is. You were-types are hard to kill, but I find that blowing the head off your shoulders pretty much does the trick." He tipped his head back, staring down his nose at me as if deciphering a puzzle. "What are you up to, Ethan?"

Despite the exterior damage to the roof, the ceiling showed no signs of leaking. In fact, the interior of the bungalow was orderly and well-maintained. *Clever.* "I came alone."

"Oh, I know that. I've been tracking you since you drove onto my island. I ask again, why? I should point out that when I say 'ask,' I mean 'demand.' That's just my way of being polite before I order Tonya to splatter your brains onto the wall behind you. Won't be the first time she's taken such drastic action. Which reminds me, Tonya: after the cleanup we really should paint that wall a dark red."

"I'll go to the store," Tonya said, eyes unblinking behind the shotgun receiver.

"We'll rob the coin jar. Hell, get some ice cream while you're at it."

"McClintock," I growled. "I don't have time for this."

"Oh, well I'm sorry about that. I'll just drop my guard and break out the Earl Grey. The last time we fought, Ethan, you said the next time I see you will be—what was it—my 'last two seconds on earth.' Tonya—"

"I'm here about Chris," I said.

McClintock studied me a moment, then grunted. At a gesture from him, Tonya took two steps back, and then lowered the shotgun to a ready position, tilted down at forty-five degrees. She kept one hand wrapped around the barrels and a finger laid against the trigger guard. From that position, she would be able to transition from guard to assault in less than a second. The old hunter pulled out two chairs from a simple square dining table, gestured to one, and then sat at the other with his legs spread wide and his hands in his lap, waiting. I would be sitting with my back to the door, and to Tonya. I turned the chair at an angle, allowing me at least a peripheral view of the front door, but she still had the advantage. McClintock rose and retrieved two bottles of beer from the fridge, popped the caps, and then placed one in front of me.

"What's she done now?" he asked, sitting.

I figured there was a fifty-fifty chance he already knew, but I was going to have to play his game. It was expected. "Chris is looking for trouble in the wrong place. Maybe I can spare her that trouble."

He made an exasperated smacking sound with his tongue and lips. "Chris and I parted ways a long time ago."

My jaw clenched. "But you still see her."

He smirked. "You never let go of anything, do you? It's nothing new under the sun, Ethan. Relationships get complicated and then they end. I hear from her from time to time, mostly just to exchange recipes. If you didn't come to carry out your threats against my well-being, I fear you wasted a whole lot of gas getting to Jekyll Island from Chicago. Perhaps you came for the fishing? Everybody does. Can't say I enjoy it much. Not really a hunter's game. I like bear, or wolf," he added, his expression suddenly cold. He glanced over my shoulder toward Tonya, but that was just to make me nervous. Probably.

I sighed, tired of McClintock's game. "The vampires in Chicago are becoming aggressive, and Chris is arming herself with silver weapons."

"Maybe it's just a coincidence," McClintock said, unconvinced. "Maybe Chris is gunning just for you."

"Our parting was mutually agreed upon."

He snorted derisively. "Tonya, what's the saying about a woman scorned?"

"Hell hath no fury like," she said.

"Ethan, you're a badass. I'll give you that. But you're not the smartest turnip in the ground when it comes to women. She may have agreed to walk away—might even have demanded it—but you still let Chris go."

Was Chris hunting me? If so, she had had plenty of opportunities to make her kill. I had no doubt Chris might accept my name as a target—for the right price—but I doubted she would pursue me for some perceived slight. "This is something else."

"Okay, Ethan." McClintock smiled crookedly over the lip of his beer, and then drank half of it in one swig.

I resisted the urge to tell him where to go just before I beat him down. "I don't want to hurt Chris, but she's into something that's going to bring us into conflict—a conflict she will not win. If you still care about her—"

"Hell, I loved her."

"Then tell me what you know, or help me find her."

"I'm old news, Ethan. Ask that Owen fella."

"No need," I said.

"Did you finally hunt him down and finish the job?"

I shook my head once. "Chris would never go back to him."

The old hunter glanced at his hands and smiled. "Being a human hunter offers an unhealthy share of risks. Everything out there is stronger, or faster, or has some special power. All we have"—McClintock gestured to himself and Tonya—"is a unique skill set. Chris is obsessed with gaining the upper hand, as I'm sure you're already aware."

"She wanted me to change her."

"And of course, you refused."

"I did."

"Well, there are other options, aren't there."

I refused to believe Chris could be that foolish.

McClintock drank the rest of his beer and then swapped his empty bottle for my full one. "Looks like you're done with your beer, so I expect you are done with your questions as well."

I rose with a smirk. There wasn't anything else to learn from the old man. "Next time," I said, gave Tonya a look that finally broke through her calm demeanor, and then strode out of the bungalow.

While I waited in my SUV, watching the ferry deliver Skylar, Josh, and Steven from Sapelo Island, my phone rang. "Artemis," I answered tightly.

"Ethan," the were-fox answered, overemphasizing the syllables as if distinct words. She had a tendency to speak as if every word that came out of her mouth was important. "I got what you're looking for." *And you're going to pay a lot for it,* her tone conveyed. Lone were-animals were fickle beasts, with no loyalty or code of conduct to ground their character, but some had their uses. Artemis was a wily character, with eyes and ears in all sorts of useful places.

"I'm waiting," I said.

"Patience buys wisdom, but neither words nor deeds. I'll sell you words, but at triple the usual price."

I growled my displeasure.

"You've got another source?" Artemis asked. "Don't mind me. I just adore wiling away my time on your behalf, and all for nothing. Aren't I generous? Your little girl is clever. Perhaps someone less reliable will find your answers for you, but I doubt it."

Given the dearth of information in my possession, I had no choice. "It had better be worth it."

Greed added excitement to Artemis's voice. "Your girl has been recruiting." She paused for dramatic effect. "Were-animals. Particularly ones who might feel a tad bit resentful of you and yours. There is a mage, as well. She must've given him a pretty penny as he initially didn't want to get involved. I guess she values his talents more than he values his hide. Now tell me those little nuggets aren't worth triple."

I scowled. "I'll make the transfer to your account."

Artemis hesitated. "Did I say triple?" she chuckled. "I believe I meant to say quintuple. Perhaps—"

I killed the call.

The ride back to Owen's was silent. Josh was pensive. Skylar and Steven appeared curious and confused. I waited until Josh and I were alone in the yard to receive his report. Instead, he handed me a piece of paper that portrayed a poorly drawn stone with a series of rings surrounding it.

"What is this?" I asked.

"At this point, your guess would be as good as mine," Josh breathed out, frustrated. "Demetrius had it on in the dreams. It's newly acquired, and I am willing to bet it's the reason for his newfound interest in Skylar. I just don't know what it is or what it's used for."

I held up the piece of paper. "That's it?"

"It's more than we knew before we got here. What about you?"

"Never mind." I folded the drawing and returned it to him.

"This works a lot better if we share." After meeting my silent stare, he added, "You don't trust me."

"This mission is on a need-to-know basis, Josh. When you need to know, I'll tell you."

"Ethan—"

"I may have been followed. I want you and Steven to take the SUV, check the surrounding roads for any abandoned vehicles on the shoulder. Get it done now."

I strode toward the house, irritated to find Owen on the porch next to Skylar—too close—staring at me with naked derision. "We are leaving tonight," I announced.

Owen stopped me as I strode into the house. "Where are they going?" he asked, gesturing to the SUV as Steven and Josh drove back down the driveway.

"They're going to meet with someone," I lied—flagrantly.

Owen tensed. He didn't like being out of the loop. "Who?"

"Don't know."

"It's not typical for a Beta not to know what's going on in his pack."

"It's not typical for one who isn't a Beta to care so much," I said matter-of-factly as I guided a confused Skylar into the house, leaving Owen behind to stew.

CHAPTER 7

$\mathcal{U}$pon our return to the retreat, the debriefing with Sebastian was a short-lived affair. All we had was the diagram of an object no one could identify—progress, but hardly a success. My visit with McClintock hadn't fared any better. There was nothing to do now but wait: wait for Josh to identify the object; wait for Chris to activate her plan, whatever that might be. Ignoring my hunger, I changed and took my frustrations out on a punching bag in the gym. I was just breaking a sweat when Winter found me.

"Just got a text message from Jeffrey," she said, holding up her phone. "Chris picked up her order."

Sparing only a glance, I kept my focus on the bag. "You trust the blacksmith to follow through on my instructions?"

She smirked. "Jeffrey just about shit his pants when you threatened him. I'd say he's highly motivated to please you."

I grunted, burying a quick combination of punches into the bag and ending with a kick.

"You know Chris is targeting you, right?"

Seems likely. I let loose with another combination of blows. McClintock had failed to give me any actionable intelligence, but he did manage to clarify Chris's attitude toward me, which he at least believed to be more hostile than I'd anticipated. Even in the best of times, I had known Chris could betray me for the right price. I had to assume now that the price had lowered considerably. While I preferred to be more proactive, protecting Skylar was the pack priority, and I had no idea where to start hunting for Chris. I would have to wait for her to act on her plan, which could prove deadly. Assuming I survived, the time to track down her employer and clarify my position on the matter would come later.

"I can hunt for Chris," Winter offered, "while you're stuck with the little girl."

There was no mistake in Winter's tone. She was offering to kill my ex-lover. Before I could object, Josh appeared in the doorway looking grim, a large book at his side. "I found it." He strode toward me, ignoring Winter entirely.

"What has she done now?" I asked. In answer, Josh held up the ancient-seeming book with both hands. Instead of a straightforward explanation, I was getting dramatics. "What is it?"

"*Symbols of Death*," Josh said ominously.

A minute later the three of us were meeting with Sebastian in his office. Josh opened the old book to a marked page that displayed a drawing of a large, red gemstone enclosed in a series of brass rings. There was no description, just a title written in a cryptic language. Josh explained, "The book is a catalog of powerful items that can be used to call forth death in a variety of manners—all nasty. In my journey with Thomas I saw Demetrius wearing this. It's called the Gem of Levage."

"What is the Gem's power?" I asked, dreading the answer.

Josh ruffled his disheveled hair. "I don't know." He gestured at the page. "The author was somewhat vague on description. The objects in this book are rare and very powerful. That Demetrius even has possession of the gem should frighten us all."

"Should I kill Skylar now, or wait until she's asleep?" Winter asked. "I vote now."

Josh met Winter's matter-of-fact expression with disbelief. "Whatever role Skylar is meant to play, the Gem of Levage is at the center of Demetrius's scheme. Killing Skylar would only slow him down, and we'd still have to deal with the Gem."

Attacking the Seethe would be risky. Most likely Demetrius would keep the Gem close, but we would need better intelligence, probably reinforcements, before considering an attack. Even if successful, the inevitable counterattack could prove challenging. Sebastian and I locked gazes, our thoughts in synch.

"Josh, is there a way to determine the Gem's power?" Sebastian asked. He was asking whether we went to war now, or waited in the hopes that revealing the purpose of the Gem could give the pack an advantage before we struck.

Josh absently bit at his fingernails as he pondered options he obviously didn't like. "Given the Gem deals in death, I'd say our best option would be to consult with a necromancer."

"No," I said flatly. I didn't trust magic in general, and necromancy was at the bottom of my list.

Josh sighed, showing his weariness. "Perhaps you'd like to consult with the Creed. I'm sure Marcia would love to help."

I scowled, showing him my displeasure. I trusted Marcia and the Creed—the ruling council of the witches—even less than I trusted necromancers. So far, Josh's options were going from bad to worse, and his delivery needed a bit more respect, a detail I planned to discuss with him at an appropriate time.

The next day, I brought up the Jeep Wrangler. Steven and Skylar climbed into the backseat, while Josh ignored my invitation to take the passenger seat. "Ethan, I can't tell you

85

where we're going." I chuckled at first, convinced that my brother was playing some childish game to irritate me, but his usual easygoing cheerfulness had been replaced by a tense, troubled expression. Reluctantly, I gave him the keys and kept my questions to myself—requiring an enormous effort on my part. As Josh drove, I found myself unconsciously tapping a phantom brake, or willing my brother to change lanes. Not knowing our destination only deepened my frustration as I recalculated the possibilities with every course adjustment. No doubt my brother noticed my discomfort but determined to withhold his usual, playful sarcasm. His mood declined with every mile.

Eventually Josh delivered us to what seemed a vacant office building in Layton, a suburban city outside of Chicago. He led us to a door, where he hesitated, his fingers drumming on *Symbols of Death* as he seemed to reconsider his plan. Having rarely seen him so intensely conflicted, I chose to keep my doubts to myself while I waited for his decision. After some deliberation, he led us inside. At my signal, Steven remained behind as Josh led us past a number of vacant offices until we reached a door labeled Nathan Green, PA. Inside, the lobby was vacant and dark except for a splinter of light that emerged from an office door that was slightly ajar. Josh led us inside, not bothering to knock.

Nathan Green was a tall man, ghostly thin, with a craggy face. He looked up with cold, purple eyes from the papers on his desk, seemingly unsurprised by our intrusion. As his gaze found Skylar, the necromancer's expression took on a curiosity that quickly transformed into revulsion, and then abhorrence, before he brought himself under control.

"Josh, is it?" Nathan asked, offering my brother a thin, jagged scowl. "I told you over the phone that I couldn't help you."

"I didn't believe you then and I don't believe you now," Josh said sharply as he opened the book for Nathan's inspection. For a moment, the necromancer refused to acknowledge the book, instead choosing to trade tense glares with my brother. Eventually resigned, Nathan gave a discontented smack of his lips before turning his gaze to the book, but not before stealing another glance at Skylar. "I found this in *Symbols of Death*," Josh explained. "It's the Gem of Levage."

"I can read Latin, thank you," Nathan snapped, scanning the picture with a casual indifference.

"I need to know what it is used for. As a necromancer, you are quite versed in the objects used for ritualistic death and the other purposes they serve. What are its purposes and why is it important to Demetrius?"

"I have no answers for you," Nathan stated tersely as he rose to his feet, rounding his desk to place his focus squarely on Skylar. A low, indistinct chant emerged from his lips. Frightened by his approach, she took a step back. Josh appeared shocked. I stepped protectively in front of her, ready to snap the necromancer's twiglike neck.

"She shouldn't be here," he said, his voice rising in anger as he continued toward Skylar, so mesmerized by her that I wasn't sure if he saw me in the way.

I growled a final warning, balling my hands into fists, when Josh rushed to intervene, extending his arm to bar Nathan's path. "Tell me about the Gem," Josh insisted, his tone threatening.

Nathan's agitation grew. "She shouldn't be here," he insisted as if Josh should understand. Nathan's body tensed. His eyes lowered as he once more started his inaudible chanting.

"Stop it!" Josh snapped. "She is not one of yours to command."

The chanting stopped, leaving the necromancer perplexed. "I sense the presence of the lifeless upon her, yet she doesn't respond to my call."

"She cannot be called by you. I need to know what her relationship is to the Gem of Levage," Josh insisted.

"Do you have the Gem?" Nathan asked, his gaze remaining fixed on Skylar behind me.

"No, but I believe Demetrius has it."

Nathan's gaze snapped to Josh, chin rising, eyes widening as fear overcame him like a wave. His heart leapt, beating with the furious intensity of a Taiko drum. Sensing an opportunity, I strode menacingly toward the necromancer. "It will be in your best interest to start giving some answers."

"Why haven't you taken her life?" Nathan's bewilderment quickly turned to a building rage. "She should not be here! You have been irresponsible for allowing her to live. Her sergence is wrong! It's all wrong. There's a void. She cannot be here!"

"Why shouldn't I be here?" Skylar demanded from behind me. I heard her start for the necromancer, but a look from Josh stopped her.

Skylar had a way of being infuriating, but I wondered what it was about her that could push a necromancer to the edge of panic, demanding her death? I saw the tension in his body just before he snatched a knifelike letter opener from his desktop and lunged for Skylar. Like all fools, he led with the knife, making it easy for me to turn his wrist, breaking his grip so that the knife clattered across the floor. Using the pressure on his wrist, I turned him and drove him to the floor, drawing his arm behind his back. Holding him there, I growled through clenched teeth, inches from his face, "You have only two options now: answer the damn question, or let me beat you to inches from death, and then answer the question. Either way, you will answer the fucking question." For emphasis, I bent his arm almost to the breaking point, but the necromancer pressed his lips together, stubbornly refusing to even utter a breath. I was going to carry through on my promise when I caught a familiar, light floral scent, followed by a velvety female voice behind me.

"Ethan, I see your skills of persuasion still leave much to be desired."

Not now. Not here. How did she get past Steven? "Chris." I turned to find my ex-lover's lethal, umber eyes staring at me over a crossbow. Her other hand held a pistol aimed at Josh. Chris was as beautiful as I remembered with flawless, toasted-almond skin. Dark brown hair tucked neatly behind her ear, drawing attention to her heart-shaped face. Instinctively, my eyes scanned her sculpted figure, remembering every inch of her.

"Ethan, now you have two choices, sweetie. You can save yourself and your brother and let me have the little wolf, or you both can die in a very painful and bloody manner—after which I will ultimately get the little wolf."

If Skylar is her target ... I grimaced, realizing who Chris was working for.

"Knowing you, of course you are going to do the heroic thing and risk injury to yourself to save your brother and the little damsel in distress." Chris rolled her eyes. "It's so textbook, Ethan, that it's rather boring. Let me warn you. I've made upgrades for you seemingly invincible were-types." She stepped closer, her movements lithe beneath tight jeans. "This cute little silver arrow is just long enough to travel to the spine, destroying all those wonderful vital organs in the process. Just for fun, it explodes into little silver shards, releasing neurotoxins that will wreak havoc on your nervous center while the silver prevents you from healing. Even Dr. Baker and his godlike talents won't be able to save you."

I caught a subtle shift in Josh's expression—confidence. I didn't know if he could throw up a ward or a field in time, or if he had some other magic prepared, but he clearly didn't feel he was in danger, which gave me some latitude to deal with Chris. First, I needed to get her off her guard. "That's counting that your skills with the crossbow have improved," I taunted her. She never missed. "But it couldn't get any worse."

She smiled. "Oh, how I've missed you, love."

I've missed you, as well.

"I'm pretty sure I can shoot you from this distance without a problem. This doesn't have to end ugly. Give me Skylar, and you and your brother get to leave with your lives. I will sweeten the deal by directing you to the guy who makes these handy little arrows—"

"We've already met. If you take a closer look at the arrow you'll find that it's not the original one you agreed to. I had him make a few little changes before I strongly encouraged him to seek another career path. He felt the need to leave the city."

While Chris's smile remained, the clench of her jaw betrayed her doubt until she finally made an exasperated sound, and then shrugged. "Oh well, then I guess I will leave you to grieve the life of your brother." She turned to Josh, adjusting the aim of her pistol at my brother's head. I rose, releasing Nathan, intent on taking Chris down, when Skylar inexplicably put herself between Chris and Josh. *No!* I wanted to scream. Josh scowled behind Skylar. Though her hands trembled, she stared down the barrel of Chris's pistol, and I knew Skylar would take a bullet for him if necessary. Her gesture was brave, endearing, baffling, and infuriating.

Chris laughed. "Oh, how cute. She values your brother's life. Isn't she the most adorable brave wolf. Honey, I just need you alive. It doesn't matter what condition I bring you in. I have no problem injuring you. Maybe if you were injured, you would be a little more compliant."

"Kill her!" Nathan scrambled to his feet, pleading. "You have to kill her! Demetrius cannot have her!" Seeing that Chris had no such intention, he moved to take the matter into his own hands until Chris turned the crossbow and shot him in his opening mouth. Nathan's head snapped back and then exploded in a shower of toxic silver shards, spraying myself, Josh, and Skylar with blood and gory debris. Skylar gaped in horrified disbelief as Nathan's body collapsed, the remaining soft tissue of his head melting down to his skull.

"You liar!" Chris glared at me, fuming. "That was supposed to be my gift to you."

I shrugged, keenly aware that she maintained a steady aim at Skylar's head. I needed to keep her focused on me. "You can be a bitch at times, but you were never thorough. You always check just one. The one to your far left. So I left you one, to humor you. I never felt you were a threat to me and mine. Contrary to what you believe, you've never been a good shot with them. I am simply amazed that you were somewhat efficient this time."

"It was that bitchiness that made you fall in love with me," Chris purred.

I crossed my arms and smiled as we stared each other down. She was in her element now, a determined predator—foiled temporarily, but she still held Skylar's life in her hands. Other hunters would have cut and run, but not Chris. Chris didn't fail. She got what she wanted, and in that moment I wasn't sure if I wanted to kill her or take her on the floor. Judging by the fiery passion in her glare, she struggled with the same dilemma. Looking into those gorgeous umber eyes, I remembered every scream, every moan, every rake of her nails on my skin. I forgot about Skylar, the Gem, and my brother as the room seemed to dissolve around me, leaving just the gravity that drew Chris and me together.

Josh let out an irritated sound, snapping me from my reverie. Ignoring the pistol, he crossed the room to stare down at Nathan's corpse. Chris tracked his movement with the weapon. "Oh, Chris, just give it a break," he snapped. "You're a hot woman, despite the fact you've just threatened to kill me and my brother. You're a bitch, which probably means you are a great lay. I suspect that's the only reason you and my brother lasted as long as you did. I don't give a crap about you and my brother's relationship, including the ridiculous unresolved feelings you two seem to have. What I want to know is how does a hunter become a lackey for Demetrius?" He stared down the barrel of her pistol. "It's rather beneath you, don't you think?"

"Lackey?" Moving inhumanly fast, Chris dropped the crossbow and grabbed Skylar from behind, digging her fingers firmly into Skylar's carotid artery as she trained the pistol once more at Josh's head. Her speed surprised us all, leaving Skylar blinking and clutching at the hand around her neck as she began to lose consciousness.

"She'll be out soon," Chris warned me. "Just let me leave with her and I promise your brother will live."

I took a step toward Chris to test her resolve and got the answer I expected. Judging by her speed, it was clear that Demetrius was offering Chris more than money—he was offering her what I had refused to give.

"Come on Ethan, it's your brother."

I glared back at her, calculating the chances I could dispossess Chris of the gun and Skylar without harm coming to her or my brother. Whatever Josh had in mind, neither of us had counted on Chris's enhanced speed, which made the situation much more dangerous. She was going to force me to make a decision—sacrifice my obligation to the pack or sacrifice my brother. I refused to give in to her demands, but I needed a solution. I needed options. I couldn't allow Skylar to fall into Demetrius's hands. Caught between awful possibilities, I noticed Steven, crouched, sneaking into the room behind Chris.

"You want me to believe that your commitment to the pack is greater than that to your only brother?" she asked.

Steven pounced, knocking the pistol from Chris's grip and throwing her backward to the floor. Skylar collapsed, nearly striking the floor before Steven caught her. "Stay down!" he barked at Chris. She sprang up and ran for the door. Surprised by her speed, Steven was barely able to grab her, but she twisted his arm and pushed him back into Skylar before making her escape.

I ran after her, emerging from the building to find her waiting in the middle of the parking lot. I charged, but she evaded me easily, stopping a dozen yards away. I charged again and once more she evaded me, this time remaining just out of arm's reach.

"Sure you want to play?" she asked coyly.

"You're feeding from him," I growled. "Demetrius."

"Give Skylar up, Ethan. Before the pack suffers. Demetrius won't stop until he has the girl, and neither will I. Sorry, love." She sprayed an aerosol at my nose, and then sped off. Before I could give chase, the aerosol did its work, burning my nostrils with a wretched, overwhelming stench that made it impossible for me to follow Chris's scent. I growled, trying to blow out and wipe off the irritant that inflamed my nostrils. Cursing myself for letting her get away, I punched the Wrangler. Not only had Chris gotten the best of me, she had nearly taken Skylar thanks to her foolish bravado.

The others emerged in a rush, but said nothing when I ordered them into the Wrangler. Once we were on the highway, Josh turned in the driver's seat to snap at Skylar. "What the hell was that?"

She squinted at him, confused. "What?"

"That dumbass stunt you pulled," I added from the passenger seat. "It's bad enough we have to protect you from the vampires, a hunter, but now from your stupidity as well. Must I give you lessons in safety and self-preservation? Let me help you with common sense: don't step in front of sharp objects, bullets, or anything in the firearm family because they can actually kill you! Or do you think of yourself as invincible?"

"Demetrius wants me alive. She wasn't going to kill me, but I wasn't so sure about Josh. While you were busy having verbal foreplay and making goo-goo eyes with your ex, I thought it would be a good idea not to let him get shot in the process. And since you feel so inclined to give me lessons in self-preservation, maybe I should give you some in appropriate choices. For instance, when your ex is threatening to kill your brother, it's not a good idea to provoke her. Just a little suggestion."

We glared at each other.

Josh sighed beside me. "The situation would have been handled."

"Before or after she used your face for target practice? I didn't realize you fancied being shot. I will remember that," Skylar snapped.

Josh rolled his eyes, while Steven suppressed a laugh.

"Just don't do anything like that again." I received an exasperated sigh in response from Skylar, which only infuriated me more.

The rest of the drive was spent in sullen silence until Josh said, "Chris has switched teams."

I nodded slowly, unable to hide my disgust. "She's trading now. I smelled Demetrius all over her. She was always too fast to be just human, but now she's ..." My voice trailed off, unable to put words to Chris's abomination.

"She's a vampire?" Skylar offered, sarcastic.

I growled.

Steven clarified in a low whisper. "She's performing blood exchanges with Demetrius. Through the exchange, she gains some of his abilities, like the supernatural speed exhibited today."

"She found a loophole, I guess," Josh added, throwing me an accusatory glance. "She always wanted the speed, strength, and advanced healing abilities of were-animals without the sun-vulnerability that the vamps have."

"Josh, don't," I warned him through clenched teeth. This wasn't the time, but of course he persisted.

"Chris was going to get what she wanted by any means. You should've just changed—"

"I said *don't*." I gave my brother a baleful glare, leaving no room to doubt the harm I would do if he continued. He got the message, begrudgingly.

Back at the retreat, Skylar went sullenly to her room while Josh and I went to find Sebastian. "Are we including the part about Chris?" my brother asked smugly.

I gripped his arm tightly, turning him. "Never withhold anything from Sebastian." I jabbed a thick finger into his chest, forcing him back a step. His initial surprise turned to resentment as we glared at each other. The intensity of my anger was misplaced, but Josh needed to understand his position. As blood ally of the pack, he carried the same obligation of loyalty that I did. Withholding knowledge that was necessary for the pack's safety was a serious offense. After what seemed an endless battle of glares, Hannah interrupted us passing by.

"Sebastian?" I growled. She gestured toward the gym, where we found him lifting free weights.

After giving our report, he announced, "It's time Skylar understood what we're facing."

"I'll take care of it," I said, turning to leave.

"Ethan." Sebastian's expression was soft, compassionate. "This can't be a confrontation."

"I'll be nice," I growled.

"Josh has some rapport with Skylar that is—shall we say —unencumbered."

I scowled from Sebastian to Josh, wishing I could knock

the smirk from the latter's lips. "You can listen outside the door," Josh offered. With no other choice, I followed him to the kitchen where he mixed two fruity cocktails, each with a healthy pour of vodka.

"You're going to get Skylar drunk?"

"Trust me," Josh said tiredly, "you may be a big bad wolf, but you've got a lot to learn about human nature."

I snorted derisively. Once Josh finished, I followed Skylar's scent to the sunroom where she stood with her arms folded over her chest, lost in reverie. I could see in her hollow expression that the events at the necromancer's office had left her traumatized. Josh and Sebastian were right. In this moment Skylar needed empathy, while I could barely stop myself from shaking some sense into her.

A wink to me, and then Josh strode into the room with drinks in hand and cheesy charm on full display. I had no idea why women responded to that, but Skylar welcomed him. "Here. You look like you need this." I heard the clink of ice, followed by a soft sip, and then a harsh cough that could only be Skylar.

Not a drinker, then. I stifled an unexpected chuckle.

When the cough had resolved, Skylar asked, "Josh, what's wrong with my sergence and why shouldn't I be here?"

Josh answered with silence. Curious, I began to peer around the doorway when I realized that my brother had positioned himself so that Skylar, facing him, was facing the doorway. For a moment, I thought she had seen me. *He did that on purpose.* I scowled. *Could have just as easily gotten her back to the door.* My brother loved his games.

"Josh," Skylar prodded.

"Nathan is—*was* very talented. Most necromancers can read your sergence—your aura. Nathan was one of the most gifted. Many of them can't detect witches and mages, but he could."

"My sergence is wrong, so wrong that he wants to kill me?"

I heard Josh take a long drink before answering, his voice troubled. "No—let's just say it's murky. No one has a sense of what you really are—it's troubling. You're a were-animal but you have a terait. In the corner of your right pupil, there's an orange quarter ring. Ethan noticed it the first day you arrived. I saw it yesterday. It's only seen in vampires and half-breeds when their bloodlust hasn't been fulfilled."

"Bloodlust?" she asked, surprised. "Should I have a bloodlust?"

"I'm sure you do. But I doubt it would overtake you as it would a vampire or even a dhampir because your survival isn't based on its consumption. I'm sure a rare steak would satisfy your lust for an indefinite period of time."

Now it was Skylar's turn to be silent, but not for long. "So what does this mean?" she asked.

Josh sounded apologetic as he answered. "By all accounts, you shouldn't exist. . . ."

"I'm not a vampire. I couldn't be cursed to be both—I just couldn't." She took a deep drink of her vodka to bolster her nerves—this time, without coughing.

"Were-animals have natural immunity and can't be changed into vampires."

"Then can you explain this terait that seems to warrant me dying for?"

"I don't know," Josh admitted, his voice thick with frustration.

"Could I be like this if one of my birth parents were a vampire?"

More silence from Josh, and then, "The probability is highly unlikely. Vampires maintain their ability to procreate about a week after being changed. Unless your mother was pregnant with you when she was changed, you couldn't be the offspring of a vampire. Becoming a vampire requires death of the human body and rebirth into the vampirism. It's a process that takes several days, and I doubt the most resilient child could survive it. To my knowledge, there aren't any known cases of a child surviving as a result of a vampire mother. All known dhampirs are the result of a new male vampire and a human mother. But if you were a dhampir, you would not be a were-animal. Were-animals and vampires/dhampirs have mated in the past, but there has never been anything documented nor even a plausible rumor that supports that an actual birth occurred. The conflicting processes kill the child."

"So I am an anomaly that shouldn't exist."

"You're an anomaly that does exist. Just like in the human world, anomalies exist all the time. Maybe not to this extent, but they do."

"Perhaps that is the reason Demetrius wants me: to either be part of his Seethe or to get rid of me because I am an anomaly?"

Josh chuckled. "I can assure you that they don't want you in their Seethe. They don't regard dhampirs. You are tainted with the blood of the were-animal. Centuries ago, they punished their own for fraternizing with were-animals, and a tryst of a sexual nature was penalized with death. That is not the case now, but they have extreme superiority complexes. They would never accept you as one of theirs. Demetrius prohibits association with dhampirs because he considers them 'deplorable half-breeds' and just as revolting as were-animals. It's rumored that Demetrius killed the children, the mothers, and the vampires for producing such half-breeds. It's rumored that he even killed his own and its mother. I assume the stories are true because new vampires are quite impulsive and reckless, yet exhibit extraordinary control when it comes to reproduction. Like were-animals, control usually comes with age and experience. I can only speculate what and who is responsible for compelling such control in young and inexperienced vampires."

Unable to contain my curiosity, I peered into the doorway to see Josh pacing, anxiously biting on his nails. Skylar followed him with her eyes, her arms wrapped protectively around herself.

Josh continued as he paced. "They tried to abduct you, not kill you, when they attacked. Under any other circumstance, you would have been under their radar and barely worth acknowledging. In my dreams, there is a distinct feeling of desire. They want you for something that will benefit them—that's the only reason they care that you exist. I need to figure out the link between you, Demetrius, and the Gem of Levage."

"And Chris? How worried should I be about her?"

"No worries. As long as you stay here, you're fine. She wouldn't attack you here."

"I shouldn't worry about Ethan's ex-lover? Then maybe I should worry about Ethan?"

Josh scowled, eyes flaring. "Don't ever underestimate my brother. He wouldn't let anything like an ex-lover keep him from doing his job well."

"Sorry. I wasn't trying ... I didn't mean to imply anything bad," Skylar mumbled.

"It's cool." Josh threw me a meaningful glance over her shoulder. "Be assured that the turbulent thing they once called a relationship won't keep either one of them from doing what they set out to do."

"What were they like together?"

Josh chuckled. "The two of them together were like watching a forest fire and a tornado consume the same space. We watched their relationship crash and burn with morbid fascination. Their fights were so intense that you wondered who was going to snap first and kill the other person. And their make-ups were so passionate they could melt the paint off the wall." He looked away, his attention focused on his empty glass as he grew pensive. "They shouldn't have been together. I think for that very reason, they tried so hard to make it work. Neither one of them was willing to admit defeat as they should. But eventually, Chris saw it for what it really was and ended it. The love or whatever you would call what they had won't prevent them from doing what needs to be done. They were always odd that way."

Not needing to hear more, I quietly walked away.

By morning, my anger at Skylar had subsided, replaced with a curious empathy. Despite the flawed logic, she had once again put her life at risk to help the pack, in this case to save my brother. She was an oddity to me, a contradiction that left me entranced and infuriated in alternating breaths. She was caught up in a world she didn't understand and that threatened to kill her at every turn. I would do better to control my anger, to show some compassion.

When she didn't appear for breakfast, I sent Steven with a tray of steak and eggs. A short time after breakfast, I discovered her lurking outside the closed door of Sebastian's office. At my presence, she appeared startled, reserved, looking to the office door as if surprised to find it there.

"How are you feeling?" I asked as sincerely as possible, though I could hardly hide my discomfort. "Did you sleep well?"

"Fine," she answered tersely, starting to leave.

"You can knock. He is in." She stopped to stare at me, as if deciding whether or not I was tricking her. Her heart was racing, not the resolute beat of anger but the rapid flutter of fear. My eyes narrowed as I studied her, noting the ready-to-go appearance of her dress. "You are going to ask to leave the retreat."

Her jaw set, suddenly defiant. "What I ask Sebastian is between him and me."

I chuckled. "Go ahead. After Chicago, there is nothing you could say to convince Sebastian to allow another foolish trip. He isn't that easily swayed." I gestured toward the door, grateful to leave her rebuke to Sebastian, and casually walked away with my hands in my pockets.

An hour later, I was driving Skylar toward her home in Chicago. I didn't know how she'd done it, and the look on Sebastian's face when he'd given me the news left no room for questions. Not wanting to vent my frustration at Skylar, I turned up the radio in the Range Rover, burying my anger beneath the grinding guitar and pounding drums and straining vocals of my preferred hard rock band. But I couldn't help myself. Beneath the music, I tapped my finger against the steering wheel to the beat of Skylar's heart, ratcheting up her irritation as she stared out the window trying to appear unperturbed.

The few times our gazes met during the journey, my attention wandered to the terait in the corner of her right eye. As we entered the Chicago suburbs, I asked, "If Nathan hadn't attacked you, would we be doing this?"

Skylar didn't turn from her window. "I don't know."

"I asked you not to lie to me."

"No."

"What do you plan to gain from obtaining these personal items? The wheels are in motion. It won't change anything, Skylar." I turned the Range Rover into the driveway of her mother's house, turned off the engine, and waited, staring expectantly at her.

"I know," she answered sheepishly.

"Then why waste my time?" As she stared at the house, I could see the sad longing overwhelming her expression.

"Ethan, I would never choose to waste your time. Any issues you have with being here should be taken up with Sebastian. I never asked for you to be my escort." She exited and cautiously strode to the repaired front door, hesitating for a moment at the top of the porch. I joined her in time to see her fingers trembling as she unlocked the door and stepped inside.

Josh had used his magic to clean the house, removing the debris from the fight along with any hint of blood, DNA, or fingerprints, but the scent of Skylar's mother remained. Skylar detected it as well. The longing and sadness in her expression were plain.

"Who came back here?" she asked, distracting herself.

"Josh put up a ward that restricts vampires and others from entering your home without an invitation. There is a similar one on the retreat."

I watched painful memories play across her countenance until she wrapped her arms around herself and sighed. "I have to go upstairs."

I remained downstairs. The house was secure, and her need for privacy was plain. I had no idea how to comfort her in her grief. Death had long been familiar to me, but I wasn't so jaded that I couldn't recognize how difficult this trip was for Skylar. Perhaps she'd brought us here to retrieve something valuable, as she'd expressed. Perhaps she'd brought us here simply so that she could grieve. I turned a couch, giving myself a view to the top of the stairs. From my vantage point I saw her open a door and hesitate. She loitered in that doorway for several minutes, seemingly working up the nerve to go inside. I heard the pained beat of her heart as if she were standing next to me. The tension in her shoulders melted just before she finally surrendered to her fear and disappeared into the room. When the sobbing began a moment later, I quietly climbed the stairway, driven more by a sense that my presence was needed than by any idea what assistance I could provide. I was drawn to Skylar with the singular, uncomfortable desire to somehow ease her pain.

I found her sitting slumped at the edge of a bed, her shoulders heaving and twitching with the ebb and flow of the sobbing that overwhelmed her. When she finally looked up, her eyes were red and grief-stricken with a pain so deep and vast that I couldn't hold her gaze. I was reduced to a schoolboy, staring at the floor and fidgeting with my hands in my pockets. There was something I should say, I was sure, but I couldn't find the words.

"I'm sorry," she said, wiping tears from her cheeks as she sniffled. "I thought this would be easier."

I stared at her, lost, until it occurred to me to fetch a box of tissues from the neighboring bathroom. I reached out from the doorway to hand her the box, as if the threshold were some sort of magical barrier to my feet. While she blew her nose, I returned to staring at my feet and shifting awkwardly.

"May I have a few minutes?" she asked.

"Of course," I said, hiding my relief. I was halfway down the stairs, eager to gain as much distance from her misery as possible, when I stopped. Reluctantly at first, I returned to the bedroom, knelt in front of her, and rested a hand on her leg, squeezing it lightly. "We should come back another time when you can handle this better," I suggested gently. "It's okay. I won't mind bringing you back later."

She shook her head, offering me a weak, gracious smile. "I'm fine." I knew she was lying. "I will be fine," she explained. "I just need a few minutes."

I nodded and backed out of the room, returning to the couch downstairs. Skylar's few minutes turned into thirty, but I didn't mind waiting. The pack had kept the house under surveillance since her rescue; I knew that Demetrius did not seem to expect Skylar's return here. When she did eventually emerge from the bedroom, she carried a stack of six journals in her bag. "Everything okay?" I asked.

Skylar nodded on her way to the front door. I followed close behind. "I need to go to this address." She handed me a piece of paper.

I frowned at the address on the paper. "Why?"

"I think she can help me."

As we climbed into the Range Rover, I had to read the address once more, to be sure. I shook my head. "That's not a good idea."

"Ethan," Skylar said, exhausted, "I can't do this with you now."

"Then don't."

She rested her head against the headrest and sighed heavily. "I am not asking permission nor will I." Her tone was matter-of-fact.

"I won't let you do this," I insisted.

She studied me for a moment, measuring my resolve as I drove us out of the city. "Okay."

Finally, she's being reasonable. My immediate satisfaction quickly gave way to suspicion, and then apprehension. I glanced at her, taking my eyes from watching the road, trying to gauge her intentions. "That was too easy."

She shrugged. "I just don't have it in me to debate with you now."

Try as I might to accept Skylar's capitulation, I found the ease of her surrender disquieting. By the next traffic light I had lost all confidence. "I don't trust that you will stay put," I said, shaking my head. I picked up the piece of paper, glanced at the address, and then turned the Range Rover around with an illegal U-turn.

"Skylar," I said, moderating the tension in my voice, "you've lived all this time not caring about what you were. Why is this now so important?"

"I did. But that was before my mother was killed,

vampires started stalking me, and necromancers started lobbying for my murder. If these things had never happened, I probably would have gone many more years not caring to learn any more about what I am. I was content with being oblivious. I'm not too proud to admit that maybe I made a big mistake in doing so. Maybe if I had made a point to know my past, then this whole mess wouldn't be happening to me now." She dismissed my response with a gesture. "Perhaps this situation was unavoidable, but I still want to know what I am. Being around you all, I realize how very different I am. Why is my sergence wrong? And the terait? I'm not moon-called—I am moon-tortured. Nathan called me lifeless. I don't know why, but I really would like to find out."

"You are doing this based on the action and the words of a necromancer," I said, incredulous. "Most necromancers are overreactive to the most minor anomalies."

Skylar wanted me to understand. "Ethan, you already admitted that something was different about me. If I'm not mistaken, you weren't too fond of it, either. I'm constantly reminded that I am different, not quite human, were, or other. I feel rejected by so many worlds. I want to know where I belong—I need to know."

I understood her need, somewhat, but answers often came with a price. Did Skylar understand what she was asking? I doubted it. Tre'ases were demons that traded in information, often at a steep price. This particular demon was well known to the pack, though we had no formal dealings with her. Josh and Sebastian would be furious if I allowed Skylar to meet Gloria, but if I stopped her now, she would eventually meet the Tre'ase on her own. At least I could monitor the proceedings, keeping her out of trouble. Perhaps Skylar might even get some answer that would appease her. "It won't change the current circumstances," I said flatly.

"You're probably right."

I parked across the street from the white house with red trim and followed Skylar out of the car. The unkempt stairs had little cracks in the concrete leading up to a discolored and dingy welcome mat. At the door, Skylar put on a brave front, but I knew she was terrified. I knocked. After a moment, we were both relieved that no one answered. Just as we turned away, the door opened, and a stocky older woman with narrow eyeglasses greeted us. Gloria. Tre'ases possessed the power to change their appearance. This version of Gloria wore long salt-and-pepper hair braided and draped over her shoulder. With her advanced age came the mannerisms that conveyed a level of wisdom presumed with age. Regardless of their appearance, all Tre'ases reeked of brimstone and lemon. Gloria was no exception.

Ignoring me, she greeted Skylar with a cool appraisal. "You're back."

"You remember me?" Skylar stammered.

You've met before? I didn't appreciate being left in the dark.

"Of course," Gloria said sweetly, "I receive few visitors."

I wondered if Gloria had worn the same appearance as before. Probably. Skylar had no idea she was already being manipulated. Rather than call the demon out, I chose to let Gloria play her game. For now.

Skylar took a breath to steady her nerves, slowing her heart rate. "Years ago you said that the change had started. What did you mean?"

The old woman stared down a crooked nose at Skylar, studying her with narrowed eyes. "Eight years and now you seek answers, hmm?" She drew her broad lips into a thin smile. "You want answers. Fine. But he can't stay."

Now she notices me. Gloria frowned as our gazes locked in mutual contempt. "Then she won't stay," I said firmly. "Thank you for your time." I took Skylar by the elbow and led her to the Range Rover, but when I opened the passenger door she held her ground. She had that determined look that

106

seemed to cause so many difficulties in my life, of late. "What?" I snapped.

"I want to talk to her."

"You heard her. She won't talk to you with me there."

"Then you will have to stay here ..."

"No!"

"The woman's like a hundred." Skylar gestured broadly toward the house. "I'm sure I can protect myself."

"It doesn't mean she's not dangerous. Most vampires are several hundred years old."

"She's not a vampire."

I shook my head, adamant. "No."

"Ethan?"

"I said no. Now get in," I commanded, climbing into the driver's seat. I glared at her expectantly. In an act of pure defiance, she turned and started back toward the house. She made it halfway to the door before I caught her arm, yanking her to me. "Must you always do the opposite of everything I ask?"

"Must you always be so dogmatic and unreasonable? We are here. What sense does it make to leave now? Just give me twenty minutes. That is all I'm asking. Please." I glared at her, relying on my anger to bend her to my will—it worked with everyone else. Why did she have to be so difficult? "We both know I will return to see her. I don't think she's dangerous, but it would be a hell of a lot better with you available, if needed."

This was my fault. I should've never brought her here. Why did I think I could control any situation that she was involved in? I raked my hands through my hair, frustrated. The moment Skylar had stated her intention to visit Gloria, I should have returned her to the retreat and locked her in a cell. Locking her in a cell was an option still, but somehow Skylar would get out. Somehow, she would have her way and come back here, alone and vulnerable. I released her, cursing under my breath. "You are so frustrating!"

"I know, but I am not trying to be," she said, sincerely apologetic. "It's that horrible side effect of being me." She forced a crooked smile as she backed slowly toward the house. "If I'm not out in twenty minutes, or you hear anything suspicious with that freakish super-hearing of yours, you have my full support to charge in and do your Beta thing and rip apart anything in your way. I know you would like that."

My fists clenched and I felt my teeth grind as I watched her back up to the porch. I didn't need her permission to intervene. At the *slightest* hint of trouble, I would kill the Tre'ase with my bare hands and destroy everything that was hers.

Skylar mouthed a thank-you, offering me a half-smile. I grimaced. She mouthed another thank-you then turned and walked to the door. Before she could knock, Gloria appeared with a self-assured look on her face. "Come in, Skylar," she said, taking off her glasses, and held the door open. I tensed as Skylar disappeared into the Tre'ase's house. Gloria gave me a crooked, insolent smile as she closed the door.

With no other choice but to wait, I set to pacing across the front yard and driveway, muttering, throwing glances at the door and the curtained front window. Looking about the quiet, middle-class neighborhood, I realized a hulking werewolf prowling an old woman's front lawn would draw too much attention. I growled, my ire rising as I limited myself to pacing a small patch of driveway in front of the Range Rover. Somehow, with her willfulness and her snark, Skylar always seemed to get what she wanted. I'd brought her to Gloria thinking I could control the situation, but controlling Skylar without handcuffs and a gag was impossible.

Aware that my anger was peaking toward rage, I paused, drawing deep breaths to calm myself as I stared at the door to Gloria's house, ready to break in at the slightest sign of trouble. Even with my enhanced hearing, I could only just pick out the volume peaks of a conversation—not enough to make out what was being said. Noticing a small gap in the front window curtains, I considered sneaking up to the window for a peek inside, but Gloria would sense my presence. I began to pace again, then caught myself as a young couple jogged by the house, eyeing me with suspicion as they passed.

A moment later, a light appeared in the window, growing in brightness until it shined like the sun. I tensed, resisting the urge to break through the front door. *It's light. It's only light.* Then came a horrific, unearthly sound, followed by a clatter as something fell or broke inside—something heavy. I strode forward, fists clenched, determined to carry out a brutal vengeance if Skylar were injured, when the door opened and Skylar rushed out, nearly colliding into me. A quick review of her figure told me she was okay physically, but badly shaken.

"Let's go," she pleaded, pulling me toward the Range Rover.

I gripped her shoulders, pulling her close enough to feel her body trembling. "What happened?" I demanded.

"I fell out of a chair."

"You're lying." I squeezed her shoulders. "What happened?"

"I fell out of a chair," she insisted, pulling away. I let her go, turning back to confront Gloria.

"Ethan, I simply fell out of the chair. Can we go, please?"

The urgency in Skylar's voice gave me pause. Glancing between her anxious demeanor and the open door of Gloria's house, I made the decision that Skylar's safety was more important. Nothing more was said between us until we had left Gloria's neighborhood. My rising anger was only fueled by Skylar's obvious fear. I was angry at her for her foolishness and angry at myself for letting her out of my sight.

"What happened?" I demanded through gritted teeth.

Skylar turned to gaze out the window. "Nothing," she answered absently, emotionally exhausted from her experience.

"Don't lie to me. If you don't want me to know then just say so."

"I don't want to talk about it."

"Did you find the answers you wanted?"

"I hope not."

CHAPTER 8

*S*kylar was placed on lockdown at the retreat while we waited for Josh to come up with our next move. I didn't expect Chris to risk an attempt to take her from the house, but I expected her to be close, waiting with the relentless patience of a predator to catch her prey unaware. I joined the patrols myself, only once catching the faintest whiff of Chris's perfume at the northern boundary of our property. After two days, Josh called a meeting in Sebastian's office. Winter joined us.

"I confess that the options are limited," Josh said, appearing tired and more disheveled than ever. "Unfortunately, Nathan's reaction to Skylar prevented him from sharing any useful information about Demetrius's plans or the Gem of Levage."

"What was the necromancer's reaction?" Winter asked.

Josh ran his fingers through his hair before answering. "He said that Skylar shouldn't exist, then tried to control her the way he would control the dead."

Winter cocked an eyebrow. "Not to rub it in or anything, but can we revisit the time when I suggested we murder the girl?"

I answered with a low growl, and Winter sighed, bored, glancing at her nails. I turned my frustration on Josh. "Taking Skylar to the necromancer was a mistake that nearly turned into a disaster."

"I wasn't counting on the violent return of your ex-lover," he snapped.

Neither was I. Now that I knew Chris was hunting for Skylar, I felt a new urgency to resolve the situation as quickly as possible. "That Chris is working with Demetrius only demonstrates his resolve to capture Skylar. Our best option is to strike now, before he anticipates an attack."

"You want to take the Gem by force," Sebastian said.

"It will be a simple extraction."

Josh shook his head. "If we knew the precise location of the Gem. It will likely be magically disguised, Ethan. The Gem could appear as a book or a candlestick or a teddy bear, for all we know."

"Then we tear the place apart."

"I know that violence feels good," Josh chided, "but you'll never find it that way."

My jaw clenched. I knew that he was right, but I didn't care to give him the satisfaction. I scowled instead.

"An open assault will start a war with the vampires," Sebastian said, tension plain in his expression.

"We can't wait for Demetrius to hatch his plan," I said. "If we cannot locate the Gem, or discover its weakness, we have to act."

"Again," Winter said flatly, "I say we just kill the girl."

Sebastian sat on the surface of his desk, hands clasped together, considering the implications.

"I have a plan," Josh said. "It's risky, but not as risky as open warfare with the vampires." He shot a sharp glance in my direction.

"I like *my* plan," Winter said, glancing about for someone to agree.

I snapped a gesture at my brother to continue.

"I can form a conduit with Skylar—a blood connection that will temporarily bind us together."

"More magic," I said contemptuously.

"It's what I do, brother. And I'll use every tool at my disposal to help the pack."

"How is a blood connection between you and Skylar going to help?"

"I'll need a third element, a power that I can use to trace the connection between Skylar and Demetrius." Josh ignored my growl. "I'll be able to discover exactly what he wants with Skylar."

"Why didn't we do that in the first place?"

"Because it's risky," he admitted defiantly. "Because that other power will also have a connection to Skylar, for a time. And"—Josh hesitated, just for a moment—"because that other power has to be Caleb."

"No!"

"As always, brother, you're overreacting before you've even heard my explanation."

"Absolutely not," I snarled. "I won't risk it."

"Ethan," Sebastian snapped. I contained myself, but barely.

"Caleb is the scion of Demetrius," Josh continued. "They were together for more than a century before their falling out. Their old bond runs deep."

"Why would Caleb help us?" Sebastian asked.

"Because Caleb is an outcast with a chip on his shoulder."

"How can you trust this vampire?" I demanded.

"I can't." Josh shrugged, offering a weak smile. "But I can trust his desire for revenge against his former master."

I folded my arms over my chest. "Too risky."

"As opposed to war?" Josh scoffed.

Sebastian interrupted. "Can you perform the magic?"

"Yes. At the slightest hint of trouble, I can break the bond.

I am significantly more powerful than Caleb. Skylar will be perfectly safe."

Sebastian considered for a moment. "Ethan," he said soberly, "we must attempt every avenue open to us before resorting to war. But the risk is Skylar's. It is her choice. If Skylar agrees, Ethan, take whomever you need to guarantee her safety." The decision made, Josh and Winter left the room. I stayed behind to further express my concerns, but Sebastian waved me away.

I left the office, furious. I wasn't confident at all that Josh fully understood or cared what he was asking Skylar to risk. Sebastian's decision was final, but that didn't mean I couldn't let my feelings be known. Not surprisingly, I found Josh in Skylar's room. I paused outside the door as he told her, "I need your help." His voice was heavy with fatigue. "I need you to come with me to meet with a source."

My fingers curled into fists.

"Okay," Skylar agreed recklessly. Of course she did. The woman would jump into a fire if Josh asked her to.

"If there were any other way, I assure you I would not have come to you." Josh's tone was soothing, comforting. That's how he got you. A smooth talker, my brother, but just as reckless as Skylar. The two of them were like a runaway train, screaming toward trouble.

"Josh," she said, "I will do whatever is needed in order to end this. It's risky isn't it?"

"Magic will be involved. Very strong magic."

Is there any other kind for you, brother? The clenching spread from my fists to my biceps to my chest.

"You don't like this source," Skylar said.

"I don't like vampires."

Time to have my say. I stepped into the doorway, surprised to find the two of them sitting together cozily on Skylar's bed. I leaned against the doorframe, my arms folded across my chest to emphasize my scowl, enjoying the joint look of surprise that gave way to dread for my brother, who looked like a kid caught stealing candy. "Josh?"

"What?" he snapped through harmless, clenched teeth.

I jerked my head up, ordering him out of the room. What I had to say wasn't for Skylar to hear.

Josh didn't budge. "Ethan, the decision has been made. Sebastian has agreed and she's agreed. Either you get on board or you can take your issues with it somewhere else."

Or there's the other option. "Out here. Now."

He slithered from the bed, his dread giving way to anger that exploded just as he crossed the threshold. No control, that was Josh's problem. That was why he needed to be checked, for his own good.

"What!" he demanded, posturing just outside the doorway. "This is getting so tiring. Do I need to ask your permission to use magic?"

Yes.

"Big brother, may I please use magic today? Pretty please? I'd be ever so grateful."

I snarled in a low voice, mindful of Skylar's proximity, "You're going into the lion's den and asking for his help. Are you insane?"

"Isn't that why you're coming?"

We traded silent glares for a long moment, mine letting him know I was almost out of patience, and he surprisingly didn't back down. "I don't like this," I growled.

"Big surprise. What else is new?"

"I'm not in the mood for your smart-ass mouth."

"And I'm not in the mood for the overbearing big brother thing. What's the purpose of me being part of this if all you want me to do is sit down somewhere and perform minor magic tricks that a child could do? Sebastian offered me an alliance because I can do things you all can't. Let me do what I do best. Okay?" Josh sighed heavily, running a hand through his hair in frustration. "Ethan, I am not going to keep doing this with you. We will not have this discussion again."

"You will have this discussion as many times as I need you to."

"No. I won't. As far as I'm concerned, you can continue this argument alone. Go with us or stay behind and pout, I really don't give a shit." He pushed past me on his way down the stairs.

"Josh!" I shouted. *Don't make me come after you.* "Josh!" I strode to the top of the stairs and shouted once more. When he didn't answer, I was forced to follow. I found him in his room, packing what he needed, petulantly slamming items into a bag. At my approach, his heard turned slightly, refusing to meet my gaze. "We're done talking about this."

I forcefully spun him about, gripping his arm. I pulled his face to within inches of my own. "Never turn your back on me," I warned and released him as he tried to brush my arm aside. "Sebastian has accepted your advice, and so has Skylar. But I am going with you, and we're doing this my way."

"Then what's your problem?" he snapped, reaching to rub his arm where I'd squeezed, but thinking better of it.

I took a moment to calm myself, drawing in my anger. I needed to get through to my brother, to make him come to his senses. As much as I wanted to tear his head off, that wasn't likely to get the job done. "Your advice is not sound. You're playing with magic because you enjoy it, and we can't afford for you to be reckless."

I watched his teeth clench, and then grind side to side before he said, "If you don't trust my advice, then why did you recommend me to Sebastian?"

"Because I wanted to protect you. And you have your uses, but your recklessness—"

"A war with the vampires isn't reckless? How many lives are you willing to throw away for your grim pleasure, Ethan?

Give me time and I'll find the Gem. I'll discover Demetrius's plan for Skylar."

"All you've accomplished so far is to put her at risk."

He took a moment to settle his own rage that was close to exploding. "Caleb was always an option," he insisted. "I know you think otherwise, but I have always had Skylar's safety in mind. But I've run out of options, Ethan. There are no more safe routes. And I'll take magic over your bloodlust any day."

"You think I want a war?" I shouted into his face, tired of arguing. "At least I'm not going to deliver Skylar into the hands of the vampires."

"But you can't keep her safe forever. Eventually Demetrius will get to her." His gaze hardened into an accusation. "Or you'll kill her to stop him."

"If necessary." I would do anything to avoid hurting Skylar, but if her death ever became necessary to protect the pack, it would be swift and painless.

Tension tightened Josh's expression, but he offered a conciliatory tone. "I know that you think I'm taking unnecessary risks—"

"Because you are," I snapped.

"You don't know when to back off, do you? Ethan, I can use Caleb to discover Demetrius's plan, which will give us an advantage. I might even locate the Gem itself. We can save Skylar and the pack. The risks are acceptable."

"And if you're wrong, we walk into a trap. Demetrius wins, and Skylar dies." I held him in my glare long enough to at least partially drill my point into that thick skull of his and then left to prepare for the journey. Three steps beyond the threshold, I realized that I had left Josh's door ajar. I strode back and slammed it hard enough to shake the entire house.

Three hours later, I leaned against the SUV, stewing while Josh and Skylar kept us waiting. Winter studied her phone in the driver's seat while Dakota paced, his unfamiliarity with his human legs apparent in his lumbering stride. We waited nearly an hour before Skylar emerged from the house with His Majesty, the warlock, in tow. She stopped short at the sight of Dakota, having not met him previously since the were-bear generally preferred his animal form. He was well over six feet tall, a hulking, intimidating beast in the form of a man. Josh explained, whispering unnecessarily into Skylar's ear. "He's a bear, a transfer from northern Montana. A couple of years ago, he had some control issues and Sebastian helped him. If he were able to tolerate his human form, he could easily be an Alpha. He's smart, strong, and a born leader, but he is turned off by his humanity. He often stays in the woods in Canada, coming out as needed. Sebastian sent for him a couple of days ago."

Skylar remained wary of the were-bear as she climbed into the back of the SUV. Winter watched her through the rearview mirror, shaking her head contemptuously, no doubt thinking how simple the situation would be if Skylar were dead. I slid into the passenger seat next to Winter, scowling my displeasure. My scowl deepened at her unrepentant shrug, and then I signaled for her to drive.

Forty minutes later, we drove into the outskirts of the city. Following Josh's directions, she parked the SUV outside a gray, two-story stucco house at the end of an eerily quiet cul-de-sac that felt as if the house had slowly strangled the life from the neighborhood. The house itself was dark, sheltered by large trees and manicured privacy hedges that funneled us single file into a narrow, easily defensible path to the front door. Skylar's heartbeat raced as her eyes darted about, wary of trouble. *Good. At least she's taking this seriously.* We were expected, but I remained alert for an ambush. It never paid to trust a vampire. Winter and Dakota kept their eyes on the hedges while I scanned the windows of the upper floor. One window was open, closed curtains swaying with the evening breeze. I remained wary of the window until we reached the door, which was unlocked.

Inside, our footsteps echoed against the marble floors. The living room was hauntingly elegant and lifeless. Too many pieces of furniture and artwork, too much elegance—a vampire's approximation of life remembered through catalogs and Internet searches. Styles varied from one vampire to another, but they all shared a taste for thick, cloying drapes that blocked even a hint of sunlight.

Josh took the lead, navigating through the house as if he'd been here before. I didn't appreciate the implication. At the top of the basement stairs, he stopped to turn on the small wall lamp that barely illuminated the upper portion of the stairway with a faint glow. We followed him down the steep steps, flanked by concrete, until the light from the top of the stairs ceased being effective and he lit the rest of the way with the camera light of his phone. The bottom of the stairway opened into a pitch-black cavern so vast that Josh's phone wasn't enough to illuminate the walls. He pulled Skylar close to him as he gingerly led us deeper into the basement.

Josh had said nothing about taking us into such a vulnerable position, but it was too late to complain. I stifled my irritation, saving it for later. Wariness required my entire focus. I had no idea of our surroundings, and the darkness left us vulnerable from every direction. The entire basement possessed the stale reek of vampires recent and passed rendering that sense useless. I had only my hearing and a truncated field of vision that could give me but a second of warning of betrayal.

A soft, glowing light appeared in the distance like a beacon, drawing us into a large room sparsely lit by muted torchlights. My eyes shifted instinctively to the tall, slender vampire blending into the shadows at the far end of the room. He stood with his back to us, partially camouflaged by black slacks and a black button-down shirt. His long, black hair was bound by a red tie just above the collar. He didn't move from what he must have thought was an artful pose. The rest of the room was shrouded in darkness, hiding any number of dangers.

I didn't like this one bit. What had my brother drawn us into?

"Josh," the vampire said formally, his back still to us.

"Caleb," Josh responded in the same manner.

The vampire turned to address us, revealing a delicate face and crimson eyes. Gaudy red lips curled back into a bloody smile. Either Caleb wanted us to know he had fed recently, or he wanted us to know we were dinner.

"To what do I owe this pleasure?" Caleb asked, taking every opportunity to expose his fangs. He walked toward us with a theatrical gait. "A gift—for me? You shouldn't have," he whispered, moving quickly behind Skylar. I took one step toward breaking the vampire's neck, but Josh halted me with a look. I hesitated against my better judgment, grinding my teeth in frustration, but the surprising calmness of my brother suggested Josh was in control of the situation, and I had to trust him. I gestured to Winter and Dakota to be ready for anything.

"You touch her," Josh stated casually, "and you won't live long enough to savor the taste."

Caleb gave us his best impression of an evil laugh. Everything from his looks to his voice to his mannerisms gave the impression of a vampire who wiled away too many hours watching old gothic horror movies. He was a clown with fangs that even the vampire world would never miss. No wonder he'd been cast out of the Seethe. Even Demetrius had standards.

A faint shuffling sound that surrounded us caught my attention. We were not alone. I stepped closer to Skylar, dropping into a defensive stance. Winter's hand went to the hilt of her dagger while Dakota growled angrily.

"Reveal them," my brother commanded.

Caleb smiled impishly. "It's okay. Show yourselves." At least ten figures closed in around us, just enough to be noticeable in the shadows.

"I see you've been busy growing your family," Josh acknowledged, the sharpness of his glare and tone a warning to Caleb. "The question is: Why are they here? Where's the trust?"

Caleb chuckled. "You, I trust. I don't trust your ill-tempered brother. His reputation of having a short fuse and a violent response is where my trust ends. You brought him into my home and I want to make sure he behaves."

I snorted. "And you think these newbie vamps can make me behave?" Clearly Caleb had no real idea who he was dealing with.

"They'll make every effort to."

They'll make every effort to die. I took several steps toward Caleb to make my point, but Josh put out his arm to stop me, giving me a look that held caution, anger, and warning.

"I need your help," Josh said to Caleb, "and have nothing to gain from violence against you."

Caleb tucked in his chin, his expression doubtful as he studied Josh from beneath long eyelashes. He remained like that for a long time, an undead statue, until he finally said, "Very well." He waved his hand and the other vampires melted back into the shadows, though I assumed they remained close enough to present a danger, if called upon.

"What can I do for my Josh?" Caleb asked in a low, suggestive voice.

Josh frowned as he approached the vampire. "I need you to answer some questions."

"Well of course you do. You never come by just to say 'hello.' Why is that, Josh?" Josh answered the vampire with a disapproving look as Caleb licked his finger then touched it to the air. "Umm, your powers have strengthened since the last time we saw each other. Exciting!"

"Demetrius has the Gem of Levage and he seems to want Skylar. Why? What is the link between Skylar and the Gem?"

Caleb waved his hand dismissively. "The Gem of Levage is a myth."

"I assure you it's not. Demetrius has possession of it and plans to use it. I need to know its function and how Skylar is involved." Josh stepped closer to Caleb, adding a hint of menace to his demand. If I had my way, we would kill Caleb's family and force his compliance. We may have come in peace, but Caleb had already violated that trust.

"How would I know what dwells in the mind of Demetrius?" Caleb challenged.

"Because he is your creator—your father, if you will. Tell me. What's your father up to?"

Caleb's gaze drifted as he began to slowly sway, as if to a violin only he could hear. I resisted the urge to scoff aloud. "You know, I loved him dearly," the vampire admitted softly. "Not the way you would a lover, father, or friend, but the way you love a god. He was indeed my creator, making me something that surpassed all that I could hope for. We spent one hundred and five years together, feeding from whom we chose, taking what and who we wanted. Every desire we could imagine was fulfilled tenfold. It was a life that others only dreamed of." Caleb's expression twisted into a loathsome scowl. "And then she came into it, Lilith. She was a controlling bitch who changed life as I knew it in the worst way. He created her but only lived to please her." He clicked his teeth in disgust, and then soothed himself, resigned to subjugating his story to the distant past. "She wasn't good for him—for us, or the family. She was slowly killing him, but he was too besotted by her to see it. When I killed her, he banished me from his family. He chose her over me!

Hundreds he has created, trying to recreate what we had together. Now he has another, but no one will ever adore him the way I did."

"Must I hear this tale every time we meet?" Josh asked, indifferent. "I grew tired of it the first time."

Caleb drew himself from his reverie to frown at Josh. "I'm sorry that I bored you."

"I need to use you as a conduit."

"What do I get in return?"

"The same payment as usual."

Usual? The vampire's red eyes brightened. His lips spread into a ravenous smile, and I knew exactly what was being offered and accepted. Josh had explained before that the blood of magical beings produced an addictive state of euphoria in vampires. Not only had my brother dealt with Caleb before, but he'd allowed the vampire to feed on him in trade. Josh's recklessness surpassed even my worst suspicions. Only my rising anger overcame my disgust. In proposing this mission, Josh had left out critical information. What else was he hiding? I'd brought Skylar into a dangerous situation I had no control of.

Josh rolled his eyes at Caleb's obvious delight, and then approached Skylar, entirely ignoring my repudiating glare. "I need to use you as well, Skylar," he said in a low voice. He took her hand into his and gave it a reassuring squeeze. Despite the fearful pounding of Skylar's heart, the look she gave my brother was one of complete, naïve trust.

Josh drew a knife from his pocket and reached for the vampire's hand. Shaking his head, Caleb took the knife and sliced it across his own hand, drawing blood, then returned the knife to Josh. Josh gently took Skylar's hand. "It will only hurt for a moment," he promised, but she shrieked as he slid the knife across her palm. I resisted the urge to step between them, to take the knife and lead her out of there. Only Josh's confidence held my reaction in check. And we needed the answers he sought. There would be a time later to express my disappointment in my brother. If his actions led to any harm to Skylar, we would have more than a discussion.

I watched, grinding my teeth as Josh cut his hand, then took the vampire's hand and Skylar's into his. He began a slow chant that quickly accelerated. His body jerked and he rose, suspended in air. A glowing, white light wrapped around him, radiating heat. Without warning, a wild sense of terror and despair rushed into the room, filling it. Josh crashed to the floor, triggering a powerful force that knocked me to the ground along with everyone else. My first instinct was to reach Skylar, to shield her from whatever danger would follow, but I was pinned by the invisible force.

"Make it stop," I heard her plead. Then she screamed, terrified by pain or fear or both. "No!" she shouted, and then became silent.

Every muscle strained against the magical force as I struggled to rise, only managing to turn to find Caleb draped over Skylar's rigid body, sinking his teeth into her wrist. Her face was frozen in horror as if paralyzed. I roared rage at the force that refused to release me, every muscle in my body straining nearly to the breaking point. Josh appeared, yanking Caleb away from Skylar, then releasing a fiery force that threw the vampire to the wall beneath the torch.

Josh knelt, taking Skylar's writhing body in his arms, attempting to soothe her. I faintly heard his whisper, "*A-na rische.* Release," and her agony stopped. The force that pinned us to the ground was lifted, but Skylar still seemed partially paralyzed, gasping for breath.

I jumped to my feet along with Winter and Dakota, ready for Caleb's vampires to make their move, but there was no sign of them as Josh crossed the room toward their master, two fingers pointed toward Caleb as he used magic to pin him against the wall. The vampire struggled in vain to break free. Before Josh could make his demands, Skylar's pain-filled shrieks filled the room, a wave of force that violently shook the house, knocking everyone but Josh once more to the floor. Struggling to rise, I watched him rush to Skylar. Gripping her shoulder, he began a chant. After a moment, she seemed to relax. The room stopped shaking as she breathed easier.

I rose to kneel next to her. A quick examination revealed no obvious physical damage. "Are you okay?" I asked, brushing sweat-drenched hair from her face.

She nodded slowly, still catching her breath.

"We're leaving," I snapped at Josh.

"You cannot leave without rendering payment!" Caleb yelled.

Josh turned to face the vampire, radiating rage with a force I'd never felt from him. For the first time, I saw my brother on the cusp of losing all control as his anger seemed to surge and pulse. A gasp from Skylar, and I realized that the force emitting from Josh was crushing her. "Josh," I said, careful not to push him over the edge. I scooped Skylar into my arms, holding her tightly to my chest. She dug her nails into my flesh as her body contorted in pain. "Josh, you're hurting Skylar."

He calmed himself, and I felt the release of pressure in Skylar's body. I stood, turning back the way we came.

"Payment forfeited," Josh declared, his tone full of venom. "You went after her. Count yourself fortunate that you are left with the sorry existence you call a life. You won't be so lucky in the future."

Enraged, Caleb stomped toward us, his fangs exposed, but he stopped at a rolling growl from Dakota that reverberated throughout the room. The were-bear grabbed Caleb with both hands and threw him into the concrete wall. While Dakota continued to express our displeasure, I carried Skylar out of the house, drawing Winter and Josh in my wake. At the SUV, we waited a few minutes before Dakota returned, his eyes no longer exhibiting anything remotely human. The hinges of the door screamed as he forcibly opened it. "As you wished, his life has been spared, though barely," he informed Josh.

The ride home was quiet thanks to the smothering pall of repressed rage that filled the SUV. My rage. I turned to glare at Josh, at the same time surveying him for any signs of damage. He appeared unhurt. After a moment, he met my gaze with a weary challenge. Holding his attention, my gaze shifted to the bite wound on Skylar's wrist, and then back to my brother, who seemed too exhausted to answer my accusation. Which pissed me off further. I was going to have my say, but not here, not in front of the others. I had no choice but to swallow my rage and bide my time.

At the retreat, Skylar headed straight toward her room until I stopped her. "You've been bitten. Dr. Baker will examine you, first."

"It's not even bleeding anymore." She dismissed my concern with a casual gesture. "I just need some sleep."

"You will see. Dr. Baker. First."

"What's the big deal? I can't be turned. It's just a—"

"For any other were, you would be correct." The doctor appeared and I directed him to Skylar's wound, to which he gave due attention.

"It's no big deal, right?" she asked, expecting Dr. Baker to take her side.

"That will take some observation. You have a terait. I'm afraid this bite puts us into uncharted territory. Let's get you to my office as quickly as possible."

"Can I sleep there?" Skylar asked, pouting as she was led away.

When I turned back to Josh, he was gone. I began to follow his scent when I decided we might both need time to cool off before I knocked some sense into him. I took my frustration to the gym. After several hours of hard work, I resolved that imagining my brother's face on the punching bag only deepened my anger. It wasn't until the evening that Doctor Baker cleared Skylar of any danger, to my surprised relief. That concern assuaged, I needed only a few minutes to find Josh in his private study on the other side of the library. He was half asleep, his feet propped onto a table, a tome open in his lap. I slapped his feet to the floor, jolting him awake. Instantly alert, he jumped to his feet. His eyes focused on me and his mouth soured into a jagged scowl.

"I am not in the mood, Ethan. It's been a long day."

"You're damn right it has!" I exploded, jabbing a finger into my brother's chest. "What was Caleb's price?"

"That's my business."

"Are you letting vampires feed off you now?"

He turned from me, circling the table to casually gather his books. What he really wanted was to put the table between us. "My magic affects my blood. It gives them a sense of euphoria." He chuckled softly. "Apparently I am quite the rage."

I threw the table aside with one hand and got into his smug face, glaring down at him. "You throw your life away on stupid risks, Josh. Smarten up, before you get yourself and the rest of us killed."

"I was in control the entire time," he insisted indifferently, as if my nose wasn't inches from his.

"Like when you knocked us all to the floor with your rage? You nearly crushed Skylar with your power. What the hell was that? You didn't have control of the situation. You told me you knew how to do conduits, and obviously, you didn't know what the hell you were doing! We could have been hurt tonight, and you could have been killed."

"Well, in theory I did know how to do it," he said far too casually for my liking. "It's not like I ever had the opportunity to practice."

"You were reckless and put us all in danger. You asked me

to trust you and let you do your job. Well, I did, and you screwed up! I should have been informed of all possible outcomes and potential risks."

Finally, Josh gave in to his anger. His expression twisted into a bitter snarl. "Why did I have to tell you anything? You couldn't have done a damn thing about it! You're just upset because my magic is one of the few things in this house that you can't control. That is the only reason you have your panties in a bunch and that is just too goddamn bad. Go cry about it to someone who gives a shit. I did my fucking job! Are you doing yours? I wasn't aware that being a ranting ass was part of the Beta duties, but if it is, you are doing a hell of a job! We have information that we didn't have and otherwise would not have gotten, information that will help us. And if I weren't down here playing around with you, I could be doing my research and finishing my job."

Every muscle in my body clenched, screaming to teach my brother a lesson he would not long forget. *You never learn. You push and you poke and you incite, yet you have no idea just how badly I could hurt you.* I snatched his collar, pulling him close enough to give him a microscopic view of my teeth as I snarled into his face. It was that or start punching. If he wasn't family ... "Don't push me, Josh. You won't like it when I push back."

"Go ahead and push." He grinned. "I've just been itching to show you what'll happen when you do."

I was considering whether to give him the satisfaction when his eyes flashed. I felt a force break my grip, pushing me back a few feet. After a second my eyes recovered from the flash and I saw Josh's smug expression, nodding at me as if he had proven something remarkable. "I did what was necessary and got the job done," he claimed. "You think you could have gotten the same results storming into Caleb's home ranting, threatening, and beating him up? Sorry, but that tactic doesn't always work. Accept the fact that I achieved something you couldn't have. If your pride is a little battered, then that's your problem!"

"You smug, arrogant son of a bitch!"

"Really. Smug? Arrogant? Surely, that is the pot calling out the kettle. Son of a bitch? That is no way to talk about our mother." Josh relaxed with the quip, returning to his infuriatingly calm, overly confident self, which managed to make him even more infuriating. Up to that moment, I had exercised a great deal of reserve, giving deference to my younger brother, but this was the last straw. Roaring my rage, I pushed him back hard enough to send him crashing into the wall, but not before he got off a spell. I easily deflected the flying chair with a sweep of my arm. In the blink of an eye, I had Josh on the floor, pressing my forearm into his chest. "I'm not fucking impressed with any of the hack magic you managed to pull over these last couple of months. It's still amateurish at best."

"Let's see what I can do about changing your mind."

Somehow, he managed to push me off. I was rising when a stronger magical force hit me, knocking me back into the wall and pinning me there. He stood with two fingers extended toward me, the same gesture he had used with Caleb. My brother had grown in power. Judging by the smirk on his face as he watched me struggle to break the field, he thought he had finally balanced the power dynamic between us, but that was unacceptable. For a moment it seemed I was trapped, but Josh wasn't the only one with a trick up his sleeve. As he swaggered toward me to gloat, I gathered myself. Focusing my intent into a single, violent scream I broke through his field and punched him in his smug lips, hoping to break his perfect teeth. While he was stunned I took him by the shoulders, meaning to throw him against the wall, but in my rage I drove him straight into the heavy door —through the door, actually. We tumbled onto the floor outside. Lost in my rage, I was up and charging him again. So violent had been my intent that I bounced off the ward he managed to cast, sending me flying in the opposite direction. But I would not be beaten by my brother. Not now. Not ever. I charged again, this time prepared. The magical ward that encased Josh's body shattered against my will as I took him by the shirt collar, snarling into his face as he gripped my collar, screaming his own rage. That's where we were when a woman screamed, shocking us both.

"Stop it!"

Still gripping each other, we turned to see Skylar near the broken door, horrified. How long had she been there?

"Ethan. Josh. Stop it! What the hell is wrong with you two?" She stepped closer, cautiously determined. And pissed.

An overwhelmingly powerful presence of authority quickly filled the room, stifling me. Sebastian. I saw his arrival in Skylar's eyes, but felt it first. It seemed our little fight had woken the entire retreat, as the rest of the pack arrived as well, responding to Sebastian's silent call. Josh and I yielded to the Alpha's authority, but not to each other, continuing to exchange glares, promising each other that this fight wasn't resolved. Sebastian stepped between us, pushing our chests apart—a simple gesture with enough power to send us clattering to the floor.

Josh sat still, meeting Sebastian's eyes for only a moment before turning his gaze to the floor in tacit acknowledgment of the pack leader's authority. I should have submitted as well, but my rage churned my blood into a furious river. I rose, eying my brother for another charge when I caught Sebastian's gaze. I held it for a moment while I struggled to rein in my anger, my behavior bordering on a challenge before I finally turned my gaze back to my brother, who glared back. *Admit when you're beaten;* but Josh was far too stubborn, challenging me with his eyes.

"Enough," Sebastian commanded sharply. "Ethan, the conduit was risky but it was necessary and you are going to have to let it go. Inevitably, some of the things Josh does will present us with unavoidable risk. It's magic. It will always have its hazards. This is not new to you and it doesn't change because he is your brother. We have to trust him and grant him the necessary autonomy to allow him to do his job. He has never failed us. You are going to back off." The pack master's tone was unmistakable. I nodded, matching Josh's glower with my own, my jaw clamped tightly shut. Finally, I was compelled to break my gaze from Josh's. No doubt Josh considered my reaction a victory, but it was the only way to bring myself under some level of control.

"And you," Sebastian said to Josh. "Stop being an ass. He's been your brother for twenty-four years, and you know how protective he is when it comes to you. Would it hurt you to give him a heads-up when you know things are going to get a little crazy? He deserves that much. You didn't give him proper disclosure, and you were wrong for that. He has every right to be pissed with you right now. When you know he's pissed with you, leave him the hell alone! Don't antagonize him. It's juvenile. This fighting between you two is no longer entertaining—it's just ridiculous and annoying. He's your brother, but my Beta, and you will respect him as such."

After a long silence, I heard Josh answer in a constrained voice. "Are we done here?"

I turned to look as Sebastian nodded, and Josh strode from the room, petulantly throwing doors open and closed with magic until he left the house and drove off in his Wrangler.

With Sebastian's permission, I returned to my room, leaving Skylar to clean up the mess of broken furniture left behind from the fight, grumbling something unpleasant about brothers in the process.

CHAPTER 9

he basement gym was divided into three workout rooms. One room was set up like a typical modern gym with cardio equipment and weight machines. The other room was old-school, equipped like a boxing gym with metal barbells and free weights, a punching bag in one corner and a heavy bag in the other. The third room, lined with mirrors, contained a large mat that smelled of old blood and sweat. In the corner stood a well-stocked, glass-front weapons cabinet. The gym was devoid of clocks and televisions.

Untold time passed as I worked out my frustration, alternating between weights, cardio, and the bags until nothing existed but the workout. I was murdering the heavy punching bag, shirtless and coated with sweat, when Skylar entered the gym in sweatpants and a t-shirt. I continued venting my frustrations into the bag, ignoring her, but then I noticed her slowly backing out of the gym. I knew that I intimidated her. There were times when that was useful, but this wasn't one of those times.

"Come in," I said as graciously as I could manage. She hesitated, eyeing the exit, then returned to the gym. Giving her space, I returned to the bag, punching and kicking in shifting patterns until I finally exhausted myself. I leaned into the bag to stop it swaying on its chain and stayed there, engrossed in my body's recovery from the exertion. After a moment, I realized Skylar was studying me while pretending to explore the gym. "Speak."

"What?"

"I can hear your heart racing and your breathing is slightly ragged. You have something to say. So say it."

"I think you were too hard on your brother," she muttered cautiously, gazing down at her fidgeting hands.

I walked toward her, picking up a towel to dry myself along the way. I stopped a few feet from her, listening to her heart and watching her fidget. When she looked up, her green eyes widened at the sight of me, and I heard her heart skip a beat. I lowered my towel, allowing her a proper look. "Was I?"

"Yeah." She nodded, swallowing, before forcibly averting her gaze. "I don't see what was so bad that would warrant you going off the way that you did."

I watched her, as much considering her statement as I was enjoying the way her eyes tried to wander for a second look, but she was determined to deny me the satisfaction. "He was rash and irresponsible," I said, finally.

"Josh is extremely powerful, isn't he?"

"He's been gifted with abilities that exceed most," I admitted reluctantly.

"You're quite modest," Skylar snarked. "I've seen him in action. He's powerful—very powerful. What would you have him do? Sit back and not use his gifts to help when needed? You wouldn't tolerate that, so why expect that from him?"

I rubbed sweat off my face, frustrated. The battle of wills between my brother and me was complex, dating back further than I could remember. "You wouldn't understand."

"You don't trust him."

"Of course I trust him," I snapped. *He's my brother.* But I

133

knew my brother's weaknesses, which could be dangerous if not properly checked.

"Then you should start acting like it. Were there other options, safer options that he ignored? Or did he do what was necessary in this situation to get results?"

I exhaled heavily. "Being a warlock isn't like being a were-animal. No matter how inept you are as a were-animal, eventually you can control your animal. With magic, there are too many unknown variables that can change the outcome. It's the little variables that you don't think about that are the difference between life and death. I don't like it." *Josh could get himself killed by a simple mistake.* I checked myself, aware that I was revealing too much as Skylar's expression softened.

"Everything has risk, including being a were-animal. He shouldn't have to deal with your anger every time things don't go as expected. It's not fair to him. I am willing to bet if things went wrong while you were in were-animal form, he would never react the way you did."

I'm not reckless. I prepared for every contingency imaginable, while my brother operated by the seat of his pants. I acted out of necessity, while Josh used magic because it excited him. Skylar's defense of my brother baffled me. Watching her, I could see the concern was genuine. "You surprise me sometimes."

She blinked. "Pleasantly, I hope."

I smiled. "What was it like, being swept into magic like that?"

Her expression tightened at the painful memory. I saw the debate in her face, heard the argument in her heart as she considered lying to me. Perhaps she didn't want to spark my anger at Josh, or was there something else she was hiding? I stepped closer to her. My fingers gently trailed along the line of her jaw while I studied her. "No need to tell your lie," I said softly, "or even the modified version of your truth. The answers are in the panic in your eyes, the rapid heartbeat of your anxiety." I stepped even closer, our chests touching as I brushed her cheek with my lips. "It's in the set of your jaw, clenching at the very idea of reliving that moment." I took her arm in my hand, gently stroking my thumb along the pulse. "Your skin, it's cool." I lifted her wrist to my face and inhaled her scent, brushing her wrist with my lips. "And fear can be sensed by a predator no matter how faint." She opened her mouth to answer me, but I cut her off. "You were going to lie to me," I cautioned.

"No, I wasn't," she stammered, rattled at being so naked.

I smiled with amusement as I brought her hand to my lips and gently kissed her palm, inhaling her once more. My other hand slipped around her waist, pulling her against me. She didn't resist. "Of course you would have. But why? Would it have been to protect Josh from his tyrant of a brother, or to ease my concerns about my audacious brother?"

Skylar shook her head lightly. "Your parents must have had hell to pay when you found out the truth about Santa Claus and the Tooth Fairy."

A genuine laugh was a rarity for me, but I laughed then. For all the frustration she caused, Skylar continued to surprise me. I bent to kiss her waiting lips when the hairs twitched on the back of my neck. An overwhelming hostility enveloped me. Josh was behind me, standing in the doorway of the gym, glaring. I knew even before I turned my gaze to confirm his presence. His expression was twisted into disbelief as he fixated on the closeness of my body to Skylar, her hand in mine, her waist in my hand. Suddenly self-conscious, she withdrew her body from mine, but remained in my embrace. I kissed her hand once more before releasing her.

"You broke my protective field," Josh stated, his tone low and sullen.

"It was just a simple ward. Not very hard to break." I shrugged dismissively, offering my brother an opportunity to save face. He was worked up, but I hoped he had the good sense not to pursue the issue in front of Skylar, who didn't need to know our family business. My efforts only served to stoke his ire.

His jaw clenched before he burst, shouting, "Don't screw with me! That wasn't just a ward. It was a protective field, and there wasn't anything simple about it. A were-animal has never been able—"

"Josh," I said softly, attempting to deescalate the situation. I tipped my head toward Skylar, which she noticed. I stepped closer to him, my demeanor deliberately calm and casual. "Your field was nothing more than a glorified ward. We break them all the time. Sebastian's broken them, Gavin's broken them, and even Hannah's broken one. It's just a broken ward. Let it go."

Our gazes locked, mine steady and his twitching, his pupils dilated. This was as much about the fight upstairs as it was about how I'd broken his field. I had spent hours expending my anger in the gym, but he had spent his time stewing. I could feel the tension in his body, unconsciously preparing to fight, but I had no interest in continuing our previous battle. I watched the tension play in his eyes, refusing to match it with my own. I remained calm, unaffected by his anger. After a moment, his rage finally broke like a fire starved of oxygen. The tension dissipated as his head tilted, considering the plausibility of my excuse. He grimaced, then gave a light shake of his head. "No. You're hiding things from me. How long—"

I turned away from him to see the fear in Skylar's eyes as she waited for my brother and I to kill each other.

"Good night, Skylar." Josh's tone was sharp, but it did the job as she left the gym, though I doubted she went far.

I stepped over the threshold and found her climbing the stairs at a snail's pace until I caught her attention, speeding her along with my glare. Only when I heard the basement door shut did I turn back to my brother, who watched me with a skeptical expression.

"Ethan, what are you hiding?"

"You can't leave well enough alone, can you," I said, walking to the free weights.

He followed. "Why won't you tell me?"

"Because some things are better left unsaid." I picked up a dumbbell and began pumping my right bicep.

"The magic that makes werewolves possible is enough to break most wards, but you would need greater magic to break a field—any field. Werewolves can't hold that level of magic. Unless you're carrying some sort of enchanted artifact—"

"You got me." I grunted as I brought the weight to my shoulder, and then lowered it. "It's my shoelaces."

He ignored my sarcasm. "You've got some magical ability. Which we both know is impossible."

"Glad you worked it out." I grunted against the burn in my bicep as I lowered the weight again. "Don't let the door hit you on the way out."

He turned, pensively stroking his chin as he walked away. I heard the low mutter of a chant just before I felt the temperature of my skin rise, creating a faint glow that seemed brighter beneath the sweat of my chest and arms and everywhere else my skin showed, which was just about everywhere. "Dammit," I snapped, letting the weight drop to the floor with a crash.

Josh turned sharply, his eyes brightening in disbelief.

"Turn it off," I growled, scratching at the heat in my chest that was just enough to be uncomfortable.

A quick gesture and a muttered phrase from him and the temperature of my skin returned to normal. "If I cast that spell on any other were-animal it would be a waste of breath. When our mother died, as the eldest you should've received her magical talent. Instead, that talent passed to me."

137

"Yes. You're a powerful warlock, Josh, let it go."

"But you did receive some of Mother's ability."

"Yes," I admitted with a tense sigh, hoping I wouldn't have to reveal the rest.

He ran a hand through his disheveled hair, bewildered. "How is this possible?"

"I have no idea."

"Can you use it? Can you cast magic?"

"No."

"I can train you. Ethan—"

"No!" I snapped. "Let it go."

"You've been keeping this a secret all along," he scoffed. "Why didn't you tell me?"

I rose from the bench to face my brother. "Do you know why you've never met a were-animal with magical ability? Weres aren't particularly tolerant of the unusual. If my ability had been revealed as a child, I would've been killed by my own kind. I've kept my ability secret as a matter of survival."

He gaped. "I'm your brother."

"There was nothing you could do to help me, Josh."

"You didn't trust me. You didn't even want to tell me now, so you still don't trust me."

I rubbed the tension building in my forehead. "I trust you. Even as an adult, I'd still have a target on my back. I don't need that kind of headache. It was just easier not to tell anyone. Just. Let it. Go."

Josh opened his mouth, but stopped. Judging by the glint of anger in his eyes and the set in his jaw, he had some objection that he ultimately chose to keep to himself. He turned, scowling, and left the gym.

That evening, a noise startled me from a restless slumber. I glanced at the clock on my antique dresser—three twenty in the morning—when I heard Skylar's agonized scream. I jumped from my bed into the hall. Sebastian and Winter emerged to follow me as I traced the horrified screams to the library, where we found Skylar rigid on the floor with Josh over her futilely pulling at a book that she clasped to her chest with the iron grip of the dead. Her skin was deathly pale and her eyes were wide open, staring at a single spot on the ceiling as if the devil itself were there. Her lips parted as she screamed again, an agonized sound that cut to my heart. For once I had no idea what to do for her, nor did Sebastian. The rest of the pack filed into the library, drawn by Skylar's screams.

"Skylar," Josh called to her, but her eyes remained transfixed on the ceiling, tears streaming down her cheeks. She screamed again.

"What's happening to her?" Sebastian asked, his voice strained.

I could only watch, helpless.

"I don't know." Josh folded his palms over her cheeks, trying in vain to turn her head. "Skylar, look at me," he demanded, but her body remained deathly rigid. Turning his attention to the book she clutched to her chest—I recognized *Symbols of Death*—he placed a hand over hers. "*A-na rische.* Release." Nothing. He tugged at the book but it wouldn't budge. "Shit!" He pulled at the book again, harder. "*A-na rische,*" he repeated, his voice growing more desperate. "Unbind." He tugged at the book until it began to glow, radiating an intense heat that touched us all. The smell of burning flesh filled the room. He released the book, horrified as he saw the blackened edges of Skylar's fingers where she touched it. "Shit," he breathed.

"Why can't you stop this?" I demanded, absorbing my brother's panic.

"She bound herself to the book." Josh gestured to it. "Somehow, she held on to the magic from earlier. I don't know how it's possible. I released her from it." He touched her face once more, trying to get her to focus on him.

"Winter," he said, looking up. "I need you to charm her. She's holding the binding and needs to release herself from it."

Winter knelt next to Skylar and whispered something into her ear. Repositioning herself over Skylar, she began a slow, gently rhythmic movement while speaking so softly that even I with my enhanced hearing couldn't make out the words, perhaps because they were not meant for me. As Winter swayed and spoke, she effortlessly shifted in and out of her serpentine form. The power to charm was unique to her animal form. I had only witnessed her charm once before. It was then, as it was now, an alien experience. She smiled invitingly as Skylar began to respond. Her eyes followed the ebb and sway of Winter's movements, locked onto her gaze. With a gentle finger, she turned Skylar's head slightly, guiding her to maintain their locked gazes as she continued her serpentine movements.

Symbols of Death seemed to tear itself from Skylar's grip, leaping into the air and landing in the middle of the room as flames ignited from the letters, and then quickly extinguished. As I returned my gaze to Skylar, I felt a rush of relief to see the life in her eyes once more as she took in our presence, confused.

"Skylar," Josh said softly, inching closer on his knees.

"Yeah," she answered, her voice hoarse.

When Josh gently turned Skylar's neck, we all saw the two bite marks of a vampire. I felt a surge of anger through my body. As Skylar explored the wounds with her fingers, she revealed similar wounds all over her arm. Bewildered and beginning to panic, she lifted her shirt to find more markings on her stomach. There were more markings beneath her pant leg, as well. Tears streamed from her eyes as the panic took hold.

Sebastian knelt beside her to examine the marks. "Skylar, it's okay." He offered her a reassuring smile. There was nothing reassuring about her wounds. "They're going away. Look." He raised her forearm to show her as the last of the wounds quickly faded away. Taking her hand in his, Sebastian placed a hand over her knee. A calmness arose from his presence, spreading throughout the room to soothe us all.

"Everything's going to be just fine," Sebastian reassured her.

Slowly, her breath and her heart rate returned to normal, but I couldn't hide the concern in my expression, not just for Skylar but for what had happened to her, which I couldn't begin to understand. Wilting under our collective stare, she self-consciously brushed a hand over her head, then over her butt, finishing with a look of relief. Was her mind damaged?

"You saw it, didn't you?" Josh asked, his voice filled with tension.

Skylar swallowed a response and bit down on her lip, drawing blood.

"What did she see?" Sebastian asked, releasing her.

Josh sighed. "Her death. She saw what they are planning to do with her." He placed his hand on Skylar's shoulder as he held her gaze. "I had to research the information further in hopes that what Caleb showed me was wrong. But"—he shook his head—"he showed me nothing but truth. The Gem of Levage is used to transfer power sources from one person to another, or in this case, from Skylar to Demetrius's Seethe."

Winter stiffened. I felt a surge of anger at my brother. Judging by Sebastian's tense expression, Josh hadn't informed him, either.

Josh continued, ignoring the thickening atmosphere. "During the ritual, if there is a blood exchange by both people they exchange abilities. This isn't anything very special for a vampire because it is one of their gifts and the very dynamics of the trade."

Skylar tipped her head back and took in a deep, calming breath as if resigning herself to her fate.

Josh took a seat in front of her, his expression growing more distressed as he continued to describe her fate. "They want her abilities, and with the ritual, there only needs to be a one-way blood exchange. Once life is drained, with the use of the Gem, the donor abilities remain indefinitely. Their Seethe, which is well over two hundred strong, will possess immunity to light, will no longer go through reversion when staked, can enter any dwelling without an invitation, and will be unaffected by religious symbols. They will also gain her strength, making them significantly stronger and faster than you all." He turned to Sebastian for emphasis. "This will be true of anyone they create thereafter, as well."

"But why her?" I growled.

"Most humans, due to their fragile nature, can't sustain life long enough to complete the ritual. Apparently, this ritual has already been attempted by Demetrius using a mage, several humans, and a were-puma. They even tried a dhampir, obviously without success. Most dhampirs have human fragility and couldn't survive the ritual. They were just fishing for candidates until Skylar came to their attention." Josh surveyed Skylar, His brow tightening in concern. "The mage was human. Though he had magical ability, he was unable to survive. For reasons unknown to me, were-animals are immune to their magic. That's why they can't enthrall or change you all and the very reason they failed when they used the were-puma. Skylar is somehow connected to them. The terait is evidence of it." He gestured toward her right eye. "That is the reason they were able to enter her home without an invitation. I don't know how this occurred but it did. An anomaly at its worst. She heals as the were-animal does and would be able to survive to complete the ritual. It is not definitive whether or not the transference will work, but since Demetrius is going to such extreme measures to get her, he must believe it is highly likely."

I wanted to run from the house and attack the Seethe in that moment. I wanted to kill Demetrius and every one of his followers with my bare hands. Winter's hand shifted instinctively to a sword that wasn't at her hip. I knew she had a different kind of violence in mind that only served to compound my building rage. I knew that my emotions were filling the room, adding to everyone's tension. I struggled to calm myself, at least for Skylar's sake. Sebastian did a much better job of controlling himself. Skylar seemed remarkably calm for someone who had just heard the prophecy of her horrible demise.

"Steven," Sebastian said, helping her to rise, "take Skylar to Jeremy and let him check her out." He gave Steven a meaningful look as he took her by the elbow and guided her toward the door. She appeared confused and taken aback as he led her out of the library. Why the burns on her fingers didn't have her in agony, I wasn't sure. Perhaps shock. The burns were healing, but slower than the shallower bite wounds. The pain would come soon unless Dr. Jeremy applied one of his special balms.

At Sebastian's signal, the library remained silent, everyone trying to control their emotions while we waited for Steven to return. The gesture was less out of respect for Steven than to allow time for Skylar to be moved outside of earshot. He returned quickly, nodding to Sebastian.

Winter began, once more laying her case for killing Skylar. This time, she was not alone. Hannah and Bryce agreed, while Steven sided with me. The argument was circular and exhausting as this time Winter refused to relent. I had reached the point where I was willing to end the argument with violence when Sebastian finally spoke. The rest of the room grew silent.

"If we retrieve the Gem, this will all go away?"

"That's a great big if," Josh answered with obvious frustration. "I know Demetrius has it, but he has a protection spell on it. He's using dark magic, and I can't find it. I've tried several times today. Tomorrow, I'm going to talk to London. She is more skilled than I am in matters like this and may be able to remove the protection spell. Once we locate it, the rest is easy."

"Are you sure she will help? In the past, she always resisted assisting us," Sebastian said.

"That's before we helped her. She owes us, and I believe she will be relieved to no longer have that debt."

Sebastian sighed, crossing his arms over his chest as he weighed our options.

Josh watched him intently. "Sebastian," he stated respectfully. "Storming into the vampires' home and threatening them until they give you the Gem won't work. A battle like that will end with a great number of dead vampires and were-animals. We would be no better off."

"I am assuming that killing Demetrius won't help, either. Is it safe to assume anyone in his Seethe can perform the ritual?"

Josh nodded gravely.

"Then kill her," Winter suggested with surprising calm considering her earlier passion. "She is the most imminent threat. At least that will give us time to find the Gem."

"She's not the threat," Steven interjected.

"Stop it with that load of crap! You can't still believe she's not a threat."

"She isn't. Nothing she's done has threatened us," Sebastian stated firmly. I felt a sigh of relief, confident now that Sebastian wasn't ready to sacrifice Skylar.

Winter gazed past me toward the library door as if retracing Skylar's departure. Her eyes narrowed, taking on a determined, murderous look. I started to follow her gaze when she turned back to Sebastian. "Her very existence is a threat. She is not one of us, and we should stop protecting her as though she were."

"Josh, what do you think?" Sebastian asked.

"She's capable of things within the magic realms that aren't typical of were-animals. But Winter can charm, which is atypical of were-animals' abilities, and she isn't a threat to us but, rather, an asset. I can't say Skylar isn't capable of being dangerous because I am not quite sure what she really is. However, she would never endanger us intentionally."

I nodded to my brother.

"I am not saying it would be intentional," Winter said, "but she is dangerous for so many reasons, starting with why the vampires wish to have her. Is anyone else concerned that we really don't know what she is? You said yourself that the necromancer got a weird reading on her. Terait, were-animal, odd magical ability, there is something terribly wrong with her. Kill her and this all goes away."

"Until they find another sacrifice," Steven broke in. "Then what? Keep killing anyone who can be potentially used? Then what form of evil do we become? She needs protection, not death. What we need to do is locate the Gem and make sure the vamps never have the chance to use it."

"Yes, sounds so very simple. However, if it were that simple, then why don't we have the goddamn thing? Demetrius is going all out for this. His Legion—seriously, when has he ever used them? He's risking the safety of his Seethe to keep the Gem hidden with dark magic and accruing a huge debt in the process. He has the Gem and we have her. It's simple. Kill her, and things get a lot less complicated."

I met Winter's gaze with disappointment. She wasn't wrong, strategically, but Skylar had proven herself. She had saved me in that alley in Chicago. She had put her life at risk for Josh, however foolishly. I recognized now that Skylar had become more than just a problem to solve by cold-blooded calculation. Much as I never wanted this, the situation had become complicated in ways that I could no longer ignore. Skylar mattered to me. I would not allow her to be simply killed out of hand—not by anyone. "Can you take the life of an innocent were-animal in cold blood, without cause?"

Winter flinched in surprise at my rebuke. "For the safety of this pack, I'll do it without hesitation. If we keep this up, there will be a battle. Lives will be lost—our lives. And for what? Her? Ethan, if you find it too distasteful for your civility, then I will do it right now."

"Winter!" Sebastian snapped as I took a step to intervene. A gesture from him stopped me.

"She's not one of us," Winter declared, confused by our reluctance. "She is dangerous. We need to kill her. It will give us time to find the Gem and not have to worry about protecting her."

Winter's resolve was absolute. Like me, she would take any risk for the pack, offer any sacrifice she believed the pack required. Once convinced of a path, she could not easily be deterred. There was murder in her eyes. Before I could warn her, Skylar said from behind me, "She's right." Only Winter seemed unsurprised to find Skylar in the doorway, wearing a resigned expression. She wore tight medical gloves I'd seen Dr. Baker use before, to keep one of his custom balms against the skin.

Skylar stepped gingerly into the room without a glance in my direction. Her entire focus was on Sebastian. "I am not one of you, and I don't warrant this type of loyalty and sacrifice. It is a lot to ask. I am terrified of what I am capable of, so I can understand Winter's concern. It would be easier to end my life, but I ask that you don't. I will leave." Despite her seeming calm, there was desperation in her tone, a plea.

"Leaving this house isn't enough," Winter declared in her coldest, deadliest voice. Her eyes stretched into serpentine slits. "Your very existence is a danger. Death is the only option for you."

"Skylar," Sebastian said, "if I thought you were capable of protecting yourself, my pack would not have intervened. You will continue to stay here under pack protection until the Gem is retrieved. Your life is protected and all members of this pack," he emphasized, glancing at Winter, "will do what is needed."

With much effort, Winter's eyes returned to their deep hazel color. "Then you are protected," she said with mechanical resignation.

"Thank you," Skylar said, relieved. This was a Skylar I had not seen before, without the snark and bravado and infuriating willfulness. At first I thought her tone was a ploy to disarm Winter's venom, but I quickly realized Skylar felt a genuine compassion for Winter, despite the were-snake's overriding desire to bring about Skylar's death—none of which mattered to Winter.

"Don't offer thanks to me. I do it because I am commanded to. If it were up to me, you would be dead right now," Winter said bluntly as she turned to leave.

Sebastian stopped her at the doorway. "You take as much time as you need. She's under our protection, and if you kill her, I will enforce the law to the fullest extent." He put a gentle hand on Winter's shoulder. "I don't want to, but I will."

Her jaw set, Winter glanced from Skylar to Sebastian. "If I kill her, the maximum punishment is exile from the pack."

"It is considered pack betrayal if a were-animal dies as a result of your direct disobedience to an order," Sebastian stated matter-of-factly. "The penalty is death."

Her stern expression softened into disbelief.

He took a deep breath, meeting Winter's entreating gaze with resigned determination. "Winter, if you kill Skylar while I consider her protected, it is betrayal. I would recommend death and see that you die at my hands. If you blatantly disobey my orders, then you are no good to me or the pack because you can no longer be trusted. You've always followed my orders loosely and interpreted our rules in ways that were questionable at best. But it was never a clear violation of my authority."

Crestfallen and in a state of shock, Winter nodded once, acknowledging Sebastian's authority. Seemingly on the edge of tears, she bowed her head and left.

Skylar seemed awestruck and confused, as if she'd never imagined Sebastian—perhaps any of us—would stand up for her, as if she wasn't quite sure his promise of protection from Winter's wrath was real. She turned to me with an entreating look, needing my response. Did she need me to challenge Winter as well? I would have, but Sebastian had done so effectively. For me to intercede now would be construed as a challenge to Sebastian's authority. Skylar fidgeted with her hands. She tugged at her shirt as she scanned the faces of the pack: some encouraging, some reserved, some angry. Finally, her gaze returned to me. As much as I wanted to offer her the reassurance she sought, I wasn't able to. By publicly rebuking Winter, Sebastian had given Skylar all the reassurance she could need to feel safe in our protection.

"You should go to your room," Sebastian suggested gently.

Skylar nodded, and then, still fidgeting, left.

CHAPTER 10

*A*fter a couple of hours of troubled sleep, I rose at dawn. The custom was so ingrained that I never needed an alarm, even when exhausted. Sebastian was the same, with much of the pack following our examples. Oversleeping was a luxury of the lazy. I rolled onto the floor and knocked out a few sets of one-handed pushups until the fog in my brain lifted, then I left my room to find breakfast. On my way to the kitchen, I passed Gavin and Sebastian emerging from his office. Gavin had been out of town attending to a personal matter and must have returned in the night.

A were-panther and fourth in the pack hierarchy—just below Winter—Gavin had transferred to us from the East Coast Pack based out of Brooklyn. He was intense and dangerous, with dark, piercing, almond-shaped eyes, hollow cheeks, and broad features. His midnight-black hair was tied loosely at the back, leaking strands of hair that hung down to the deep, tawny-colored skin of his neck. He was slim, built for the agility and stealth that suited his panther. Judging by his grim, angry expression, he had just been briefed on the current situation with Skylar and Demetrius. We acknowledged each other in passing, then he went downstairs to the gym while Sebastian climbed the stairs toward Skylar's room.

My thoughts turned unbidden to Skylar—a very common occurrence since I'd brought her to the retreat. After the events of last night, I would be surprised if she'd slept at all. Or perhaps she'd rested peacefully for the first time since her arrival, having finally embraced our protection.

In the kitchen, I was sifting through the cuts of steak in the fridge when a wave of fury swept through the house, originating from Skylar's room. The package of meat in my hand dropped to the tile floor with a wet smack as I raced to the stairs just as Sebastian, the epicenter of rage, emerged in a rush, his wolf lurking just below the surface. I worried that something else had happened to Skylar, but then I knew what had happened even before Sebastian began barking orders.

"Ethan! Bring her back!"

Steven and Hannah emerged half-dressed from his room, joined by Gavin rising from the basement.

"Go!" I shouted, snapping a gesture toward the door. They picked up another wolf, Marko, on the way out.

Josh emerged from his room, groggy and disheveled from sleep. "What's happened?"

"She ran," I growled.

"Oh, no." He understood the gravity of the situation as much as I did. He darted back into his room and returned with the keys to his Wrangler. He wouldn't be much use finding Skylar, but a warlock might come in handy if we found trouble. Knowing Skylar, trouble might already have found her. If nothing else, Josh could carry her corpse back in the Jeep. At that moment, I didn't care if she lived or died. By running, she'd put the entire pack in danger. Sebastian would be well within his rights to strip her protection and order her death, which seemed almost certain to be the outcome. As much as I wanted to protect her, I couldn't save Skylar from herself.

I exited the house to find Gavin had changed into his panther form. Hannah and Marko had transformed as well, sniffing about for Skylar's scent, while Steven remained in his human form. It was Steven who first picked up the scent. Tracking her through the dense woods, it became obvious that she was keeping parallel to the driveway as a guide from the property, while attempting to mask her scent among the strong odors of the oak and pine trees. I could've admired her strategy, but it was taking all the control I could muster to hold my anger in check. I gestured to Hannah and Gavin to guard our flanks.

Her agonized scream pierced the quiet of the woods. I ran toward the gut-wrenching sound, picking up the scent of Gabriella and Chase along the way. Another scream. I charged through a copse of trees, the others just behind me, to find Skylar with her back against a thick pine tree. A wooden stake—her stake—had been driven through her right shoulder into the tree, pinning her. A knife similarly pinned her left hand. At her feet lay the fresh corpse of a young girl, blood coagulating over bite wounds on her wrist.

Skylar's initial relief at my arrival turned to fear as I approached. I contained my anger at her, but barely. Until we returned safely to the retreat, we were all in danger. She tensed as I took the stake in one hand, the knife in the other. "Inhale," I whispered. She took a ragged breath. "Now exhale." As the air slowly escaped from her lips, I pulled stake and knife out simultaneously, releasing her from the tree. She let out an agonized wail. A gush of blood spewed from the wounds onto my shirt as she fell against me, catching her breath, but I offered no comfort. Once she seemed sufficiently recovered, I released her, stepping back from her. The wounds were serious. She did well to remain on her feet, but I wasn't in the mood to offer accolades. Just as I was about to order our return, she doubled over to vomit. Gavin, still in his panther form, showed his displeasure with a low, snarling growl.

"Look to see if there are others," I commanded. Steven, the dingo, and the wolf moved quickly to obey, spreading out into the surrounding woods. Gavin remained behind, eyeing Skylar with the gaze of a hungry predator. He snarled again, then licked his lips greedily. The panther's short black fur glistened in the sunlight as he stalked toward her, drawn by the intoxicating smell of blood and fear that emanated from her. Steven returned to stand protectively with her.

"Gavin, she's under our protection," I declared firmly, but he continued, mesmerized by Skylar. Surprised at his lack of discipline, I stepped into his path and dropped into a fighting stance, calling my wolf to just beneath the surface. Skylar might well lose her life before the day was out, but the decision was not Gavin's. I growled a final warning, tensing for violence. The panther hesitated, confounded by my determination, then brought himself under control. He lowered his head in capitulation and backed away.

Skylar fell back against the tree, relieved. She tested her shoulder, grimacing as she rolled it several times in succession. Satisfied, she turned her attention to her left hand, touching each finger to her thumb in turn. When she finished, relieved, I gestured sharply toward the house. She relented, taking the lead with the dread of a condemned woman. I followed close behind, directing the others to protect our flanks. More than once Skylar glanced back at me, her expression fearful and perhaps regretful beneath her obvious discomfort. It was too late for regrets. Actions spoke for themselves, and she'd been given more than enough chances. Her fate was in Sebastian's hands now, and I had never seen him so furious.

Josh's Wrangler appeared on the driveway. We emerged from the woods and I directed Skylar to the passenger seat. I took the seat behind her, and then directed the others to scout the area. With any luck, the vampires were gone and we would once more survive Skylar's foolishness without casualty. Josh raised his eyebrows at her wounds, but said nothing as he turned the Wrangler around. Watching her shrink in the front seat as the house came into view, I felt my ire rising. She hadn't just betrayed the pack's trust, she'd betrayed mine. I was out of the Jeep before it came to a complete stop.

"Chase and Gabriella left a body on the property," I told Josh as he emerged from the driver's seat. "All evidence of it needs to be removed. You need to do your thing." I waited for Skylar to ease herself out of the Jeep. When her gaze met mine, I felt a rush of furious anger. Thankfully, Josh saw the storm building and stepped between us until I finally forced myself to turn away. I strode into the house, greeted at the threshold by the oppressive force of Sebastian's fury that had only grown worse since I had left the house to retrieve Skylar. Dr. Baker greeted me with an anxious expression, shaking his head as he glanced over my shoulder, presumably at Skylar.

I strode directly to Sebastian's office where I found the Alpha pacing, himself struggling with his composure. Seeing me, he paused, tensing in anticipation.

"She is wounded, but alive. Chase and Gabriella had her, but we arrived in time."

Sebastian's eyes narrowed to amber slits. His jaw set. "Anyone injured?"

"Skylar was injured badly. No one else. Dr. Baker is tending to her." A part of me considered pleading on her behalf for mercy, but my anger couldn't be brushed aside so easily.

I moved aside as Sebastian strode out of the office, and followed him. Skylar sat on an exam table in the medical station, her shirt torn and cast aside, leaving her in a sports bra as the doctor filled a syringe from a medicine bottle. Neither of them noticed as Sebastian stopped in the doorway.

"I don't think what happened between Gabriella and I today could remotely be considered a fight," Skylar told the doctor, too casually. "If so, I think someone should explain to me what a fight is. I thought it involved two people trying to best one another in a physical confrontation. What occurred between Gabriella and I was a smackdown and I was the only one being smacked."

Dr. Baker's chuckle transformed into a laugh until he noticed Sebastian and me. He walked into the room, meeting the doctor's gaze. From the doorway, I saw Skylar's shoulders tense as Sebastian rounded the table. When his gaze met hers, his surging anger erupted into the room like a shock wave. Skylar smartly turned her gaze to the floor in a submissive gesture, instinctively shrinking.

"How does it feel?" Sebastian asked coldly, without hint of concern.

"Hurts like hell," Skylar answered cautiously.

"Good."

Her head snapped up. I hoped she had the sense to recognize that her usual snark and willfulness could now get her killed. I found myself holding my breath until she lowered her gaze to the floor once more.

"She's not going to have efficient use of her left hand and right shoulder for a day or two," Dr. Baker said softly, trying to diffuse the tension in the room. "There's serious soft tissue damage."

Sebastian let out a disgusted grunt, his anger unappeased as he observed Skylar's wounds. "You allowed yourself to be injured by your own weapons. I will tell you again. You are our responsibility." He was working hard to suppress his wolf.

Gaze still downcast, she eased herself off the table and

tried to back away. Sebastian roughly grabbed her face with hands that seemed giant against her skull. Forcing her to meet his gaze, he said through clenched teeth, "You realize the severity of what will take place if you are caught by the vampires? You've seen it and felt it almost firsthand. Mayhem will ensue and I could very well lose a large number of my pack trying to stop that shit! You do realize that your death will give them strength and power that will surpass ours, leaving them virtually unstoppable, giving them free rein to act in any reckless manner they choose. Unnecessary deaths will occur, and who will be there to stop them? We will try to stop the rampage, and possibly be successful, but will suffer great losses. I will lose people that I watched grow up all because you continue to act recklessly against us."

Though I couldn't see Skylar's expression, I heard her heart racing to the breaking point of terror as Sebastian's eyes turned the amber of his wolf. Dr. Baker quietly left the room, joining me in the doorway. We exchanged a glance, but didn't dare speak.

Sebastian pulled Skylar's face close to his. "Do you want to die or are you really this fucking irresponsible with your life? If death is what you long for then I can make that happen right now." I tensed as he shifted one hand to her throat and lifted her off the ground, choking her effortlessly. Her feet twitched, scrambling uselessly for purchase. She clutched at the hand that slowly tightened around her throat as she gasped and sputtered for breath. The bones in her neck cracked.

He is going to break her neck. But then I saw the slight release of pressure that allowed Skylar to catch a single breath. Was he in control, or simply toying with her? When it came to matters of death, Sebastian was efficient, perfunctory, and never cruel—but I had rarely seen him this furious. I had no intention of standing by and watching Skylar be tortured, but my intervention would be a challenge to Sebastian's authority. My response would have to wait until the last moment. For now, I had to trust that Sebastian was in control of himself.

Her single breath expired, Skylar began to choke again, straining uselessly to break Sebastian's hold. He turned her enough that I saw the terror in her eyes, tears streaming down her cheeks. My fists clenched and my jaw set. I had one foot into the medical bay when Sebastian seemed to recoil from his own aggression, dropping Skylar to the floor. She landed in a pile and climbed slowly to her knees as she caught her breath. The crying continued, and I had the sense there was more to her tears than the fear of death at Sebastian's hands.

His anger subsiding, Sebastian lowered himself to the floor and knelt in front of her. "Look at me."

She took a deep breath before obeying him. Staring into her eyes, he sighed. "Skylar," he said, his tone softening further, "you don't deserve to die because of what you are. It's not your fault. I am not holding you accountable for it, nor should you. I want to protect you, but you are making it painfully hard ... eyes up here. I don't understand you, and I don't wish to. Maybe you are depressed about your mother, or you're one of those emo-chicks with a strange obsession with death, or perhaps you are just tragically stupid. Either way, I can't bring myself to give a damn. If death is what you want, then there is no need for my pack to waste any more time protecting you. I can no longer continue to waste resources that could be better spent finding the Gem of Levage. I will ask you once, and I expect an answer now. Do you want to die? If so, I will give it to you now, swift and painless."

I was sure Skylar would say "yes." Judging by Sebastian's posture, he expected the same. After a long, tense moment, I felt a rush of relief as she shook her head. "I'm afraid," she whispered.

"There isn't anything wrong with fear unless you allow it to control your actions. I want you to survive this. You are protected and that order extends to you, as well. You will do whatever is necessary to keep yourself safe from harm. Don't run away again, because if you do . . ." Sebastian left the obvious threat unspoken. There would be no more chances.

She nodded.

As Sebastian helped her to her feet, I left the room, choosing to wait in his office. He arrived a few minutes later, unsurprised by my presence. "Ethan," he said, waiting.

I chose my words carefully. "Was that necessary?"

He turned on me with a sigh. "You know I'm right. She doesn't know she is suicidal or she doesn't think her life is worth saving. If she continues on her path, she will get any number of us killed. I can't allow her to put the pack in jeopardy, and you know that."

"I understand that."

"Then what's the problem?"

"Was it necessary to choke Skylar to make your point effectively?" He stared back at me, surprised, but I continued. "She's not a combatant. When we kill, we do so out of necessity. We've never been cruel."

"It was necessary," he said sternly. I let my silence challenge him. "Skylar's problem is that she doesn't know she's suicidal, Ethan. Do you think a gentle explanation of the stakes was going to convince her this time? She needed to taste death so that she could make an informed decision."

"It was extreme," I said carefully, "and unprecedented."

"I understand your objection, Ethan. You're correct. I don't tolerate cruelty. I never intended to torture Skylar, but it was necessary to force her into making a decision that I believe was long overdue. If she had chosen death, it would have been as swift and merciful as promised, as it will be if she runs away again."

After a long, silent exchange, I nodded. I wasn't

convinced that he hadn't lost control of himself in his confrontation with Skylar, but I did believe it would never happen again. I wouldn't tolerate it.

"Since Skylar has demonstrated a fascination with windows," Sebastian said, "it would be best to dispossess her of the temptation. I want Steven to share her room until further notice. She responds well to him."

I scowled at the idea, but it was for the best. Steven would elicit the least reaction, and it would not be wise to leave her another opportunity to run. Leaving Sebastian's office, I felt it best that I stayed away from Skylar until my anger subsided, but I couldn't shake my concern for her.

I entered Skylar's room without knocking and found her supine on the bed, her eyes closed, fresh from the shower and wrapped in a towel. Her shoulder and hand were bandaged, but nothing covered the fresh bruising around her neck. With her naturally fast healing, the bruises were already transitioning from red to purple. She shifted on the bed, the pain of her wounds obviously discomforting. My gaze remained fixed on the bruising of her neck, a frustrating mix of anger and concern tightening my chest.

Sensing my presence, she snapped her eyes open.

"Sit up," I commanded. She remained supine, watching me. I released the tension in my jaw, careful to soften my tone. "Now."

She rolled into a sitting position on the edge of the bed, drawing the covers with her. Her voice was hoarse. "If you've come to reprimand me, I can assure you I've been appropriately chastised and frightened by Sebastian. If you came to threaten to kill me, Sebastian beat you to it, as well. And if you came to yell at me, can you please wait until tomorrow? My ears are still ringing from my encounter with Sebastian."

I watched her tense as I lowered myself to the hardwood floor and knelt in front of her. As I reached out to touch her, she recoiled slightly, but then allowed me permission to

158

gently cup her face in my palms. I turned her slightly to inspect the bruising on her neck, lightly brushing the imprint of Sebastian's thumbs with my fingertips. "You shouldn't have run again," I whispered.

She sighed. "It was stupid."

I exhaled a deep breath. "It was dangerous." I sat back. Staring into her eyes, I felt a returning surge of anger toward her and chose to focus my attention on the wall behind her shoulder. Despite my empathy for her, I couldn't escape my anger at her for running, for doubting me. After Sebastian had assaulted her with his rage, expressing my anger could only be self-serving. "I don't know what is more insulting: your belief we have no honor and would go back on our word to protect you, or your fear that we are so craven that we would attempt to kill you while you sat unknowingly in our home. We are animals, it would be against our natural sensibility to hunt a captured prey."

"My running was by no means a reflection of my thoughts of your honor or integrity as a pack or a hunter. There is validity to Winter's argument, and I can honestly see how you all could agree with her. The pack is your family, and I expect you to take necessary precautions to keep them safe. If the roles were reversed, I couldn't say that your lives would be safe at my hand. If any of you had been an imminent threat to my mother, it would be nothing less than dishonest to say I wouldn't have taken your lives to protect her."

"The same would be true with us. If your presence in our lives were to put us in imminent danger, I couldn't say that your life would hold much value to us, either. Our pack is in no danger at the vampires' hands. This is not the first time we've had less than favorable dealings with the vamps, and I assure you that it won't be the last."

"Winter thinks I am a danger to the pack."

"She, along with the rest of us, is concerned with your

159

unique characteristics. But at this time, you aren't a direct risk to us. If things were to change, then we would revisit the situation. But for now you are safe."

"In other words, if I were a direct risk to the pack, then I would have cause to fear for my life."

I nodded and moved closer, tenderly resting my hands against the exposed skin of her lower back where the sheet failed to cover her. The warmth of her skin sent a small shiver through my hands. "You would be treated like any other threat," I said as delicately as I could manage. "But you are under our protection and that is something we do not take lightly."

I found it best to change the subject. "It is a good thing that you didn't kill Chase. The vampires lust often, but love infrequently. Chase and Gabriella are *lynked*, similar to being mated. He created her, and they have been together for, I believe, fifty-three years, never straying and never parted. They vowed their existence to each other. If you kill one, you must kill the other or suffer the wrath of the survivor. Whatever you saw in your vision would be nothing in comparison to the torture you would have endured at Gabriella's hand if you had killed him. She wouldn't care about any consequences because he is her existence and she is his. Once, a hunter tried to make a name for herself, caught Chase, tortured him, and left him for dead. Horror tales evolved around the torment she endured once Gabriella found her."

"I thought vampires had an aversion to light. How were they able to walk in the light like that?"

"Borrowed source. The older ones can walk in light if they consume enough to sustain them. Usually it takes about three lives to give them twenty minutes of light. There are only a few vampires who can travel, but Gabriella and Chase aren't gifted in that manner. This means they must be feeding from an elf and accumulating a large debt to do so. Elves do not help without getting much in return. I am curious to find out the specifics regarding that debt. The vampires have accumulated a great deal of debt on your behalf. You are important to them."

"Yeah, I get the point. Chase and Gabriella have made it painfully obvious."

"Even more reason for you to start making wise choices. Skylar, please understand if you keep pushing us, we won't have any other option—" The words caught in my throat. I wasn't sure if it was anger or fear, but I didn't want to express either—not in front of Skylar, not in an uncontrolled fashion. I rose without meeting her gaze and left the room.

That evening, while taking my frustrations out on the free weights in the gym, Winter joined me on the bench. Her hazel eyes appeared sad and defeated. I continued pumping while she contemplated the weights.

"I don't understand," she said finally.

"Sebastian made his wishes clear."

"But why? Why take the risk in protecting the girl? We've always put the pack first."

I grunted at the burning tension in my bicep as I slowly lowered the weight. The motion complete, I set the bar on the ground and picked up the towel next to me to wipe sweat from my face. "The pack always comes first."

"Killing the girl is the best move for the pack's safety," she insisted, but there was an underlying question.

"Skylar's death will not dispossess Demetrius of the Gem."

"It solves the problem of her being stupid. She's going to run again. Next time Demetrius gets her and completes his little ceremony, and we're all fucked." She considered for a moment. "How does keeping Skylar alive make sense, again?"

"We're not like the vampires," I stated plainly. "We're animals. We're not evil. Sebastian protects Skylar because she does not deserve to die. She doesn't understand our world, doesn't understand the consequences of her choices."

"But she makes *bad* choices," Winter said sternly.

"Skylar may well force Sebastian's hand, but that time hasn't come. Winter, Sebastian has stated his position unequivocally. Do not test him." I met her gaze directly. "Or me."

She sighed, disappointed. After a moment, she glanced wistfully at the sparring mat. "Want to fight?"

Hours later, I went to bed sore and satisfied, sleeping well for the first time in days.

The next morning I showered, then went in search of Skylar. I found her in the library, presumably searching for Josh. Just how often were they meeting? Not finding him, she appeared anxious.

"He left early this morning," I said, announcing my presence. She turned to me, and I saw the bruising on her neck was barely noticeable. "He believes Caleb had something to do with what happened to you last night. Josh was quite infuriated by the betrayal. I hope Caleb lives through the meeting." She frowned at me, ignoring or missing the sarcasm. She seemed distracted. "How are you feeling?" I inquired casually, stepping closer to her.

"As well as can be expected." Her nose wrinkled as if she had caught a disgusting odor. "How's Winter?"

Her sense of smell is improving. I smiled playfully, enjoying Skylar's apparent jealousy. She had the wrong idea, but I didn't feel the need to correct her. "Winter does her job so well I often forget how young she is. She can be quite emotional when provoked. She doesn't like you. I had to talk to her last night. On rare occasions, I seem to be the only one capable of reasoning with her. She feels things quite deeply, whether it's love or hate."

Skylar ignored me. She seemed to contemplate something distasteful, then blurted, "I've been marked."

My smile faded as she turned around and raised her shirt, showing me a new, raised, rough mark resembling the Gem of Levage on the right side of her lower back. I knelt, my fingers fanning out across her stomach while my thumbs carefully probed the mark, ignoring the chill bumps that rose on her skin beneath my touch. I took out my phone and called Josh. The voice mail picked up. "Josh, come to the house when you're done, I need you to look at something."

CHAPTER 11

*S*kylar spent the next few hours in her room, watching television with a numb expression. Recognizing she was overwhelmed, I checked in on her, but otherwise left her alone until Josh finally returned. He didn't mention Caleb, and I didn't ask. Rather than explain, I led Josh directly to Skylar's room. She rose expectantly to greet him. At my urging, she turned slightly and raised her shirt, showing him the marking on her lower back.

He only needed a glance, as if confirming what he already suspected. "She is bound to the Gem. It will go away once the Gem is destroyed. It's not a good idea to bind yourself to such things, Skylar."

"It wasn't my intention. I ..." Her gaze shifted sheepishly to the floor as she lowered her shirt. "It called me."

"You held on to magic." Josh was clearly intrigued.

Skylar shrugged. "I guess."

I looked at Josh, waiting for an explanation.

"Binding yourself to things is something were-animals can't do," he explained to Skylar. "It falls in the realm of magic—quite advanced magic. It's the reason I can use others as conduits. The only explanation for what happened is that you held on to the magic you were exposed to at Caleb's house. When Caleb bit you, it was enough of a blood exchange for you to attain a bond with him and me. That is why you experienced what you did the night before last. You were still bound to him by blood and magic, but he couldn't call you." Josh slowly paced the room, his mind racing with possibilities. "If I had been aware of your magical abilities, I would have done a different unbinding spell." He grew angry. "It was Caleb's intention to draw enough blood to call to you last night, forcing you to respond to him. Once you did, he would have given you to Demetrius with hopes of returning to the family. In the past, he has been a reliable source, but his betrayal has made him a liability."

Caleb's still alive? I preferred not, but I wouldn't mind killing him myself. Josh approached Skylar, took a deep breath, and then touched her arm. After a moment, she drew back with a shocked expression.

Josh stepped aside, gesturing to me. "Touch Ethan," he instructed her. She hesitated, then slowly approached me and touched my arm with a single finger. I wasn't sure what he had in mind, but I felt nothing but her tentative touch.

"Ethan?" he inquired. I shook my head. He studied Skylar a moment, bewildered and pensive. "I just wish I knew what you were. When I met you, I didn't sense magic. Now there is a weak presence."

"You need to find out," I insisted, and then left them in the room.

I wandered the house, lost in troubled thought. I could restrict Skylar's movements, limit her proximity to physical danger, but I had no power to protect her from her own ability to use magic, and that riled me. It also left me completely useless, relying on my brother to come up with a strategy. A short time later, I got a call from Josh. His voice was conspicuously calm. "Ethan, I need you in here."

I entered Skylar's room to find her with her back to me,

staring out the window. She had her arms wrapped around her chest, constraining the shudders that randomly rippled through her body. Her head twitched slightly, uncomfortable on her neck. She radiated fear. Like our first encounter at her mother's home, she was at a point of maximum stress. She was instinctively calling her wolf, but holding it back at the same time.

"What the hell happened?" I demanded.

"Nothing," Josh equivocated, backing toward me and lowering his voice to a whisper. "She's just having a little trouble dealing with some new information. I'll explain later."

Skylar dropped to her knees and quickly transformed. Within seconds, her gray wolf was anxiously pacing the room, claws clattering on the wood floor. In another circumstance, I would have guided her outside to let her run off whatever anxiety drove the transformation, but I couldn't risk allowing her out of the house. We had to assume now that the property was under watch by vampires at all times, even in daylight. Trapped, Skylar paced, then just as suddenly transformed back into her human form. I watched her struggle in pain as the transformation triggered itself several times in quick succession until finally she sat on the floor, exhausted and trying to catch her breath. After a moment, she collapsed, giving in to unconsciousness.

I knelt next to her, gently lifting her eyelids to verify her eyes had not rolled back into her head. Her breathing was anxious, but otherwise unobstructed. I carefully covered her up to her chin with the henna-colored, paisley-patterned duvet from the bed. Turning, I found Steven and Hannah watching from the doorway. While Hannah appeared calmly curious, Steven wore a concerned expression. "She'll be fine," I told him. "Watch her."

Steven nodded, bringing Hannah into the room with him.

I drew Josh into the hall, noting a stack of books in his hand. "What happened?" I asked in a controlled voice.

His face screwed up with anger. "You took Skylar to see Gloria." Obviously, she had told him. I had never asked her not to, but expected some discretion on her part. "You left Skylar alone," he continued. "With a Tre'ase!"

The meeting had turned out to be a mistake. I couldn't fault Josh his anger, but my patience was limited. "If I hadn't, she would've gone on her own."

He stepped in front of me, his face inches from mine. "Were you at least in the room when they met?"

I swallowed my irritation, and then said carefully, "It did not go as I had planned."

"You've always been a controlling bastard. Never mind that you took Skylar to see a Tre'ase in the first place, how could you let Gloria lock you out of the meeting?"

"It was"—I ground my teeth in frustration—"complicated." Everything with Skylar was complicated.

"Skylar said that no bargain was made. I find it hard to believe that Gloria would use her abilities without exacting something in return."

"Skylar told me the same. She did not lie."

He turned, restraining his frustration. "Who knows what game she's playing. I don't know if she knows, either," he muttered, and then turned back to me. "Ethan, I realize you don't understand."

"What don't I understand?" I snapped.

"A Tre'ase is not your typical trickster demon. They don't just make bargains, they distort the truth. They sprinkle the truth with tidbits of deceit to trick you into striking a bargain. But nothing the Tre'ase promises is ever what it seems. And once you become indebted to a Tre'ase, there is no escape. Think of the worst legal contract you've ever seen and add a demon's magic."

My jaw clenched. If Gloria had tricked Skylar, I would personally see that their bargain was annulled.

Accepting my reaction, Josh gestured to the books. "As it turned out, the rest of your trip proved fruitful. Sebastian needs to hear this."

A few minutes later, we were in Sebastian's office. I closed the door before Josh continued. "These are journals kept by Elena, Skylar's adopted mother. I've only had a short time to review them, but they are solely focused on Skylar, her development, and"—Josh paused for annoying effect —"her origin. The story Skylar knows is that Elena happened upon the murder of Skylar's parents by a vampire. The father was already dead, but Elena managed to kill the vampire before it finished feeding from the mother. Before the mother died, Elena performed an emergency C-section to save Skylar." He gestured to the journals. "As it turns out, the truth is somewhat different." Josh opened a journal and began to read. "The woman whispered part in English and part in Portuguese, 'This life you shall have. This life I shall take.' The fanged creature exhaled, hardening before he crumbled into dust." He closed the book with a dramatic snap. "Somehow, Skylar's mother killed the vampire with a death curse. I don't know if she was a witch or just a human with gifts. It's an amateurish spell, and the penalty for performing it is death. You can see why it's something done as a last resort."

"She sacrificed herself to save her daughter," I said.

"It's more complicated than that. The vampire was not trying to kill Skylar's mother. He was turning her."

"Turning a pregnant woman?" I scowled. "The vampires would never allow such an abomination."

"A child born into vampirism would never be able to fend for itself," Sebastian said. "It would remain dependent on its creator—an eternal burden. Once discovered, the vampires would kill the infant, the mother, and the sire."

"I never said this vampire was intelligent," Josh said. "As an innate werewolf, the conversion to vampirism was already killing Skylar. No were-animal survives that."

Sebastian and I exchanged glances. "And yet Skylar is here," I said.

"The death curse the mother used was more than just a curse. I believe the mother possessed a spirit shade that she transferred to Skylar, which saved her life."

I frowned at my brother, not quite following his logic. Sebastian struggled as well, but did a much better job of managing his patience.

"There is a tale told among witches that describes how the Tre'ases obtained their powers."

"How is this relevant?" I demanded, wanting Josh to get to the point. He ignored me.

"Most have viewed the story as a myth, while some have believed it a cautionary tale. There was once a very powerful witch, Emma, who was distraught over her daughter, Maya, who died at two years old. Driven by sorrow and desperation, Emma struck a fool's deal with a Tre'ase. In exchange for her daughter's life, she gave the Tre'ase her gifts of morphism and foresight. The Tre'ase brought Maya back to life as promised, but not the body to store it in." Josh focused his attention on me. "As I said, Tre'ases are the worst kind of tricksters. Maya became a spirit shade, cursed to wander bodiless through this existence. A sorrowful existence," he emphasized, "unable to touch, to feel, to truly experience life unless through a host, but the host must be willing.

"I believe Skylar's mother was Maya's host. She saved Skylar's life by inviting Maya to transfer to Skylar. Since she was unborn, her mother's permission was probably enough to allow the transference."

"Gloria was the same Tre'ase that Emma went to?" I asked, incredulous.

"Witches, elves, fae, demons—their gifts are transferred

169

through lineage but also can be gifted to others upon death, though many chose not to do so. Gloria has the powers described in the story, which seem unique to her. She may be the Tre'ase from the story. It's also possible Gloria is the offspring."

After a long, heavy silence, Sebastian folded his fingertips into a pyramid. "What is Skylar?"

"Just a werewolf with gifts. And a spirit shade."

"Can you exorcise the shade?" I asked.

Josh frowned. "If Maya were to leave, Skylar might cease to exist. Understand, Maya is almost entirely at Skylar's mercy. She is neither evil nor good. She merely takes on the characteristics of whomever hosts her life."

"But Maya is her own entity," I said, seeking clarification. "She has a consciousness that is separate from Skylar's."

"Yes, but Maya cannot exert control over Skylar."

"Can she influence Skylar?"

Josh ran a hand through his hair, scratching his scalp as he blew out a heavy breath of air. "I don't know."

A knock at the door interrupted us. I opened the door to find Steven, anxious. "Something is happening."

I led the way back to the room to find Skylar asleep on the floor where I had left her, but her body was encased by a soft golden glow. Josh pushed past me into the room. He placed the journals onto the dark mahogany nightstand next to the bed, and then knelt next to her, taking in the glow of her body. He reached out tenderly to touch her face, then abruptly pulled back as if shocked. At his gesture, Hannah, Steven, and I backed up to the doorway.

"*A-na rische mendu*," Josh said over Skylar, but when he reached out to touch her, his hand snapped back again.

"What's happening?" I demanded.

Ignoring me, Josh repeated his chant, then reached out once more. Once more, he was repelled. "*A-na rische mendu*," he said, emphasizing each syllable, but got the same result.

His expression shocked, he was about to explain when Skylar stirred, waking slowly at first, and then bolting upright. Her eyes had turned a sickly white, the pupils and irises completely drained of color. Hannah gasped behind me, but I couldn't take my eyes from Skylar. She blinked and glanced at the clock.

Josh stepped back from her. "Are you okay?"

Skylar nodded, conspicuously noting his distance.

"Are you sure?"

"Why?" she asked in a tired voice.

"Your eyes are an ugly white color. And there's a field of protection around you. I've brought it down three times, but you keep putting it up each time we approach you. Can you release it?"

"Of course I can," she responded sarcastically. "I'm on it."

"Okay. I got it." Josh smiled, purposefully conveying calm for Skylar's sake. *"A-na rische mendu."* The gold shimmer faded from around her body. He inched closer to her without obvious resistance.

"And my eyes?" she asked, blinking dramatically.

"Back to emerald and gorgeous," Josh flirted, but with a hint of apprehension. Skylar turned to me, and I saw that only her right eye had returned to normal. She blinked rapidly and the other eye changed as well, but my uneasiness remained. Hannah shook her head, disgusted, and left.

"Josh," I said with forced calm. "What was that?"

"She was still holding on to magic," he said, keeping his eyes on Skylar. "She just lost control, but she should be fine." If he meant to sound confident, he was doing a poor job of it.

"She can do the same type of magic you can?" Steven asked.

Skylar glanced between us, absorbing our apprehension.

"Yes, as long as she holds on to my magic. But she doesn't know how to control it."

As if managing Skylar isn't difficult enough. "How long is she

171

going to be like this?" I snapped. "The last thing we need is her using powerful magic she can't control."

Josh didn't answer at first. He remained with his back to me, staring at Skylar. After a moment, I caught a very soft chant. He slowly reached out toward her and flicked his finger at her. She yelped in pain.

"Stop it!" she snapped, indignant.

Josh turned to me. "I can't find any other magic sources here. I think she used it all."

You think? I stared at my brother, taking his measure, then nodded. He was as sure as he could be. I hated magic. A blade, a fist, a bite from sharp teeth—those were absolutes. With magic, nothing was ever simple.

"I'm going to borrow these," Josh informed Skylar as he grabbed the journals from the nightstand and left. Steven lingered, concerned, until he caught a look from me and left as well. I remained, leaning against the doorframe, studying Skylar.

"I need to get dressed," she said, seemingly agitated by my presence.

I shrugged. "Then get dressed."

Sitting on the cold floor, holding the comforter around her, Skylar continued to stare, indignant, until I begrudgingly turned in the doorway. Her sense of modesty was annoying. "How did you live as you did?" I asked, listening to her rifle the dresser.

"I'm not sure what you are asking."

"Living in the unknown and being content with it. I operate best when I know all there is to know about things. If I was in your position, there would not be a source I wouldn't investigate to find out about myself." I turned to find her standing before me, dressed in t-shirt and jeans.

"You won't understand because you don't seem to understand fear."

"I understand fear just fine, just not as a recipient," I stated.

"Then you won't understand me or any explanation I try to give you."

I took a seat in a corner near the door and waited. "Try me."

After a moment's hesitation, she dropped onto the edge of the bed as if a heavy weight drove her down. Her gaze lowered to a spot on the floor. "Early on, I knew Elena wasn't my mother, even before she told me. I didn't need her to tell me. There was something different—something wrong with me. I thought I was protecting her by not discussing it but deep down I knew I was protecting me." She glanced up at me from beneath her eyebrows.

"But why not confront the fear?"

"Because of the night terrors. At six, I had nightmares of creatures much like the were-animals, but angrier and more frightening than you all could ever be, which is saying a lot because you all are very scary." She caught my half-smile. "They attacked me in my dreams and I could make them disappear, but I didn't know how I did it. I would just imagine them gone, and poof, they went away. They never injured me but just terrorized me for months. It wasn't until one clawed me and I awoke with this mark, that I realized it wasn't just night terrors." Skylar pulled at her shirt to reveal a scar on the top of her shoulder that resembled a claw mark. "I killed him—well, in the dreams I did, but after that, I never had them again. When I told Elena, she cried. That was something I had never seen her do before. I made her cry. Can you imagine what that did to me? I was a freak that had odd dreams, weird abilities, and she didn't know how to help me. I did that to her and I never wanted to do it again. After that, I made it my goal to be as normal as possible, at least until my change into my wolf. Now, knowing what I do of my birth, I guess she was frightened for me and not of me."

173

Skylar met my gaze, fearful of judgment. Seeing that I had none, her shoulders fell as if relieved of a heavy burden. She seemed grateful, but there was still a fear that she had revealed too much. Aware that my steady gaze might be increasing her self-consciousness, I leaned back into my chair, turning my eyes to a spot on the wall. I frowned. "So when you changed, you thought you had become one of the monsters that terrorized you as a child?"

"I didn't want to be that creature. I just wanted something about me to be normal. Changing into an animal once a month was far from normal."

Considering her nightmares and Josh's story, I rose from the chair and sat next to her. Her body tensed as I gently pulled her shirt back from her shoulder and lightly brushed my finger over the mark. A subtle shiver passed through her body as she slightly raised her shoulder to meet my touch.

"Do you feel like a monster now?"

She didn't answer.

"At one time, we were all monsters, creatures of the night that were nothing more than living nightmares. The vampires, were-animals, witches, and demons commanded the night in bloodshed and terror. We all have evolved throughout the centuries—some more than others. Evolution had to occur, some by force, others through adaptation, and many through their connection with their humanity. Those weren't your night terrors. They were Maya's memories. The memories of those times in which she lived in people whose lives were nothing more than a nightmare in living form. She seems to exorcise the horrors of the lives she lived when you sleep. That explains why your nights are so restless. I often hear you in your sleep, but I always assumed it had to do with what was going on now."

Skylar gave a little ironic smile. "I never had problems sleeping until now."

"I'm sure that's true from your viewpoint, but what do the

174

people say who sleep on the other side of your bed or in the house with you?"

She chose not to answer, self-consciously turning her head and brushing her shoulder with her chin.

I rose to stand at the window, gazing out at the pine and oak trees that populated the retreat. The woods called to me, always calling my wolf to join them.

"Why didn't you tell your brother we went to see the Tre'ase?" Skylar asked.

"I forgot," I lied, without the slightest shift in my heart rate, my breath, or the timbre of my voice. Yet when I turned to Skylar her expression betrayed her disbelief. *She's learning.* I suppressed a satisfied smile.

"Have you been there before?" she asked.

"No."

"Are you lying?"

"You shouldn't go back to the Tre'ase. It wouldn't be safe." Judging by Skylar's disgusted reaction, that was a concern I could put to rest.

"You didn't answer my question. Are you lying?"

"If I were, answering that would defeat the purpose of doing so." I walked out the door, stopping when she blurted, "The magic you're able to do, did she tell you about it?"

I turned, my expression a mask of indifference. "Breaking a ward is hardly witch magic. Were-animals break them all the time. It would be beneficial if you learned to do so, as well, or you will find yourself denied entry into many places you may want to be." I left before she could interrogate me further.

CHAPTER 12

$\mathcal{I}$ spent the afternoon in wolf form, patrolling the retreat grounds with Gavin and Steven, both in their animal forms. More than once we caught the scent of vampires near the house, but never closer than two hundred meters. Each time the vampires had briefly lingered in the woods, and then hurried off the property, probably to escape the sun. None of the scents were fresh. After tracking several of these incursions, I was going to signal the end of our patrol when I picked up the sickening scent of death and sweet flowers intertwined as if the two odors could not bear to separate—Chase and Gabriella. The scent was fresh, perhaps an hour old. Gavin picked up the scent as well, and then Steven. We tracked it toward the house, where it lingered in a copse of trees. Standing in the very spot Chase and Gabriella had stood together, I looked up to Skylar's window just ten meters away. Judging by the lingering scent, the vampires had waited here for some time before leaving. A low, angry growl escaped my lips. I sent Gavin to confirm the vampire pair had left the property, while Steven and I returned to the house. I gave him instructions to tighten up our patrols, and then went off to check on Skylar.

I followed her voice to the library to find her with Josh. He reclined in a chair, his feet up on a table, while she stood next to him. He was flirting with her. Always flirting. I noticed what appeared to be Elena's journals before him. Neither of them noticed my presence in the doorway.

"You will be using me as a conduit, which means you will be bound to me," Josh explained as he stood up.

Skylar appeared anxious. "Will the same thing happen to me as before at Caleb's?"

I tensed.

"Yes, but it won't be as intense," Josh promised, comforting her with a grin. "We will be bound, connected. I can hear your thoughts, so keep it PG and no more name-calling. And any impure thoughts you may have about Ethan's strong, muscular arms around you should be kept under wraps."

"All comments were made under extreme duress. I was out of my head at the time."

"Okay, let's pretend that I believe that."

I raised an eyebrow, but remained silent as Skylar raised the cuff of her jeans on one leg to reveal a sheathed knife attached to her calf. *She must have learned that from Chris.* I was impressed by Skylar's initiative, but I didn't like where this was headed. Was Josh teaching her magic, or merely trying to impress her?

She drew the knife, handing it to Josh. After examining the blade, he cut a thin, shallow red line across his palm. He cut Skylar's palm next. Unlike in Caleb's house, she accepted the pain without reflex or sound. Josh set the knife on the table, then clasped his hand to hers and began chanting. Their silhouetted bodies became luminous until he ceased his chant, and the glow suddenly disappeared.

"Your turn," he said.

I considered intervening. Teaching Skylar magic was dangerous, but if she could learn to protect herself with a simple defensive field, the risk might be worthwhile, but then magic had a way of getting out of control. And Josh had a compulsion to use magic, which is what made him reckless. Could he show the wisdom and self-control necessary to train her to protect herself? I had my doubts, but chose to wait and observe.

"How do I do it?" she asked, doubtful.

"There's no spell for this. Defensive magic is at my command. Will it and it will manifest."

She closed her eyes, settling herself. He waited patiently until she gave up a moment later, frustrated. "I can't do it."

"Skylar, feel what I am doing." He muttered the chant again. The glow of his protective field returned, and then faded away. He released her hand. "Now you do it."

She closed her eyes, her brow tensing with concentration, until a shimmering gold field flickered into existence around them. She opened her eyes, satisfied at the results of her effort. "Cool," she whispered.

Josh frowned at the field, then pushed his hand straight through without resistance. "It would be even cooler if it weren't just a glamour. It works fine as an illusion, but if someone's trying to hurt you, then you are screwed. Make it stronger."

She closed her eyes again. After a moment, she reached out and easily passed her hand through the glamour. She frowned, shoulders slumping in defeat.

"Skylar, protect yourself," Josh insisted.

"I'll try."

He took a few steps back from her, his expression tightening. "Protect yourself, Skylar," he commanded, his tone more urgent. A drinking glass flew at her from the table. She reflexively dropped to her knees so that the glass passed over her, breaking against a bookshelf. A book flew at her next, nearly hitting her before she sidestepped it. Next, the table itself slid across the floor until she physically stopped it.

"Josh, stop it!" she shouted.

"No," he stated firmly, barking, "Skylar, protect yourself." With a wave of his hand, he pushed her back and pinned her against the wall. He held her there, continuing his chant despite her obvious anxiety. Her trust in him turned to naked fear as she stared at her arms, reacting as if in pain. She opened her mouth to scream when he sent her crashing to the floor with a simple gesture.

"You are hurting me!" Skylar shrieked through clenched teeth.

"Then make it stop," Josh insisted.

"I can't."

"You're not trying."

"I don't know what to do!" she cried.

"It's in you. Command the magic to do what you will. You want me to stop, then make it stop."

She squeezed her eyes shut, trying, but remained trans-fixed in the grip of his spell. "I can't do this," she cried, exasperated. But Josh didn't stop. I wondered if he had lost all control.

"Just leave me the hell alone!" Skylar shouted, her face flushed with anger and humiliation.

Remorse came over Josh, as if he'd just realized what he'd done. With a quick wave of his hand, he released the force that held her. She instinctively scrambled to her feet. Realizing she was safe, she backed up to the wall and slid to the ground, exhausted as she caught her breath. "You're a jerk," she rasped, wiping tears and sweat from her face.

"Sorry, that was very wrong of me. It has been my experience that most perform better with a noxious stimulus and high stress situation. Are you okay?"

"I'm not 'most.' I don't want to do this anymore. It was silly to ask."

"It will get easier," Josh promised. "I apologize if I scared you, but don't let my stupid behavior prevent you from exploring your potential."

"I can't do this right now. We just need to hold off for a while."

"Of course," he agreed quickly, offering her a hand. She hesitated, giving him a dark look before accepting. The moment her hand grasped his, his body became rigid. His eyes rolled back and his breathing sped up. "Skylar," he gasped, "let go of me." She gaped at their clasped hands, as if unable to break her grip. I straightened, prepared to intervene, though I had no idea what was happening.

"Skylar, let go!" Josh cried in a strangled voice.

"Josh!" I snapped, but neither of them heard me. My body tensed. My fists clenched, but they were useless. I needed to take charge of the situation but had no idea what I was dealing with.

"I'm trying," Skylar complained. "What am I doing? Tell me how to stop it!"

Josh's eyes darkened the way they had at Caleb's. Heat filled the room, emanating from their grip. I reached for a chair, prepared to break their grip on each other by force, when I was struck by a shock wave that knocked each of us backward. Only I remained on my feet, striking the wall behind me. Skylar collapsed against a wall, while Josh struck a bookshelf, books tumbling down around him. They stared at each other, wide-eyed.

"We need to help you control the way magic affects you," he said through ragged breaths. "I guess I got what I wanted —you protected yourself."

"Sorry."

He shook his head. "Nothing to apologize for. You're right. We should stop experimenting until I have a better understanding of your abilities with magic." They stood up slowly.

"I agree," I said dryly from the doorway, glowering at

Josh. "What good is it to save her from the vampires, only to let her kill herself with magic?" My point made, I turned and left the library before Josh said something we would both regret.

"I think you're in trouble again," Skylar told him as I left.

I chose to walk off my anger by making my rounds of the house, contemplating my brother's dangerous obsession with magic. Like magic, there was no way to control him, which left me furious. "Ethan," Sebastian said, drawing me from my reverie. I found myself in front of his office. "I would like to review the performance of the pack's investment portfolio from the previous quarter." I hesitated, needing a moment to tamp down my residual anger, and then nodded and followed Sebastian into his office. A short time later, Josh and Steven appeared, excited.

"We have an idea how to get the Gem," Steven said.

Sebastian closed the investment spreadsheet on his computer, then gave his full attention from his desk chair. Standing, I crossed my arms over my chest and waited.

Josh began. "We've been worrying about Skylar's link to *Symbols of Death*. What we haven't considered is that the link works both ways. Skylar—"

"No more magic," I insisted. "Haven't you learned your lesson?"

"Not magic," Josh snapped petulantly. "At least, not new magic. This spell has already been cast. We just need to manipulate it to our advantage. Skylar isn't just linked to the book. She is indirectly linked to the Gem itself. If she were to get physically close to the Gem, she will be drawn to it."

"You want to take Skylar to the home of the Seethe," Sebastian said.

Josh opened his mouth to reply, no doubt with a smart-ass remark, but I cut him off. "No." I had more to say, but Sebastian cut short my rebuke with a sharp look. In the Midwest Pack, everyone was allowed their say, even if their ideas were foolish. I grimaced, but had no choice but to endure Josh's recklessness.

"We've already established that the Gem will be disguised by magic"—Josh gave me a defiant look—"but Skylar's link to the Gem cannot be fooled. If she is in proximity to it, she will be drawn to it no matter how it is disguised."

"It's impossible for us to search the home of the Seethe without being detected," I growled, schooling my brother on the obvious. "Even during the day, while the vamps rest, they retain the sense of smell as well as the ability to act. Inside their house, we'll be at their mercy. We might as well put a bow on top of Skylar's head and hand her over to Demetrius."

"There is a window of opportunity," Steven said. "I've reviewed our surveillance of the Seethe over the past year. They are most active at the end of the week."

"You want us to go at night?" I asked, incredulous.

"If we go on a Friday or Saturday night, we should be able to get in and out before they return. At the end of the week, they hunt longer and use that time to satisfy their other desires, as well."

Tonight, then. I considered Steven's plan. Unlike my brother, Steven was not prone to recklessness. He was a cautious, experienced vampire killer. "It might work," I admitted begrudgingly.

A few hours later, well into the evening, I drove the SUV to the Seethe's home on the outskirts of Chicago. Where the pack preferred privacy, the vampires preferred proximity to their prey. I turned down a street lined with extravagant European-style homes. Had I not known better, I wouldn't have believed that vampires lived there. Which was the point. Unlike Caleb, Demetrius didn't draw attention to his Seethe by feeding on the neighbors. I parked in front of a palatial brick house. The lawn was meticulously manicured with small shrubberies, gently outlining the path to the house. No privacy hedges and obscuring trees, here.

Approaching the house undetected was a simple matter. Most streets in the area were lined with lights; this one was lit by just one light on each end. While the Seethe chose to blend into the neighborhood, they also preferred that their comings and goings were not closely observed. I emerged from the SUV, directing Steven and Skylar to follow. Josh and Gavin remained behind—reinforcements to cover our retreat, should our incursion become a battle. Their instructions were specific. Rescuing Skylar was the priority, even at the expense of Steven's life or mine. But if she could not be rescued, Skylar could not be allowed to fall into Demetrius's hands, at any cost. Josh might not be able to follow that order, but Gavin would without hesitation.

I heard Skylar's heart beat faster with each step as we approached the house. Not surprisingly, the front door was unlocked—an open invitation to an unexpected meal. I entered the house first. As with Caleb's home, the living room was another lifeless showroom, though more contemporary. A fully furnished kitchen completed the ruse, but nothing lived here. The house reeked of fresh linen and blood.

Standing in the foyer of the house, I turned to Skylar for direction. She closed her eyes. Her lips pursed in concentration, and then she shook her head. I frowned as she stepped farther into the house, paused, and then crept up the stairs to the second floor. I followed close enough to scoop her into my arms and run at the slightest hint of trouble. She hesitated next to a door that was slightly ajar, then gently pushed it open, the hinges faintly creaking. Light-filtering blinds barred even the moonlight from the windows, but the residual light from the hallway barely illuminated an opulent, king-size bed, decorated with richly colored pillows and a duvet, set against the far wall. The rest of the room was unfurnished.

I watched Skylar closely as she continued down the hall, looking for a sign that she was following the pull of the Gem rather than just blindly wandering through the Seethe's home. *We should leave.* I had already trusted her this far, though, and would give her a few more minutes—at most. At the end of a hall, I caught the scent of Demetrius. Skylar noticed it as well, though I didn't think she could identify the stench that emerged from the master bedroom. The room had an exotic feel, decorated with artifacts and mahogany furniture. Stylistic art hung on cinnamon walls. There was another scent here, entwined with that of Demetrius. Chris, I realized, suddenly revolted. On the verge of losing myself to fury, I backed out of the room, leaving Skylar to explore alone. I already knew that Chris allowed Demetrius to feed on her. I didn't need to know that their relationship had developed further.

At the sound of thumping drawers, I peered into the room to find Skylar on hands and knees looking under the bad. She rose and searched the closets, slamming the doors shut in frustration. This wasn't working. We needed to leave, before something went wrong.

"Skylar," I hissed, "we are not here for that." Sensing her frustration, I placed a hand lightly on her shoulder, over the scar. "Demetrius is smart. I doubt he hid it in his underwear drawer. Just do what we came to do, okay?"

I followed her out of the room and into the next. Through six more rooms, she detected nothing, her desperation growing. As we moved through the living room, kitchen, and dining room, I caught her searching through drawers and closets when she thought I wasn't paying attention. She was determined to leave no hiding place unturned.

We were approaching the stairs to the basement when I heard movement in the shadows. Something approached.

"We need to leave," I whispered. When Skylar didn't budge, I took her by the elbow, pulling her toward the front door. "Now."

"Unexpected guests," said a calm voice with a north-eastern accent. I turned to find the silhouette of a man leaning against a nearby wall. One of the Seethe's garden, I assumed, hearing the man's surprisingly faint heartbeat. He pushed himself up from the wall and emerged from the shadows, revealing unblinking, fluorescent green eyes. His lips curved slightly into a forced smile until he saw Skylar. His smile vanished. His entire focus directed at her. I tensed, fists clenched, wary of an ambush, but the man seemed alone. Killing him would be an easy feat, but I preferred not to. Our incursion was an offense to the Seethe, but killing one of their own in the Seethe's home was an offense on an entirely different level.

Something about the man was off. His heart continued to beat, yet there was no sound of respiration. Sensing my confusion, he offered a forced smile, exposing the tips of his fangs. Neither fully human nor fully vampire. Whatever he was, I was significantly larger, yet the vampire-man remained poised. The beat of his heart betrayed no fear, no emotion at all. *Why isn't he hunting with the rest of the Seethe?*

His gaze shifted back and forth between Skylar and me. "It's her. The one that our Master desires," he whispered, seemingly surprised. Over the man-vampire's shoulder, I saw Steven stealthily approach, grabbing it in a chokehold. He also thought the creature was a human in need of breath.

"Steven, release him," I commanded softly. "Take Skylar to the Tahoe. I will be there in a moment. I need to talk to ..." I raised an eyebrow at the man-vampire, waiting for a name.

He rubbed a hand across his neck. "They call me Quella Perduta, Quell for short," he said, pronouncing his name with an awkward Italian accent.

I recognized the name, by reputation only. Quella Perduta

was an amusement designed for Michaela's enjoyment, with short brown hair and regular features. "They call you 'the lost one.' I dare not ask why," I observed calmly, not wanting to escalate the situation with Skylar in the room.

A devious smile crept onto Quell's face. "Good, because I dare not answer."

"What were you called before?" I asked.

"It doesn't matter because he no longer exists. Since my creation, I have been Quella Perduta." He offered another wan smile. "I may indeed be considered the lost one, but they value my existence tremendously. My Mistress and Master will be quite saddened if it were taken. I guarantee revenge will be sought," he said plainly, fearlessly. Quell seemed to have a very limited capacity to express emotions.

"You should have no fear of that," I answered. "I dare not attack you in your home without cause. You refrain from violence against me and I will do the same."

"Very well, then how may I be of service to you?"

"I need you to relay a message to your Master." I turned to Steven, nodding in the direction of the Tahoe. "I will find my way back to the house."

Steven hurried Skylar out the door.

Once my offer had been made, I disposed of my clothes in a neighbor's trash and then transformed into my wolf for the journey back to the retreat. A hunger came upon me during the journey, but I couldn't spare the time to hunt. Once home, I sent Marko out to keep watch on the Seethe, then quickly showered, dressed, and joined Steven, Gavin, Josh, and Winter in Sebastian's cramped office. While I explained the offer made to Demetrius, I noticed that Steven appeared uneasy.

"You have something to say?" I asked him.

"Skylar did not immediately return to the SUV," he admitted.

My jaw clenched. "Were my orders not specific enough?"

"I got her out of the house and she ran around to the back before I could stop her," he explained evenly, giving a report rather than offering a confession, which I appreciated. "We went inside, to the basement."

Winter made a disgusted sound, while Gavin grimly shook his head.

"You allowed this?" I asked, holding my anger in check.

"I thought she had a hit on the Gem." Steven gave a slight, helpless shrug. "She convinced me."

"This girl seems to have that effect on people," Gavin said tightly.

"You noticed?" Winter asked.

At a signal from Sebastian, Steven continued. "Once we were inside, I realized she was just snooping. There were no signs of vampires, so I decided to give her a minute. She didn't get a hit on the Gem, but we found a room decorated with ritualistic drawings and runes on the wall."

"The site of the ritual," Josh interjected.

I saw a look pass between Steven and Josh. There was more to the story, something Skylar did that neither of them wanted to mention. Given that she was already on thin ice with Sebastian, I decided not to ask. Whether or not Sebastian noticed, I couldn't tell.

"And still we let her live," Gavin said in his Brooklyn accent. "She has a terait, strange magical abilities, a sergence, and the uncanny ability to make the entire Seethe unbearably powerful through her ritualistic murder—an abomination of oddities."

I uttered a low growl, letting Gavin know his place. He gave a faint nod in disgruntled obedience. He was exactly the kind of were that would have called for my head as a child if he had discovered my magical abilities. Anything abnormal was an abomination better destroyed than understood. I considered beating some sense into him, but doubted his ability to fully appreciate the message. He was a good leader, but headstrong—there was a reason he had left the East Coast Pack. Sebastian had already made clear to Gavin that Skylar was protected. Asshole that he was, Gavin wouldn't disobey the Alpha—not directly. I would have my own word with the were-panther—privately.

The offer I had made to Demetrius was agreed to as a matter of formality. As the pack Beta, I had the right to negotiate on the pack's behalf without consultation when the necessity arose. Nothing to do now but wait for the vampire's reply.

Starving, I made my way to the kitchen, where I found Skylar waiting with an anxious expression. I wondered what she had done at the Seethe's home that Josh and Steven had chosen not to share—something reckless. "Yes, Skylar?" I asked roughly as I retrieved a pair of tenderloins and a chicken breast from the fridge.

"Go ahead." She sat down at the table, observing my every move. "I can wait till after you've eaten."

How considerate. Trying to ignore her, I plated the food, heated it in the microwave, and then sat at the table.

"I know you identify with the wolf," Skylar said, frowning at my plate, "but your human half needs vegetables."

I looked at her, then walked to the refrigerator, broke off a small stalk of broccoli from the produce drawer, took a tiny bite, and swallowed. "Satisfied?"

She shrugged. "It's your health."

I finished my meal under her watchful gaze. My mood somewhat sedated, I pushed the plate aside and waited patiently for her to speak.

"What happened with Quell?"

Not the conversation I want to have with you. I considered not answering. "We are trying to negotiate with Demetrius."

"Negotiate? For what?"

"We asked for the Gem, and in return, we would overlook certain indiscretions that we haven't in the past."

188

"Indiscretions?" Skylar said, disgusted. "What type of indiscretions? Did you agree to let them kill a certain number of people while you turned a blind eye? Do they get to kill expectant mothers now or maybe children? Can they now turn children and kill whomever without any recourse? Or will you provide carry-in for them once a month?"

I didn't bother to hide my disappointment. Even after the time Skylar had spent with us, she still didn't understand pack life. While the pack often curtailed the activities of the vampires and other supernaturals in our territory, we operated strictly in the interest of self-preservation. Humanity was largely unaware of the supernatural world, affording us the privacy and discretion to live as we chose. The vampires were less careful, but their limitations forced some discretion. Should the vampires complete their ritual and shed their limitations, the resultant debauchery and carnage would draw the attention of the human world. The pack would likely be exposed, as well. Skylar had been with us long enough that she should have been able to understand how we operated; I wasn't in the mood to explain again. There were hard lessons for her to learn. Survival didn't always fit into a pretty, comfortable box. My refusal to answer furthered her rising ire. "Skylar, you need to calm down."

"No, I won't calm down! What the hell did you do?" She rose to her feet.

I rose as well, resisting the urge to slam my fists onto the table in the process. I approached her carefully, willingly suppressing my frustration. "This isn't a good situation. It is a necessary evil. It is a much better alternative than them actually gaining possession of you, and all boundaries that restrict them being lifted. I assure you, they won't stop until you are theirs." My anger taking over, I found myself backing her into a wall. I planted my hands on either side of her, pinning her in place. When I tried to meet her gaze, she turned from side to side, avoiding me. Finally, she slid down the wall until she sat on the floor and pulled her knees to her chest.

"I know this is a bad situation," she admitted, close to tears. She had the look of someone caught in a moral dilemma that would drive them mad. She was wrong to think of this as a moral dilemma. It was a matter of survival.

My anger melted at the sight of her distress, but I held on to the frustration, resisting the urge to kneel next to her. I sighed, but it came out more like a growl. "The cards are dealt and we have to play with what we have. You can't wish them away nor will tears wash the situation away."

I watched her body tense as the tears dried up in a single, defiant sniffle. "I'm sorry that loss of life is so frivolous to you." She looked up at me with a stern dislike that bordered on hatred. "We can't all be as callous as you seem to be."

I stiffened. "If I were as emotional as you are, I could never perform my job. Sitting on the floor overwrought with emotion is a luxury this pack cannot afford. We have to make very hard decisions. Decisions I wish came with a better resolution, but we must weigh them all and go with the one that is easiest to live with."

She defiantly held my gaze, finally blurting, "Sucks to be you right now, huh?"

The weight of protecting the pack, protecting Skylar, who was prone to foiling my every effort, was challenging. But that was my role. I was the pack Beta and I would not fail. Not ever. Suddenly tired, I leaned against the counter. "I would love to go into their home and just wipe the place clean, rid us of all the bloodsuckers. But that would guarantee a war that would leave far too many casualties." I shook my head.

Skylar's expression softened, the fight in her body fading. As she considered what to say, I saw her shoulder twitch as if she wanted to reach out to me but decided better of it.

Instead she rose and left the kitchen. At least now I could be alone. My phone rang. Marko informed me that he had seen Chris leave the Seethe with six others. Two of them he recognized, lone were-animals known to sell their services. The rest appeared to be human. Finally the information Artemis had given me fell into place. If Chris had wanted security, she would have brought vampires. She was coming to deliver Demetrius's reply, and the answer was "no." She had no intention of leaving empty-handed. She'd been preparing for this sort of assault all along, and I had given her the pretext she needed to put her plan into action.

I gathered the others with Sebastian and a plan was made. Skylar was to remain where she was, upstairs. There was no reason to inform her what was happening, but I placed Steven in position to watch the stairs and prevent her from descending. Josh and Gavin took key positions in the house, while Winter distributed the rest of the pack on the grounds. "There will be a mage," I warned them. "He may be of use to us, if he survives."

This is it for Chris and me. This was Chris's plan unfolding, and once it was over, we would likely never see each other again. My thoughts turned to the memory of her skin against mine, the heat of her flesh. I remembered the taste of her lips. I was reliving our last intimate encounter when I heard the front door open. The intruding breeze brought the familiar, light floral scent from my memories, but entwined with the corrupting reek of Demetrius. I scowled. Chris was already lost to me. She just didn't know it. Sebastian and I greeted her in the entryway as she strolled casually, defiantly into our home. The fitted white button-down and jeans showed off her figure splendidly. Quell watched calmly from just behind the threshold of the open doorway. Marko had not been entirely accurate, then; Chris had brought a vampire, after all, but in Quell's case the mistake was understandable.

Steven appeared from a neighboring room. I caught a

flick of his eyes toward the stair and saw Skylar crouched there, spying. Shifting slightly to block Chris's approach to the stairs, I made a subtle gesture to Steven, sending him out of the room to another, less-used stairwell. Chris stopped before Sebastian and me, basking in our condemnation.

She smiled demurely, gesturing toward Quell. "He's harmless," she told Sebastian. "Ask your Beta."

"Maybe so, but a vampire will never be invited into our home," Sebastian said. "It is our misfortune that you don't require one."

Chris's smile broadened. "Demetrius received your message," she stated as she stepped closer to me. "He wasn't too thrilled about your little visit to their home. I think his exact words were, 'That damn wolf entered my home and left his stench in the house.'"

"If I can stand his, he surely can stand mine."

"That is not the point," Chris said, amused. "You all know better. How dare you! I don't believe you to be this stupid, so I assume the little doe-eyed wolf with all the gumption was behind this plan. She's too new to this world and doesn't know—"

"I made Demetrius a proposition," I snapped. "What was his decision?"

"And it was quite a proposition, but regretfully he declined. In fact, Quell, what were his exact words?"

Quell's expression remained void of all emotions as he spoke softly. "I apologize. My Master never responded but his declination was implied."

"He laughed, sweetheart. Your offer never even got a response. It's over. The fact you all are sneaking into their home and making bargains shows that you know this as well."

"I assure you it is not over," Sebastian said confidently. "Attempting to provide a civil resolution to a rather distasteful situation was our intention. If failure is what Demetrius desires, then it is what he will receive."

"Certainly you don't value the little wolf's life so much that you will risk the safety of your pack?" Chris asked in disbelief.

Sebastian sneered, taking several steps toward her. Her eyes widened in mock alarm. Very few could stand before an angry Sebastian and remain calm. I admired her fearlessness, but she knew we would never harm a messenger without direct provocation. "Her life has very little to do with this," he said. "It is the life of the many that we are concerned about. What would the body count be if the vampires were allowed the freedom that the powers of this world saw fit to deny them? We would all be drawn into the light."

"When the were-animals' restrictions were removed, not less than a century ago, the vampires' should've been, too. At one time, the were-animals were tied to the Moon, Mercury, and Saturn, like children. Now your kind are no longer slaves to that which calls them. Instead, you all are allowed to take animal form at will. This is something that more than a century ago was unthought of. Back then, when the animal was unleashed, it was a vicious murderous creature unable to control its primal impulses. Were-animals were nothing more than death that traveled on four legs. Now you feel that you are superior to the vampires because you all somehow evolved to a lesser evil. *Pshaw!* You all are no better than the vampires. Dwelling just below the surface still remains that wild, ferocious animal—no matter how hard you try to assume domestication. Why do you think lone were-animals still exist? Because some of your kind still long for the primitive ways—to be the very embodiment of death. They are what you used to be in its purest form—raw, uninhibited, merciless—true predators."

Sebastian answered with a contemptuous scowl. "I am by no means domesticated or presume to be. We are predators and that will never change. We have evolved over the years, making our existence easier. However, restrictions still exist. We still have to answer to that which once restricted us like the vampires to the night and you to whatever demonic force that holds your interest. We still have something that we answer to. Centuries ago, we formed packs when our kind chose to not kill for entertainment and to stop being the things that nightmares were made of. Our restrictions were modified because of the penance we paid. Perhaps the vampires should learn from our example. I don't know why these restrictions exist, are modified, or even removed. Nevertheless, they are our restrictions—our rules. Demetrius doesn't get to spurn his restrictions because they are hard and he lacks self-control to deal with them."

"Please trust that Demetrius will practice discretion and self-control with the new freedoms. He just wants his people to enjoy the same privileges that are given to others."

"Really? You expect us to believe that Demetrius and his Seethe know anything of control? That's your compelling argument? Far too often, Demetrius has been known to kill his donors. After being a vampire for over a hundred and sixty years, he still manages to lose control when feeding. His control is quite limited, and it is wise that you remember this and be careful as you trade with him—or maybe not. Maybe we would be better off if he did lose control."

Chris's casual bravado finally cracked, irritation creeping into her smile. "I don't really care what you believe. Your pack members will die if you continue with this. I know you like to think that you are more powerful than the vampires. In the past, they were content, allowing you to hold this belief because you were too insignificant to challenge. But now he grows tired of the pack's intrusions. You have been warned. I advise you to take this seriously and not be as foolish as your Beta," she stated boldly, shooting me a look.

"What do you get out of this, Chris?" I demanded,

frowning as I stepped closer to her. I already knew, but I needed to keep her distracted. "You really seem to be determined to make this happen. What are you getting out of it?"

"It's a job." She shrugged. "I take my jobs quite seriously."

"You've always been good at your job, a quality I greatly admire about you. But you are not speaking as a hunter doing an exceptional job." I allowed a half-smile, which caught her off guard. "He's agreed to turn you, hasn't he? He turns you right before the ritual and you get to have what you've always wanted with no penalties. It's a win-win situation for you. I guess then you can stop being his blood whore." I glared at Chris, unblinking, as my accusation spread through her like a resentful wildfire. She was about to answer when Steven appeared, descending the stairs to join us.

"It's done," he stated in a rough voice. Gavin and Josh emerged from other areas of the house. Gavin's shirt was covered with blood, the lust for more plain on his face. He nodded at me. Josh did the same.

I turned back to Chris. "You had five people with you, hiding outside: a mage, two lone were-animals, and two members of the garden. The were-animals are dead; pack law would not allow us to spare their lives. The members of the garden are dead, as well. You can give Demetrius and his Mistress my condolences. The mage's life was spared, but he will not be returning with you."

Chris shrugged as if she couldn't care less. "Casualties of war. Something you too will soon experience."

She didn't miss a beat. I loved her bravado. It took a great deal to break her confidence. I stared at her, taking in every inch of her for the last time. She stared back, defiant at first, but then it seemed she recognized the finality of my attention. I stepped closer. She gave a surprised but inviting smile. Inches apart, I lost track of the others around us—not that I cared. For a moment, there was just Chris and me and the passionate love we'd once shared. I slowly reached out a hand and gently stroked the back of her neck, while the other hand pushed away strands of hair from her face. Her lips parted as I leaned forward and gently kissed her cheek. Then I turned and kissed her ready lips, our passion fed by our time apart, concentrated now into a single, all-encompassing kiss. When it was over, I brushed her cheek with my own. I inhaled her scent—ignoring that of Demetrius—then brushed my lips against her ear.

"You are usually quite wise in your decision making," I whispered. "But this time you've chosen the wrong side. Leave tonight. You can no longer be part of this. You are welcome to return when this is over. I've warned you far more times than you deserved because of the love we once had for one another. Now you can only repay my consideration with your life. Tomorrow I go for a hunt and you are the prey. If you are found, then your life is mine to take."

Chris stumbled back a step, her arrogant veneer finally cracked. She stared at me, her expression frozen in mirthless humor, taking my measure. Slowly, fear settled on her as she realized I was telling the truth. I would hunt her. I would kill her. She straightened, taking in slow, steady breaths to regain her composure. She gave me a sly smile, assured that she could manipulate me with her charm.

"Casualties of war," I stated coolly.

I could hear the confused beats of her heart as she backed toward the door, staggering over the threshold. Gathering her dignity with a final sharp glare, she turned to leave. Quell followed, expressionless. I closed the door behind them.

The next day, I left the house to hunt for Chris. I explored the grounds of the retreat and the surrounding areas. No trace of her remained. At least we had been able to say a proper good-bye.

CHAPTER 13

The next few days were frustratingly quiet. Chris's absence felt like a loss, the end of our relationship played out for the second time. I wanted nothing more than to cleanse my grief through combat, but Demetrius refused to comply. I increased patrols, frequently joining them, but the vampire incursions onto the retreat grounds had ceased. When not on the grounds or tending to pack business, I exhausted myself through extreme workouts and sparring with Winter and Gavin. I kept my distance from Skylar. It seemed inappropriate to share my grief with her, and she would not understand. She hardly noticed, enjoying Steven's company instead. Since he had been ordered to sleep in her room to prevent another escape attempt, the two had formed a curious bond. Often I heard their rapid-fire conversations and laughter extend deep into the night.

While they took advantage of the peace to deepen their relationship, I knew the quiet wouldn't last. Demetrius would be furious at Chris's failure, but not deterred. He would make his next move soon, but tonight was a full moon. An ancient agreement existed between the vampires and werewolves; even during our most bitter conflicts, the sanctity of the full moon had never been broken.

Returning to the house from a morning patrol, I arrived to find a delivery vehicle pulling away. Steven, wearing loose-fitting jeans and a white t-shirt, accepted an extravagantly wrapped package. He was on his way with it to Skylar's room when I stopped him to examine the parcel. The card, smelling faintly of geranium and sage, simply read, "Skylar" in stylized print. Steven watched, his objections silent as I expertly opened the package in a manner that would be easy to disguise. Inside, I found a rolled canvas that contained an eerily lifeless portrait of Skylar, devoid of color or vibrancy. Her expression seemed fragile and naïve. I growled at Owen's signature at the bottom right of the canvas.

"He calls her sometimes, to check on her," Steven said, unimpressed as well.

Resisting the urge to shred the portrait, I carefully returned the canvas to the box and handed it to him. "Seal it before you give it to her," I said, and then left to shower before lunch.

As the day progressed, I shared the rising anticipation of the pack's canidae as moonrise approached. Though we were no longer slaves to the full moon, it beckoned to us from our ancient past, drawing us to our most primal urges. For some, the full moon was a curse. A few weres spent their entire lives resisting their animal nature, as if those ancient urges could be absolved through academic study or meditation or sheer will. But the power of the full moon could not be denied. Our animal nature emerged, to horrific results for those who resisted. Other weres surrendered their entire lives to their animal impulses. For them, control was a foreign concept, but it was not the animal that lost control— it was the person inside. It was their desire to be led only by primal urges. I'd never known that lack of control. I embraced the cleansing glow of the full moon as an opportunity to embrace my animal nature.

I wondered if Skylar would participate in the run. Despite her recent, tentative acceptance, she still saw her wolf as a separate entity, to be managed and suppressed unless needed. For her, the full moon remained a dreaded symbol of her perceived curse. She might not feel safe on the retreat grounds, either. After we'd finally instilled in her a healthy fear of presenting herself on a platter to the vampires, Skylar might not understand the ancient pact that held the Seethe at bay this night. The decision was hers. I was determined not to interfere.

Those of us drawn to the moon—wolves, coyote, dingo—watched it rise over the treetops, gently illuminating the night with a soft glow. I waited among them until Sebastian left the house, drawing the rest of us onto the lawn. Thirty of us gathered, eagerly anticipating the start of the run. From across the lawn, I watched Skylar, tentative but excited, emerge from the house at Steven's side.

Sebastian was the first to strip off his clothes and change into wolf form. I followed, along with the others. Through my wolf eyes, I watched as Steven offered a word of encouragement to Skylar, and then changed effortlessly, showing her how simple the change should be. I padded toward her, expecting to assist her transformation, when she quickly and unexpectedly transformed on her own. I smiled at her progress.

Sebastian howled, drawing a crescendo of melodious howls that resonated throughout the thick woodlands, and then ran, drawing us behind him. We bounded across the wooded grounds of the retreat, enjoying the thrum of the grass beneath our paws as we darted between trees, embracing the unbridled freedom of our animal nature. The pack swayed as members nipped and chased and tackled one another, basking in our collective ebullience as we followed

Sebastian's lead. I caught a glimpse of Skylar chasing Steven into the heart of the pack. Deciding to leave them be, I raced toward the front, pulling just short of Sebastian's right flank. Joyous howls erupted sporadically as the Alpha led us over grassy terrain, weaving our way through the woods for the simple pleasure of running.

The chorus of howls suddenly ceased, dowsed by a sudden, oppressive wave of anger that arose from Sebastian. He growled just as I caught the scent of vampires in the woods before us—dozens of vampires. The entire Seethe had come to break the ancient truce between werewolves and vampires. They had come for Skylar. I growled at the wretched scent before us, lusting for the kill. In animal form, we were more than a match for the Seethe, but Sebastian turned the pack about. As we raced toward the retreat, I glanced back to see Steven guiding Skylar into the center of the pack while the others surged protectively around her, but her gray coat was unmistakable.

Vampires emerged from the woods ahead of us, armed with crossbows, swords, and guns. Crimson eyes glowed with the anticipation of blood. The moonlight that was ours reflected off pale faces and bared fangs. Sebastian charged the nearest vampires, tearing the throat from one in a bloody spray, and then mauling another with his claws. I took down two others in quick succession. In a matter of seconds, we took out several vamps, nearly clearing a path to the retreat when I heard a chant rising from the woods to my left. My body seized in pain. Struggling to stay on my feet, I saw four hooded figures, witches, in a nearby coppice, chanting in unison. I stumbled toward them, but collapsed onto the ground next to Sebastian. Panting, convulsing, I resisted the call to change that was being forced on me, but the reversion spell was too powerful. Knowing I was most vulnerable in transition, I accepted the change, which came quickly.

Once in my human form, I jumped to my feet, naked, and

charged the witches, determined to reach them and kill them at all costs. I lunged at the nearest witch, but the four suddenly vanished. I roared in fury at the empty air, and then turned back toward the pack. The witches had completed their task. The spell had been massive. Skylar, in her human form, stood confused amid a ring of writhing figures. Most of the pack lay on the ground, resisting the protracted transition, while the rest stood, confused and naked, still absorbing the situation. Surprisingly, the vampires waited. We were naked, weaponless, and vulnerable, and the vampires were enjoying it.

While I gathered the others, directing them to gather around Skylar, an overexcited vampire charged. Sebastian killed it easily, snapping its neck with his bare hands. Even in human form, the Alpha's power was formidable, but we were about to be overwhelmed. As the vampires began slowly pressing toward us, Winter broke from the trees at a dead run with her katana in hand. At full speed, she was faster than any were-animal or vampire. She leapt over Skylar, brandishing her katana and severing a vampire head as she landed. Continuing her motion, Winter dropped into a crouch, cut the legs from another vampire, and then rose to decapitate it on the backswing. She finished by dropping into a combat stance. With a defiant look, she dared the closest vampire to come forward. The vampire obliged, along with another. While I preferred the thrill of brute force, I couldn't help but admire Winter's elegant gestures with the sword, a martial exercise in graceful efficiency as she cut the two vampires down with a single, fluid motion. She was ready for more, coolly prepared to take on the entire Seethe in ones and twos, but then an unseen, oppressive force entered the battlefield.

The vampires closest to Winter parted like the flesh from a fresh wound, making way for Demetrius as he entered the battlefield, a heavy, two-handed sword gripped in one hand.

The ends of his wavy midnight hair bounced on his shoulders with each stride. A hint of red glowed like hot coal in his black opal eyes. An arrogant, thin smile stretched across his lips, highlighting his sharply defined jaw and cheeks. The vampire leader radiated an unnatural terror.

Winter's confidence melted in a way I had never before witnessed. She dropped back into a defensive posture, and I saw the tip of her katana tremble slightly. Demetrius's lips spread into a sadistic smile. Without breaking stride, he swung his massive sword. Winter deflected the blow with her katana, but barely. The vampire followed up with a series of blows, sending her stumbling and fumbling backward as she barely deflected them until the blade of her katana finally snapped just above the wrist guard. The next blow came so fast she had no choice but to try and deflect it with the wrist guard. While she managed to turn the main force of the blow, the blade cut into her shoulder. She screamed, a cry of pain that quickly transformed into a roar of gritty determination.

She dropped down and kicked Demetrius's legs out from under him. His sword tumbled to the ground. Before she could follow through, the vampire leapt to his feet, grabbed her with one hand, and tossed her back several feet as if he were discarding a toy. Before Sebastian and I could intervene, a handful of vampires broke from their line, charging toward Skylar. Like the weres around her, she remained engrossed by Winter's fate, oblivious to her own danger. The Alpha and I charged into the vampires, tearing them apart as we fought our way toward Skylar.

Demetrius retrieved his sword and was advancing toward her when Steven, somehow still in coyote form, lunged at him. The vampire leader swung his sword upward, piercing Steven's torso, and then slid the blade through his abdomen as though it were cutting through butter. Steven cried out in mortal agony, and then fell to the ground. He lay panting hard as he changed back into human form, exposing the full gruesome details of his wound. Gripping the pommel with both hands, Demetrius pushed the sword farther through Steven's stomach and then twisted. Steven's face trembled. His body shuddered but he did not cry out again. I wasn't sure if he was alive or dead. With a pleased look on his face, Demetrius withdrew the sword and started toward Winter.

Josh suddenly appeared, popping into existence with a crossbow, a large cross, and an armful of weapons. From the looks of it, he had grabbed anything and everything in sight. He tossed a sword to Sebastian, who snatched it from the air. Reaching out, he called for another and Josh obliged, tossing one of Winter's katanas. Sebastian twirled both in unison, demonstrating his exceptional swordsmanship. Brutal anger settled on his face as he stalked toward Demetrius, who relished the challenge.

I froze with the rest of the battlefield, captivated by the elegant dance that followed, a masterful display of swordsmanship on both sides that ebbed and flowed as the two leaders circled, pressed, and maneuvered each other, at all times pressing for deadly advantage. Like a pup, I allowed myself to be distracted. I failed to notice Skylar edging toward Steven—away from her protectors.

"Skylar!" Winter called frantically, jerking my attention from the fight.

I turned to see Skylar and Winter running toward each other. A blur appeared, a vampire at full speed. Only when she stopped to grab Skylar did I recognize Michaela, the Mistress of the Seethe. Gavin charged, but too late. I saw her victorious grin just before she disappeared from the battlefield, taking Skylar with her.

I turned to my brother with an anxious fury. "Josh!" I roared.

He tossed the remainder of the weapons he'd been distributing to the ground, keeping a knife in one hand and the cross in the other, and then disappeared. The rest of the vampires charged, flowing around the still raging battle between Sebastian and Demetrius to kill the rest of us. They grinned, the anticipation of easy blood in their expressions. I charged, bare-handed, meeting the vampires halfway. I heard the thump of a crossbow as a bolt whined past me, piercing the nearest vampire through the cheek. I snapped the vampire's neck with two hands, drove the bolt through the brain, pulled it out the backside of the skull, and then drove the wooden bolt into the heart of the next vampire. Beside me, Hannah drew her knife across the throat of another vampire, while Winter and Gavin defended Steven's body with swords.

I couldn't be sure if Sebastian knew anything of the battle around him, but there was an added urgency to the blows he rained down on Demetrius. The vampire fell back under the assault, defending from his heels, while Sebastian relentlessly pressed the advantage. Demetrius was on the cusp of defeat, but then his lips spread into a satisfied half-smile just before he vanished. Sebastian roared in fury, and then charged into the vampires' flank, severing heads and limbs with both blades.

The battle continued. After a few short minutes, we seemed on the cusp of total victory when I realized the vampires were running, withdrawing in stages. We were fighting the rear guard that covered the retreat. The last of the guard fell. I picked up a fallen sword and roared, intending to pursue the others back to the home of the Seethe and rescue Skylar. The pack surged forward to follow my lead until Sebastian called us back. I turned my fury on him, but Sebastian gripped my shoulder hard.

"Ethan! We are too weak for a counterattack. We have to regroup."

No!

"Josh will get Skylar back! We have to get Steven back to the retreat while we can."

I turned to see Winter kneeling next to Steven. He was alive, but barely. The rest of the pack was ready to carry on the fight, but many of them were wounded. Exhaustion, exacerbated by the reversion spell, was plain in their expressions. I jerked free of Sebastian's grasp, took two steps after the Seethe, and then stopped. I wanted to bathe in vampire flesh and blood. I wanted to save Skylar. Now.

"We could be charging into a trap," Sebastian continued.

He was right. Barely bridling my rage, I dropped my sword, strode to Steven, and gently lifted him into my arms. Sebastian directed the others to guard our flanks and rear as I ran, carrying Steven back to the retreat. Winter opened the door in front of me. As I entered, I felt a rush of relief to find Josh and Skylar sitting with their backs against the wall. A bloody knife and a cross that reeked of burned flesh lay at his feet. His shirt was drenched in blood. Judging by my brother's obvious exhaustion, his magical abilities had been stretched to his limit. A bruise was forming on Skylar's face. She gasped at the sight of Steven in my arms as I carried him past her to the infirmary. Behind me, Dr. Baker stopped her at the door.

"She can stay," Sebastian stated as I carefully laid Steven onto an exam table. Ragged, shallow sounds emanated from him as he struggled to breath. The muscles of his face and neck strained with the effort. Dr. Baker examined the wound, revealing the full horror of it. I knew by his grim expression that there was nothing he could do for Steven. For the sake of the others, Sebastian and I maintained our poise, radiating calm as we were able to, but Steven's wounds were difficult to behold. We lived in a violent world, but nothing could prepare even the most jaded of us for the horrific sight of pack members—family and friends—dying in such a gruesome manner.

I prepared myself for the pain to come, as did Gavin and Winter.

Skylar appeared at Steven's head, the anguish raw in her expression as she forced herself to stare at his gory wound. Gavin made a disgusted sound as she began to sob. Ignoring him, she gingerly placed her palm on Steven's chest just above his wound. Her face tightened. She fought back tears as she watched his breaths steadily grow shallower.

Sebastian placed his hand over Skylar's, surprising me. It was not her place to participate in the ritual, but I saw the deep compassion in her eyes. Steven was right about her. Perhaps Sebastian would be able to utilize the obvious bond between them. He would need every support available. Judging by the scowl on Gavin's face, he didn't agree with Skylar's inclusion, but said nothing. As Sebastian created the link, I felt the heat radiating from his chest as he began to absorb Steven's wound. That heat spread to myself, Gavin, Skylar, and Winter as we each absorbed as much of the energy from Sebastian as we could. Some wounds Sebastian could heal alone, simply by taking them into himself, but Steven's wound was a mortal one. In order for the Alpha to survive the ritual, the rest of us needed to share his burden.

As Beta, I took more than the rest. The heat in my chest began to burn. The others experienced the same, to varying degrees. Unaware of what was happening, Skylar tried to jerk her hand free, but Sebastian's grip was unyielding. The pain in my chest accelerated. I felt Demetrius's sword stab into me. I doubled over, struggling to keep my feet. Gavin and Winter collapsed, and I followed them. I didn't know how Sebastian remained standing, but Skylar kept her feet by leaning against him.

For what seemed an eternity, I knew nothing but blinding agony. When the pain finally subsided, I lay on my back. Sebastian stepped back from Steven, exhausted. Slash marks identical to Steven's wound covered his stomach. A glance at my own chest revealed no such marks. Sebastian had spared us the worst of Steven's wound, taking the bulk of it upon himself. Sebastian's breathing was hard and raspy, and his eyes switched quickly between his human and animal forms until he finally accepted the transformation. A massive, dark brown wolf collapsed to the ground, panting. Winter knelt next to him, giving Skylar a warning glare as she did the same. Offering soothing comfort, Winter gently rubbed her hands through Sebastian's fur. Frightened and no doubt in shock from what she had just witnessed, Skylar rose to her feet, barely composed herself, and then quickly left the room.

A new hope in his eyes, Dr. Baker diligently tended to Steven. I rose, relieved to see that Steven was conscious, his eyes open. The grimace on his face spoke to the intensity of his pain, but his wound had diminished significantly. If he lived, it would be a testament to the strength of our Alpha. Satisfied with the results of the ritual, I stumbled to one of the beds in the infirmary and collapsed into an exhausted sleep.

I awoke sometime later to a wave of fury coursing through the house. I found Sebastian at the epicenter as he paced one of the larger communal rooms, intermittently throwing chairs and chaise couches as he vented. Each time his temper flashed, a fresh wave of anger spread through the house, the shock wave of an emotional earthquake, driving the younger members of the pack into a rage many of them had no ability to control as their animals responded. I could see several pack members struggling to resist transforming. Winter lurked on the edge of the room, keeping out of Sebastian's path while exuding calm to the others, but she was overwhelmed. For all her talents, she did not possess the power I had. The two of us combined were unable to match Sebastian's power, but we managed to keep most of the pack in human form. I didn't need a house full of enraged were-animals.

"They violated the rules," Sebastian shouted, triggering another shock wave as he flipped a couch across the room. "You never attack during the call of the moon!" Demetrius had done more than lie or break a pact; he had attacked the very heart of order. Eventually, Sebastian's fury abated, withdrawing within him and leaving the rest of us exhausted. In a final outburst, he threw another couch across the room to crash into the wall just a few feet from Skylar, who looked terrified. I had no idea how long she had been standing there, obviously drawn by the same energy that had drawn us all. Without a word, Sebastian strode into his office and slammed his door shut.

Skylar glanced about the room, shocked, and then went back upstairs.

After calming the rest of the pack, I found Josh studying some old text in his room, barely able to keep his eyes open. I asked him to fill me in on what had happened to Skylar after she'd been taken. "Michaela took her to the Seethe home. By the time I arrived Skylar had already escaped," he stated, impressed. More than likely, Michaela had allowed Skylar to escape to toy with her. "I cut Michaela's throat, but it was really just a distraction. She'll survive." He sounded disappointed.

I studied his haggard look. "You did well. Get some rest."

"Sleep." Josh's weak smile quickly turned into a yawn. "Wish I could remember what that's like. First I need to try another locator spell in the Chasm. If that fails, I'm leaving in the morning to see London."

As far as I knew, locator spells were simple, but I'd never heard Josh mention the Chasm. "Explain."

My brother rolled his eyes at me, but was too tired to offer much resistance. "The Chasm is the space between natural and dark magic. It's a bit of an overlap. Witches go there sometimes, when we need to poke at the darkness." He quickly cut off my objection with a dismissive wave of his hand. "Honestly, Ethan, I'm too tired. The Gem is dark magic, and it's being hidden by dark magic. I'm not new to the Chasm. It's not a big deal, big brother. I just need to put a foot a bit further into the darker side, just long enough to take a good look."

"You're not exactly inspiring confidence," I snapped. "I forbid it."

"Here we go again. Ethan—"

"You're exhausted." *You'll make a mistake and get yourself killed.* I cut off the urge to bark further commands, and then sighed. "Just take one day."

Josh rested his head back against the wall. "Skylar doesn't have time."

"One day," I insisted. "Demetrius will need time to regroup."

"He won't wait long. The best option we have is to locate and recover the Gem. If I can't locate the Gem on my own power, there's still a chance that London can disenchant it through its link to *Symbols of Death*, but getting to London will take time. If I need London, I have to leave in the morning. I know the Chasm sounds risky, but it's a hell of a lot safer than my fallback plan." He cut me off with a simple gesture. "Don't even ask about my fallback plan."

"One. Day."

"Not possible. I have to try before . . ." Josh bit his nails, allowing his voice to trail off.

Before Demetrius captures Skylar again. "Forget the Chasm for now." This time it was my turn to cut off an objection. "Go to London in the morning. If that fails, come back, rest one day, and then try your locator spell in the Chasm."

Josh pushed his fingers through his hair as he exhaled slowly. "Sure," he surrendered. "Fine. I'll agree to that."

That was the best I could hope for. I nodded, rising, and then stopped at the door. "Promise me you won't do any more magic until you've rested."

He lay back onto his bed, folding his hands over his chest and closing his eyes. "I won't do ... I promise. I'll ... I'm ..." He muttered the rest, falling fast into a deep sleep.

A soft knock on the door, and then Dr. Baker entered. "Steven is awake now." I nodded, grateful, and followed him out of the room, gently closing the door behind me.

I stopped to eat something in the kitchen first.

Steven had been moved to one of Dr. Baker's recovery rooms. As I approached, I heard him laugh. Skylar sat beside him in a chair that had been pushed up to the bed. I hesitated in the doorway, unnoticed. The smell of blood and antiseptic lingered, but Steven appeared to be doing well. He clutched his stomach, wincing as he laughed. "Still hurts."

"Well, it happened just a couple of hours ago," Skylar scolded him. "A gut wound like that, even for you super-furries, is going to take time to heal."

"I know. I've never been injured this badly before," he admitted, putting on a brave face, but I heard the fear in his heartbeat. Steven knew just how close to death he had come. "Farmer's market, huh?" he said with a grin, returning to some earlier discussion I had missed, or had they developed their own shorthand? "That's what every were-animal wants to hear. I sound really hardcore, a menace for all to fear." Another attempt to laugh left him wincing in pain.

Skylar laughed. "I assure you—you are quite scary. Speaking of scary, I met Michaela today."

Steven's mouth twisted in surprise. He studied Skylar. "Well, you're here, so I assume the meeting didn't go well for her."

"Did you know she likes to feed from children?"

He nodded, frowning.

"She found me amusing and wished she could keep me as a pet."

"That's not unusual. Gabriella and Chase are similarly amused with Winter and had the misfortune of expressing it on several occasions. They even asked if she would consider joining them in their bed." He scowled. "That was a bad day for them. One of his tattoos is covering a scar Winter gave him as a result of that lewd proposal."

"Aside from the fact Michaela wants to murder me so she can go around feeding from children, she seems like a big bowl of crazy."

Steven chuckled. "Demetrius likes his women to be eccentric, with a certain level of passion."

"You realize *eccentric* and *crazy* aren't synonymous."

"For them, it seems like a very fine line. From what I hear, she is actually more palatable compared to his former Mistress. She was touched in the head and tap-danced on the line between sanity and crazy every inch of the way. Apparently, she was quite the menace."

Skylar leaned forward and laid her head on the bed next to his leg. "If I never see another vampire in my life, it will be too soon." She let out an exhausted sigh.

Patting her on the head, Steven said, "You're not a very good wolf. The challenge should be exhilarating."

"What about me ever gave you the impression I was a good werewolf? I am probably the worst ever created," she whispered into the side of the bed.

He chuckled. "Worst ... that's a stretch. You're just not a very good wolf yet, but I assure you, I've met worse."

"Sleep," she insisted, exhausted.

Steven reached out to gently stroke her hair and fell asleep, a few strands of her hair interlaced through his fingers. Skylar placed a hand just over his knee and slept with her head on his bed next to him. I scowled at the two of them. I blamed my rising irritation on my own exhaustion, and then quietly backed out of the room.

CHAPTER 14

I spent most of the next two days checking the grounds and coordinating around-the-clock patrols. Demetrius knew we were ready for him, and I doubted the vampire could currently launch anything more than a conventional night attack, but I wasn't going to get caught by surprise again. I should have anticipated the full moon assault. All the signs were present that Demetrius was throwing everything he had into capturing Skylar, whom he seemed to prize above any other trophy. The sustained effort, the wealth he was willing to spend—all the evidence was available that Demetrius wanted her at all costs. The full moon presented his best opportunity. He had spent an enormous amount of resources on the reversion spell, and for a brief moment he had Skylar in his grasp. Were it not for Josh, he might still have her. I had lowered my guard for one night and nearly delivered Skylar and the pack to an unprecedented catastrophe.

While the pack recovered, Skylar seemed determined to learn how to defend herself. Out of either bravado or recklessness, she chose Winter as her trainer. I wasn't sure if Winter agreed out of a desire to see Skylar protect herself or to take the opportunity to beat her up. They spent eight hours a day, nearly every day, sparring in the gym. I kept my distance, resisting the urge to be involved in Skylar's training, but made a point to inconspicuously check on her after each session. Each day she emerged from her training bruised, battered, and deflated. Each day Winter left the gym unmarked and wearing a satisfied smirk. After observing the damage done by Skylar's latest session, I was on my way to find Winter when Sebastian drew me into his office for a report on the retreat's security.

After I finished, he stated, "Skylar is training with Winter."

"I noticed. I intend to review their training regimen."

He sat on the corner of his desk, studying me. "Ethan, this is good for Skylar."

"I agree that she needs to learn to defend herself. Perhaps another teacher would be more appropriate."

"You don't have time, Ethan," Sebastian said softly. "And neither does Skylar. Winter is the best choice. She is neither the biggest nor the strongest of us, yet she is third. She knows how to use her disadvantages, of which Skylar has plenty."

I felt my jaw clench and forced it to relax. "In other circumstances, I would agree. I hoped Winter could control her revulsion for Skylar, but the results of their training suggest otherwise. The sparring mat offers a perfect opportunity for an ... accident. Perhaps with supervision—"

"Winter knows what she's doing," Sebastian said definitively. "And she understands the consequences. Ethan, Skylar sought Winter out. Skylar has chosen to live. Learning from and beating Winter is emblematic of that choice. Let this play out."

I nodded and left, unconvinced. Winter might be the right choice as a template for Skylar's training, but I doubted her ability to set aside her hatred and train Skylar properly. I chafed at the order, but had no choice. I would wait for further developments to present my case again.

I found Steven reading in his room. The bandages on his chest were growing smaller by the day, but Dr. Baker was taking a cautious approach by keeping him on bedrest. He started to sit up, but I gestured for him to relax as I pulled out the wooden desk chair and straddled it backward, my arms folded over the top of the chair back. "How are you?" I asked, studying him. Despite his experience with mortality, Steven retained his deceptive look of youthful innocence. I wondered if Skylar was charmed by his dimples and olive green eyes.

"Improving," Steven answered eagerly, throwing a longing glance toward the trees that stood outside his window. "I can't wait to get out of this room. I've been catching up on my reading, but I'm going a little stir crazy in here. A couple more days and I should get the all clear."

"Light duty, first." I uttered a small, satisfied grunt at Steven's disappointment. "Your wound was severe." He nodded solemnly. "Were-animals tend toward a sense of invincibility." I smiled grimly. "The truth comes to us all, eventually. Some don't survive the lesson, while others prefer to ignore it."

Steven reflected, glancing at his palm. "To say that being gutted by Demetrius was a surprise would be an understatement." He met my eyes steadily. "But I get it."

I held his gaze for a moment, and then nodded. "Rest now while you can. There will be another fight, sooner rather than later. Skylar will need you," I added, rising. "She spent the night with you in the infirmary. According to Dr. Baker, he found her in the morning quite close to you."

"We've become friends," Steven said carefully.

"Friends," I stated, waiting for him to explain.

He thought for a moment before answering with a smile. "I like her. She has the self-preservation skills of a bunny, but she's unusual for a were-animal. Kind. Our world hasn't tainted her yet. She actually cries. I can't remember the last time I saw a were-animal cry."

"Sebastian selected you to keep close to Skylar to make sure that she doesn't get herself or the pack into more trouble. It's important not to get too close," I said softly.

"I know. My friendship with Skylar doesn't change my obligations to the pack. I'll do whatever I can to keep her safe, but the pack comes first."

I nodded, pleased. "Rest while you can," I said, and then left him to his reading.

The next few days, I made a point to be at the top of the stairs at the end of Skylar's training sessions. Each day, Winter appeared, unscathed, followed by a bruised and dejected Skylar. Finally, I had resolved to intervene when Winter crested the stairs wearing a swollen, bloody nose, a black eye, and some minor bruising on her arms and face. She smiled, showing bloodstained teeth as she passed me. Skylar appeared a moment later, bruised and beaten as before, but wearing a confident, self-satisfied smile.

After allowing some time for her to shower, I knocked on Skylar's door and opened it to find her wrapped in a bath towel, proudly examining her newest bruises in the mirror. Her hair was still wet, smelling sweetly of apple-blossom shampoo. I frowned at the purple and yellow splotches that tattooed much of her figure. "How bad does it hurt?" I asked, gently brushing a finger over a large purple mark on her cheek. She cringed at the touch, and then forced a smile through swollen lips.

"I've never been hit by a car but I'm willing to bet it feels a lot like this."

Steven walked into the room unannounced, offering a cold pack to Skylar. "Put this on your face." If my presence surprised him, he offered no hint. Instead, he made a soft whistling sound at the extent of Skylar's injuries, and then held the cold pack against her lips.

"You should see the other guy," she muttered.

"I have seen the other guy, and unless Winter is suffering from internal injuries, then she fared well. Have you gone to see Dr. Baker?"

"Not yet."

"Make sure you do," Steven said, frowning his concern. "I can't begin to imagine what you are going to look like in the morning." He raised his voice to a conspicuous volume. "No matter how good you are, you will never beat Winter. She has to win at all costs and cheats when she begins to lose."

"I do not!" Winter retorted from somewhere in the hall. She walked into the room holding a jar of Dr. Baker's medicine. Any hint of her injuries had vanished.

"Winter, you do cheat," I taunted. "You changed to animal form when we sparred, and that, my dear, is cheating."

"Really. I'm a snake, how is that cheating?" she responded with a playful smirk.

"It wouldn't be cheating if you went into midform and were just a cute little four-inch snake, but when you change to true form and I'm fighting a five-foot venomous snake, then that is cheating. And don't forget the fact that you poisoned me."

Winter smiled coyly. "It's still not cheating if the person you're fighting is over five feet."

"You poisoned me!" I laughed.

"I was there. I don't need the recap. It happened six months ago. It's time to let it go. Besides, you were paralyzed for like, what ... five minutes? No need to whine about it." She handed me the jar, started to walk out of the room, and then turned back to Skylar. "I'll meet you in the gym at noon. You need to convince me it wasn't a fluke." Winter left and Steven followed.

I opened the jar, wrinkling my nose at the pungent odor. "Are you sure you want this stuff on you?"

"Does it work?"

"I've never been bruised to the point I needed it. And if I were, I doubt I would care."

"Look at me. I am willing to try anything." She warily sniffed the cream once more and frowned. When I started to lift her shirt, she pulled away. "I can do it," she said, taking the jar.

"What about the bruises on your back?" I grabbed the jar. At my urging, Skylar turned around and pulled up her shirt, not quite sure if she trusted me. "Do you feel better now that you have been Winter's whipping girl for the past week or so?"

"How many fights have you had in your life?"

"I have no idea."

"Technically, I haven't had any. I have been pounced on by Gabriella and Michaela, and I killed a human because of my unfair advantage. I've been brought into a world that I eagerly await to leave, but until then, I don't like being the victim. When trouble finds me, should I wait around for my knights in furry armor to swoop in and save me?" She took the ointment and began smearing it on her face.

"I swoop?"

"Yeah, but it involves a lot of growling, snarling, and making your trademark angry face. And I must not forget the eyes, the scariest thing of all." She touched her cheek as her grin became a wince.

I took a seat on the bed, wondering if there was enough of the cream to cover all of her bruises. She stared at me as though I had broken some unspoken rule. Did she want to be alone? I didn't bother to ask. "You look terrible," I said. Unable to further witness the damage done to her, I averted my gaze.

"Apparently that's the general consensus." Skylar took a

quick look in the mirror, and then returned to slathering the cream on so thick that it formed a pasty layer on her skin. She found an aspirin bottle in the dresser and swallowed a handful of pills without water.

"You know what drives Winter to be as good as she is?" I asked. "She's a lesser species and a very attractive woman. She thinks that everyone underestimates her because of it. It really pisses her off."

"Well, do you?" Skylar asked earnestly.

"I've known Winter for a very long time. I knew what she was capable of then, and I have seen what she is capable of now. Only a fool would underestimate her. There are very few fools in this pack, but quite a few exist in the world. Those who do underestimate her, do so at their peril."

"What drives you to be the way you are?"

I raised a brow, surprised by the directness of her question. "Do I interest you?"

Skylar shrugged. "Among other things, I find the were-animals quite interesting. Yes, it interests me that you maintain your position among a group where being the most dominant matters. What drives you to do this?"

"I am not challenged often because I make it known that the challenge for my position is to the death. Most are not willing to wager their life that they will beat me."

She smiled, surprisingly at ease with the notion. "Like in a game of poker where you raise the ante enough to force the challenger to fold."

I tensed, suppressing a surge of anger. "That analogy implies that I am not playing with a winning hand. And that I buy myself out of the situation with the threat of potential death. I am in my position because I earned it, not because I bluffed my way into it. If the penalty was just an ass-kicking, then I would be challenged constantly. Every young member who has something to prove would challenge me. Frankly, I would get bored. There isn't much pleasure in fighting someone whose skills are markedly inferior to yours."

"Winter seems to find immense pleasure in fighting me," Skylar pointed out.

"She thinks you are weak." I studied her for a moment. Like Winter, I had expected Skylar to give up on her training on the first day. The next two days I attributed to pure stubbornness, but I still expected Skylar to throw up her hands and give up. That she could take such debilitating, successive beatings and still demonstrate the tenacity to achieve victory was more than I had expected from the frail little wolf-girl I had rescued from vampires just a few weeks ago. "I do believe she's changed her mind about you," I said.

"Do you think Winter will ever challenge you?"

The question took me aback. "Maybe," I admitted, frowning, "but it wouldn't change how I deal with challenges." Skylar appeared mortified. She still saw the pack as a treacherous group organized around the principle of mindless violence. There was much she didn't understand about us. Our hierarchy, however brutal it seemed from the outside, was what made us strong. While some were-animals might challenge me out of a desire for advancement or pride, a challenge from my friends would be indicative of my own abject failure as a leader. I didn't relish the idea of killing my friends. "I would never jeopardize this pack," I said carefully, wanting Skylar to understand. I was a violent beast, just not the violent beast she thought I was. "If I was no longer fit to be Beta, I would step down. If Winter or Steven were ever to challenge me, they'd do so because they saw weakness that would compromise the pack. If they see it, so will others outside of this pack. If stepping down is the best thing to do, I will." I rose and left the bedroom without looking back.

CHAPTER 15

A few days later, I saw Josh's Jeep Wrangler parked in the driveway. I found him in a common room, leaning back against a sofa, resting an arm over his eyes to block out the light. Skylar arrived just as I did.

"It's been done," he stated in a weary voice. "London believes she disenchanted it, but there is really no way of knowing, except to see the Gem in action. She wanted me to let you know that this clears her of all debts and we are never to ask her for assistance again. It was pretty bad. She's a tough girl and a great teacher. Far more knowledgeable than even the level ones I know. Next time something needs to be disenchanted, then I will do it." Josh moved his arm. He saw Skylar first, offering her a surprised, weak smile. The look he gave me was more meaningful, knowing I didn't share his evaluation. I decided now was not the time to express my opinion on the matter.

"I called Claudia," I said. Josh sat up quickly. His mission with London had left him even more exhausted than he had been after Demetrius's assault. Had he even slept? Dark rings circled his eyes and his five-o'clock shadow looked something closer to the beard of a sixteen-year-old. "She's expecting us at two o'clock."

"You are always one step ahead of me." Josh smiled. "Skylar, you're coming with us."

A trip to visit my godmother was a special event requiring a special ride. My collection was modest, but every vehicle had a story. Since the advent of the Internet, most collectors had traded the fine art of the hunt for instant gratification. Nowadays, almost anything could be found somewhere in the world with a handful of Google searches. I preferred the hunt, scouring local newspaper ads, visiting dealerships and car shows, putting out the word and waiting for that phone call that paid off my anticipation. Here, before me, was the prize of my latest hunt, waiting patiently for her maiden voyage.

Skylar and Josh waited at the front of the house as I pulled up in my new, forest green Hummer. "Nice ride," Skylar said, scowling as she climbed into the passenger seat. I looked to Josh for a more educated opinion, but he lay down on the back bench, too exhausted to bother. "I bet you it's great on gas and a reasonable choice for navigating through the jungles of the interstate and war-torn suburban neighborhoods," Skylar quipped.

I stared back at her, appalled at her lack of taste. We spent most of the trip in welcomed silence. My gaze drifted repeatedly to my brother. I worried for him. He had been working relentlessly for days, seemingly without sleep. He was putting himself at risk, but his commitment to the pack was unimpeachable. I had recommended him with some reservations, but he had proved himself worthy. Eventually, Josh caught me checking on him.

"Just like college," he grinned. "All night partying and still making it to class in the morning."

I grinned back. "Yeah, but I was ashamed of your behavior then. Not so much now."

Skylar rolled her eyes for an inexplicable reason. I looked to Josh for an explanation, but he had already closed his eyes again.

Fifty minutes later, I parked in front of Claudia's enormous art gallery, a large brick building just off the city's main street. Inside, track lights illuminated the exquisite modern and abstract art that dotted the textured white walls. Uniquely styled benches and sofas were strategically placed between sculptures and installations on the crackled cement floor. Chicago's most sought-after artists showcased their work here.

Realizing I had lost track of Skylar, I turned to find her captivated by one of Claudia's paintings. Josh noticed her attention just as I did. We exchanged a perplexed look as Skylar studied the portrait of two boys. The smaller of the two, with short ruffled hair, lay on a bed in peaceful slumber, his expression angelic, while the other boy protectively knelt close by. Hs brown hair was flecked with gold and his deep blue eyes were somber and intense, displaying a wariness beyond his years as he watched over his sleeping brother. Behind him, a shadow loomed just to the right of the slightly ajar doorway as flecks of light filtered into the room. Skylar stared searchingly at the portrait. She was more observant than most, and I wondered what she saw. Thankfully, our godmother had left the portrait unsigned. The less I needed to explain to Skylar, the better. Josh slipped his hand behind her and urged her forward.

We found Claudia near the center of the gallery, holding court with a handful of patrons. After making sure we were seen, we respectfully waited until she was able to gracefully extricate herself. "Ethan, Josh," she greeted us warmly. She was a slender woman in her midfifties, but she seemed timeless to me, like royalty. Her necessary satin gloves matched her dark blue business suit. Her delicate, brown hair was back in a bun.

"It's South African, dear," she said to Skylar, smiling, referring I assumed to her accent, which some had a hard time placing. I never thought much about it. "It's such a pleasure to see you two." She leaned in and kissed the air on each side of my cheeks, in the European style, and then did the same for Josh. She took our hands in hers, glowing at us. "It's been far too long. How have you been?"

"Please accept my apology. I've been very busy," I said regretfully, aware that my excuse, however sincere, was unacceptable. Josh offered a similar feeble apology. To her credit, Claudia betrayed no disappointment. Skylar gaped at me as if just discovering I was a stranger.

"We will make a better effort in the future," Josh promised.

"No worries." Claudia directed her attention to Skylar. "I see why you've been so busy. She's absolutely lovely. Whose is she?"

I stifled a laugh as Skylar's expression hardened. "She is lovely, but she is neither of ours. She is the pack's responsibility." I hesitated, just for a second, before adding, "And we need your help."

The smile quickly vanished from Claudia's face as she looked at me, and then Josh. He nodded. Claudia knew we would never ask for her help if we hadn't run out of options. She bowed her head, her expression solemn. She approached Skylar warily, slowly removing her long satin gloves. Drawing her lips into a gentle but forced smile, she took both of Skylar's hands. "Relax, dear," she urged, holding Skylar's gaze. Slowly, Claudia's gaze grew distant. I watched, unsettled, as her expression became sorrowful, and then terrified, and then grief-stricken. She suddenly dropped Skylar's hands as if they were toxic. Claudia gently touched

Skylar's cheek before a tear ran down her face. "I'm sorry, dear.

"Good-bye, Ethan," Claudia stated coolly without looking at me. She turned to face Josh, her voice commanding as she said, "You need to take care of this—all of it. Do what is necessary. Hard choices need to be made and they need to be done rather quickly." Josh stared back at her as if he had been slapped.

"What should I do?" he entreated, despondent.

She stepped closer to him, touching an ungloved hand to his cheek. "Josh, you know what needs to be done, you've always known. You will do what is necessary because you always have." She offered him a compassionate smile.

Josh's shoulders sagged under the weight of her expectation, his expression sullen and troubled. Still avoiding my gaze, Claudia turned sharply, raised her chin, and walked swiftly toward the back room. Chastised and guilt-stricken, I started toward the exit. Josh took Skylar's hand, interlocking his fingers with hers, and pulled at her to follow, but she refused. "Claudia!" she shouted across the busy gallery, much to my horror. My godmother continued on, ignoring the outburst. I rushed to her to apologize, but she stopped me with a simple, commanding gesture.

"You come to visit me as much as you please," she snapped, "but don't you ever do this to me again without warning."

"I'm sorry." I lowered my head and slowly backed away from her.

"No need for apologies. Just don't do it again. I expect better from you, Ethan. Next time such rudeness won't be forgiven."

"I'm sorry," I muttered again. It would never happen again.

. . .

The long trip to the retreat began in silence. While Skylar fumed, Josh and I pondered the guilt of our offense along with the troublesome results of Claudia's reading. *Was it worth it?* I would ask Josh later what she meant. Whatever it was, it weighed heavily on him.

"Who and what the hell was that?" Skylar finally broke the silence.

"Our godmother," Josh answered dryly. "She has the gift of foresight. We rarely come to her for assistance because it is too hard on her. We don't know if she is an empath, but she feels things too deeply not to be."

"They are going to kill me," Skylar said with an air of finality. "Nothing we do is going to stop that."

Unable to offer her comfort, Josh turned to stare out the window. I had nothing to offer, either.

"Josh?" she pressed, waiting until he finally met her gaze. The pain in his stare saddened her. "I'm going to die. Right?" she asked, frightened.

He nodded once. "Yes."

CHAPTER 16

*W*e returned to the retreat and a somber Skylar went directly to her room.

"What did Claudia mean?" I asked Josh.

His expression became grim. "Sebastian needs to know." A few minutes later, we were in the Alpha's office, along with Winter, Gavin, and Steven. Steven wasn't a member of the pack leadership, but Josh had requested his presence because of the bond he held with Skylar. With all of us waiting, Josh hesitated, shoulders slumped as if the weight of the world were crushing him.

"There is no way to be sure that London's attempt to disenchant the Gem was successful. Based on Claudia's warning, we can't afford to wait to find out. Our priority should still be to locate and retrieve the Gem. Sooner, rather than later. Much sooner."

"You haven't been able to locate it," Gavin said bluntly.

Josh answered with a tired smile. "I have one more trick up my sleeve."

The Chasm. I expected Josh to put up a battle over our agreement to take one day of rest first, but he would not win.

Josh continued, avoiding my gaze. "The dark magic protecting the Gem is very strong. To find it, I need stronger dark magic. I'm going to ask Pala for help."

Sebastian's face tensed. Winter cursed. Gavin scowled, and Steven appeared worried. I was furious. "You said you would try your locator spell in the Chasm, first," I insisted.

Josh's eyes met mine, and I knew the answer before he spoke. "I already tried. At London's."

My fists clenched. My brother had directly disobeyed me, and broken his promise. "You agreed to wait," I said tightly.

"Ethan," Josh said wearily, "there just wasn't time to convince you. It had to be done."

I fought to unclench my jaw. "You took an unnecessary risk."

"I did what I had to do for the sake of the pack," he snapped back.

"Why Pala?" Sebastian asked, cutting off my retort.

My brother took a deep breath before answering. "As a servant of Ethos, she has the greatest source of dark magic available. I'm going to use her as a conduit. By binding myself to Pala, I will be able to use her dark magic in the Chasm to locate the Gem."

No one knew exactly what Ethos was—demon or warlock—but he was the most powerful purveyor of dark magic known to us. Those who aligned themselves with dark magic were duplicitous and dangerous. "You will give Pala control of your body—of your mind?" I demanded.

"Only for the length of the spell. And it will be done here. I don't think Pala will try one of her tricks surrounded by angry were-animals."

"No."

"This is my absolute last resort. I assure you, I wouldn't take this risk if I knew of another option. We can mitigate the risks."

"No!" I shouted, but I knew by the grim determination in my brother's eyes that there was no stopping him short of beating him unconscious, throwing him into the back of my SUV, and driving as far away as I could as fast as possible. But then he would wake up and teleport himself away. Was he hell-bent on getting himself killed or just contrary?

"I've already called her. Pala is on her way."

"There is no way in hell I am going to let you do that!" I stormed out of the office, and then the house, with Josh following me. I stopped just outside and turned on him, more than happy to fully vent my anger, but he wasn't his usual, arrogant self; he stood motionless, conflicted, almost desperate for me to understand. His expression was full of doubt. This wasn't reckless Josh. He knew the risks, was calculating the odds, but I couldn't let go of my anger. "I don't care what you have to say," I stated firmly, "I am not going to let you do this."

Josh's troubled eyes lowered. He was actually showing me deference, which infuriated me further.

Skylar. He's going to get himself killed for Skylar. I wanted to shout at Josh, shake him, force him to listen to me, but he wouldn't. Without his resistance, my rage collapsed. I simply didn't have the energy to fight a losing battle. I stared at him for a moment, until I finally turned my back on him. "You owe her nothing," I said softly, listening to the call of the woods.

"I don't," Josh said behind me, his voice determined. "But I owe you. I owe this pack. You know Demetrius won't stop. If it's not her, then it will be someone else. He hates you and despises Sebastian. When Demetrius succeeds, it won't be long before he comes after you. What happens if the person he uses is stronger than Skylar and imbues him with strengths and gifts that exceed anything she offers? Then what?"

I turned to see the plea in my brother's eyes, and felt no empathy. Josh had lied to me about the Chasm. Bargaining with Pala and Ethos might get my brother killed, but it was his choice and I had no way to stop him. For the first time in my life, I felt truly powerless. If Josh didn't want my advice or protection, then he could face the consequences of his actions alone—even if it meant his death. I washed my hands over my face, wondering just how I could walk away, but I had to. "Don't do this to protect me," I whispered. "I can take care of myself."

"If things get so bad that you can't?" Josh asked, emotion catching in his throat. "You wanted me to become 'blood ally,' because this pack is a force most won't oppose, to ensure my safety. I'm trying to ensure the safety of all of us."

I exhaled a long, ragged breath. "This is dangerous. You've never tried anything at this level before and there is nothing I can do to help you if it fails," I admitted bitterly.

"The favors that we curry, the alliances we have formed, the power we enjoy are all the results of our successes. If we don't stop this, our failure will be apparent, our weaknesses exposed. The fae trust us, and the elves have given us their unyielding respect because of what we have achieved. This one failure will ruin it—will ruin us, and you know it." Josh sighed. "You are going to have to let me do this."

I know. But I don't have to like it.

We studied each other, taking in every detail as if this might be our last moment together. I gently gripped the back of my brother's neck, and then pulled his forehead to mine. "Okay," I finally said, and then released him. I turned and strode into the woods without looking back, stripping my clothes along the way. Once naked, I transformed into my wolf and ran.

I ran until I had lost any sense of time, crossing and looping the grounds while staying clear of the house. Grass raced beneath my paws as I embraced the simple, raw power of my wolf. What else could I do? Eventually, the urgency dissipated and I slowed to a trot. My stomach growled as I sniffed at a deer scent in a recently flattened patch of high grass. My thoughts turned to Josh. By now, Pala was at the house. The ritual might already be underway, if not completed.

What if Pala betrays him? Josh was smart to bring her to the retreat. Would Pala risk Sebastian's wrath? A physical foe wouldn't dare, but magic brought too many variables to the equation—dark magic was even more dangerous and unpredictable. *I should be there.*

I followed the deer's scent trail into a copse of trees. Josh didn't want my protection. If he wanted to make his own choices, devoid of my advice, then he could damn well face the consequences. *If something does go wrong, and I'm not there ...* The deer burst from its hiding place at a run. Distracted, I had allowed myself to get too close, unprepared for the kill. I started after the deer, but I couldn't shake the sense that I needed to watch over my brother.

I came to a halt and glanced back over my shoulder, in the direction of the house. I growled my frustration. *Josh believes he is protecting me, protecting the pack.* He'd pushed himself too hard. In his state of exhaustion, he could easily make a mistake. In magic, mistakes kill. My brother was risking his life for me, and I had abandoned him. I ran at full speed back to the house, transforming on the front lawn. I quickly scooped up my clothing and dressed. The driveway was clear. Either Pala had come and gone peacefully, or she had transported herself to the house, which made for an easy escape.

Winter met me at the door in a rush, a wild look in her eyes. "Pala's—"

"Where?" I demanded.

"The infirmary."

I pushed past Winter, running through the house. She followed. Skylar greeted me just outside the double doors, her expression anxious and relieved. Before she could explain, I burst through the door to find Josh lying on the floor, thrashing violently. A lightly bloodied knife lay at his feet. Pala sat next to him, her hand gripping his tightly. She was a short blonde in a compact curvy body, with the round supple face of a doll. Her eyes were closed, but popped open at my entrance, exposing pupils that were absent of all pigmentation, cold and piercing. Her true nature revealed, Pala reminded me of the doll that every child imagines is possessed and buries in a closet, or hides from under the covers. She shrieked, making a loud, reedy sound that filled the room with a chilling power. We covered our ears simultaneously, bracing against the onslaught to our senses. The only person who seemed unaffected was Sebastian, who had just entered the room. At the sight of him, Pala stopped screaming and a calm came over the room. Josh's thrashing ceased. He lay motionless, but I knew by the sound of his heartbeat that he was alive. I could just make out his shallow, ragged breaths. His body seemed intact, but possessed of an absence, as if Josh wasn't wholly there.

"Release him," I commanded through clenched teeth.

"I am not finished," Pala responded in a sharp, sinister tone—the kind of voice expected from an evil doll.

"Ethan—" Sebastian started.

I lunged at her, but he intercepted me, forcibly pushing me back several feet. I glared at him. Had Pala possessed Sebastian? It didn't seem possible, but Josh was in danger and I wasn't going to take the time to find out. I crouched and snarled at Sebastian, baring my teeth in warning. This was not his business. He responded in kind, dropping into an aggressive stance. A fight with Sebastian was a fight to the death. I didn't want that, but nothing was going to keep me from saving my brother—not Sebastian, not Pala, not the entire pack. If she had gained control of them all, I would kill them all to stop her. My wolf rose to the surface in a rolling growl that came from my gut. In response, Sebastian's eyes became amber as his carnal nature rose to the challenge.

Our primal rage filled the infirmary as we shifted for position, snarling at each other. Sebastian was an imposing figure, at the peak of his power, but I didn't care. I never expected to challenge him like this, but in the moment I didn't care. He was big and strong and in my way. He took one step closer. I responded in kind, ready to pounce, when Winter intervened. She stepped between us, her movement uncharacteristically slow and timid as she gingerly reached a hand toward Sebastian. "Sebastian, please. It's his brother," she said soothingly, radiating calm, but I smelled the fear in her. I didn't need her protection, but in my current state I didn't know how to cast her aside without hurting her. "He's just trying to protect Josh," she pleaded while Sebastian's gaze fixed on mine with murderous intent. "I know you understand that." Winter spoke slowly, gently caressing the Alpha's cheek. "He's not challenging you. You know he would never do this to you. Not like this. Sebastian." She tried to turn his head toward her, but he stubbornly resisted, his gaze fixed on mine. "Sebastian, please look at me. It's not a challenge." She tried again, this time drawing his gaze to hers. "It's not a challenge," she whispered, her tone unnaturally soft, almost submissive. She was playing Sebastian, breaking through his aggression in the only manner possible. It was working on me, as well.

"It's his brother and our blood-bonded ally," she continued. "Ethan's aggression is misdirected. You know he would never do such a thing if his brother wasn't involved. Sebastian, it's not a challenge," Winter assured, keeping eye contact with him. The tension in Sebastian's body slackened slightly, but his wolf remained close to the surface.

Pala did not have control of him after all. I turned my gaze to Josh, who remained still, his hand in Pala's grip. The spell remained in progress, I realized. It occurred to me that I might have overreacted, but the aggression and passion in me remained with nowhere to vent.

"Ethan," Sebastian said calmly, drawing my attention. "We need Pala alive for now. It would be better if you stepped out. Seeing him this way may be too hard to handle. I will protect his life as though it was my own," he promised.

I took a deep, but strained breath, barely calming myself. I nodded, and then backed out of the infirmary. Skylar followed, watching me closely, but I ignored her. I remained at the double doors, fixated, staring through the windows, ready to intervene if required. Josh appeared sickly and unresponsive. Unable to restrain myself, I reached for the door, but Skylar took my hand instead, squeezing it. Full of pent-up rage, I turned on her with a violent sneer, daring her to stop me as I stepped forward to push through the door. Surprisingly, she pushed me back.

"Move," I barked. She only glared at me, her expression concerned but determined. When she didn't answer, I stepped towards the door.

"No." She pushed me back once more. "Not until you calm down."

I glared down at her, but she stood her ground. She lacked Winter's cunning, but Skylar had her own strength—her unimpeachable determination that could infuriate and confound anyone that crossed her. Her dark green eyes glared up at me, burning with an emerald fire. I stepped back from her, shaking my head at her willfulness, and began pacing the hall in an attempt to calm the anger and frustration that coursed through my body. This was not her place. She had no right to intervene between Josh and me.

Skylar exhaled softly, obviously relieved. "I understand—"

"What exactly do you understand?" I barked, suddenly in her face.

"I understand what it's like to feel you are responsible for endangering others who feel obligated to protect you," she insisted, refusing to back down. "I understand how infuriating it can be to wish you were the one dealing with Pala instead of standing idly by watching Josh take a risk that should be your own. I understand what it feels like to be so angry that all you want to do is curse, fight, and kill, but know that it won't make things any better. I understand more than you care to know," she added softly.

I remembered her helpless anguish over her mother's corpse, her struggle with grief when she was sitting on her mother's bed. Skylar had suffered at the hands of an enemy in a world she had known nothing about. My anger at her melted, but the raw intensity of my emotions remained, searching for a new avenue of expression. Already close, I felt myself drifting toward Skylar as my eyes traced the lines of her slight nose, drawing my gaze from her green eyes to her deep-set cheekbones, and then to her supple lips that parted for me. I leaned in, resting my face in the crook of her neck. My lips parted, brushing her olive-toned skin, and I felt the pulse of her blood beneath them. Her heart raced with excitement, matching mine almost perfectly. She made no effort to pull away. We remained like that, our breaths rapid.

"I am sorry," she whispered. "I know it doesn't mean anything to you, but I wish I hadn't come into your lives and created such problems."

"It's not your fault," I said, lightly brushing my lips against her cheek. "It's not your fault," I repeated so softly I wasn't sure she'd heard me. Perhaps I was comforting myself. I brushed her lips with mine until I felt her lips reach out, and then I kissed her firmly. The kiss quickly changed to something ravenous, sensuous, and intoxicating as my anger and frustration transformed through her passion. Grasping fistfuls of her hair, I pulled her body to mine.

For a moment, we remained lost in each other, but then Skylar suddenly pulled away, slipping past me to stand several feet away. A mix of emotions appeared on her flushed face. I stared at her, wanting her, watching her want me. "I need to see how things are going with Josh," she stammered, ending the awkward silence.

Josh!

I nodded, stepping back from the door, and then followed her into the infirmary. Josh remained supine with Pala attached to him, while Winter and Sebastian looked on. Sebastian turned to me, his gaze an intense warning. I heard Skylar's heart begin to race in anticipation of violence, but I had no such intention. I brought my hand to my chest and extended it in nonverbal apology. It was the best I could do, under present circumstances, but Sebastian deserved more.

The tension left his body as he shook his head. "If the roles were reversed, I would look to you to save me from myself."

"Something's wrong!" Winter shouted.

"He's strong," Pala admitted, making little effort to hide her pleasure. "I couldn't resist having him for myself." Winter grabbed her, but Pala retained her firm grip on Josh's hand. With her free hand, she grasped Winter's wrist. The room dimmed. Winter grimaced before being thrown back, crashing into the door.

Pala's lips spread into an ominous smile. Waves of darkness emanated from her that stifled the air. Before I could act, Skylar grabbed the knife that lay at Josh's feet and slashed her palm. She turned Pala's wrist, forcing her to release Josh. Blood welling in her hand, Skylar grasped Pala's cut hand to bring their blood into contact, and then said something in a commanding tone. I thought it was nonsensical, at first, but then I recognized the words that Josh had used to bind himself to Caleb, and later to Skylar in the library. The moment the last word fell from her lips, Skylar's body became rigid. Her expression became anguished. Pala bucked, screaming out as she tried in vain to break Skylar's grasp. She muttered phrases in strange languages. Finally, in a desperate bid, she called in a hushed, reverent tone the name of her master, "Ethos."

An ill breeze blew into the infirmary, delivering a promise of pure evil. Drawn curtains that isolated the infirmary from the beds billowed as the ceiling lights flickered and then dimmed. A dark cloud drew itself from the shadows, sending a shiver of fear through the room as it engulfed Pala and Skylar. I tried to reach for her, but the cloud radiated a scorching heat. Inside, I could see she maintained her grip on Pala even as the cloud wrapped itself around Skylar's wrist and arm. Once more I tried to reach her and was repelled. I roared in frustration as Sebastian was repelled as well. A desperate fury overcame me as I was once again helpless in the face of magic, with nothing to kill.

Josh rose to his knees, shook his head, and then came to his feet. As he uttered a chant, a gold glow surrounded him. The evil wind seemed to focus on Josh, trying to push him back, but he held his ground as he reached into the black cloud and grasped Skylar's shoulder. Sparks flicked around him as his magic deflected the cloud's attempts to burn him. I could see Josh's lips moving rapidly, but couldn't tell what effect he was having, if any. For a moment, I thought he could save her, but then the cloud enveloped them both, swallowing them into darkness.

A long, desperate moment later, the wind dissipated. The dark cloud withdrew back into the shadows, revealing Skylar and Josh supine on the floor next to each other, their eyes closed. Pala had vanished. Josh blinked, beginning to move as if waking from a deep slumber. Skylar's skin was deathly pale, but she was alive; I could hear her heart beating at an erratic, panicked rate. Her body twitched. Her expression tightened as she faced some sort of inner struggle. As I moved to help her, her lips parted, and she released a banshee-like scream. In one violent explosion, glass vials and jars and cabinet faces exploded, wood splintered, and the curtains ripped. A dark wind answered her call, picking up and swirling the debris around us. I shielded my face with my arms, as did Sebastian and Winter as they backed out of the room. I pushed forward toward Skylar and Josh, but a layer of whirling shrapnel threatened to shred my flesh. I shouted Josh's name, hoping to wake him to help as I backed out of the room.

His eyes blinked open. Absorbing the situation around him, Josh turned and climbed on top of Skylar. His lips moved, as did hers, but once again I wasn't able to hear their chants. A light shimmered around Skylar, but failed. A protective glow appeared around Josh, transferring to Skylar as he pressed against her. He took her hand and continued chanting until she finally stopped screaming. The wind dissipated, the darkness faded, and then the room became eerily calm.

To my relief, Skylar opened her eyes, rolling them at Josh's flirtatious smile above her. When he didn't move, she said, "Um ... I think you can get off me now." He grinned, turning just enough for Skylar to scramble out from under him. For once, I didn't mind my brother's inappropriate behavior. All that mattered in that moment was that they were both safe. Dr. Baker and Steven arrived behind me.

Skylar climbed to her feet, frowning at her torn shirt and the cuts on her arms. She was about to complain when she finally noticed the condition of the room, which was almost entirely destroyed: while one of the double doors remained intact, the other hung limply off the hinges; hospital beds were flipped upside down and on end; room dividers were crumpled, bent, and torn; the medicine cabinet was smashed to pieces; anything that was glass had shattered, and chunks of plaster broken from wall and ceiling lay strewn about. Skylar stared at a chair embedded in the wall just as the chair shifted and collapsed to the floor, bringing down a large portion of wall with it. She stared through the now gaping hole to the latrine on the other side, and blinked. "I did this?"

Josh nodded slowly.

"I can fix this," she said, her tone doubtful and anxious, and then ran from the room.

The rest of us stared after her in a state of shock until Winter finally broke the silence. "What. Was. That?"

"Did you find the Gem?" Sebastian asked Josh.

My brother took a deep, troubled breath before answering, "Yes."

In a closed meeting, Sebastian made it plain by omission that now wasn't the time to discuss what had happened to Josh and Skylar. For that, Josh was grateful. He had successfully divined the location of the Gem of Levage in the home of the Seethe. The time to act was now, while his information remained valid. The plan to capture the Gem was formed quickly. When the meeting ended, I followed my brother into the kitchen.

"Don't you people eat anything besides steak?" he shouted, digging into the contents of the fridge. "Kelly and I actually need fiber, you know. Maybe a bean and cheese quesadilla once in a while."

"Josh," I said behind him.

He half turned. Seeing me, his shoulders slumped, the depth of his exhaustion suddenly apparent. "Ethan. If you agree to wait until tomorrow, you can yell at me as much as you want. I might even listen to you for a moment, but my answer to your overbearing nature is always going to be the same; you don't control me. If I need to—"

"This is not going to be a discussion," I said.

Josh slammed the fridge door shut, frowning.

"It was your call," I continued before he had a chance to piss me off. I felt my jaw clench and forced it to relax. "You are reckless, but you've more than demonstrated your skill set, and your character. It's never been my intention to control you." He blinked at me as if in shock. I cleared my throat and glanced about the kitchen. "I can be ... protective. I won't apologize for that, but perhaps I can ... moderate my efforts."

"Okay," Josh said, looking at me as if he might take my temperature. "Does this mean I have to be less obnoxious? I'm not sure how that's going to play out."

"I'm sure you will eventually go back to being as obnoxious and inappropriate as ever. But for now, you could just say, 'Thank you.'"

"Thank you," he said softly, his tone bewildered but sincere.

I nodded and left the room. After a tour of the house, making sure Pala hadn't left any surprises, I decided to check on Skylar. Her door was open. Before I entered, I heard voices inside.

"Why did Pala attack your magic that way?" Skylar asked. "It's not like she could use it."

Josh answered. "Most of it she wouldn't be able to use, but there is a small part of dark and natural magic that are *respicts*. It is magic that has no boundaries and can be done by both holders of dark and natural magic. If she had taken any of my magic, it would have just enhanced the respict magic and killed me. The only way an exchange of magic can be made permanent is that the donor must die. Pala's pretty strong. We don't want her stronger. She wants more power than Ethos will allow her to have. Skylar, you are able to do some really cool things with magic. I think we should explore your effects on it more."

That didn't take long.

"No thanks."

"No?" Josh asked, surprised and offended. "Why? Aren't you the least bit curious about what you are capable of?"

"No. Not really. If the Tre'ase showed me an inkling of the truth—even if there were some deceit, I have a connection with Ethos and some very dark things. I don't want any part of it. Did you ever stop to think that the reason I can affect dark magic is because I am strangely connected to it? No. I don't want to explore it. I don't want to unlock any potential gates to that world and find out I am something horrible—evil."

"She showed you a version of the truth."

"Really? Josh, I was the one there. I experienced it. I don't want to be your science project or some type of magician's apprentice," she stated harshly.

I heard the creak of the bed, followed by a protracted silence. "Okay," he whispered, his tone unexpectedly intimate. "But I think one day you will want to explore it, and when you do, know that I am here to help you."

I strode into the room to find Skylar sitting on the edge of the bed. My brother stood hunched over her, his hands gently cradling her face and his lips less than an inch from hers, as if they had just kissed. I resisted the urge to clench my fists. Josh had no idea what had occurred between Skylar and me outside the infirmary, I reminded myself. "What part of her 'no' did you not understand, Josh? Don't pressure her into dealing with things that she really should avoid," I said sternly. Skylar appeared surprised, as if caught red-handed committing a crime. There was a gloom about her, the remnant of the dark magic she had borrowed from Pala. I wondered if Josh was attracted to Skylar or the magic. My brother answered my greeting with an impish smile while remaining close to her, his hands still cupping her face. My eyes narrowed as I focused on his hands until he finally lowered them and stepped back. My eyes followed his reluctant retreat across the room.

I returned my attention to Skylar. "Thank you for saving Josh's life."

"No one in this pack should ever thank me for anything," she said earnestly. "I am still alive because of you all."

"We did not intervene to protect you. If you were just a person that Demetrius desired, we would have never intervened. I wish I were ashamed, but it is our truth. Your death would have given them power that we could not allow them to have. That is the only reason we protected you," I admitted.

"I know. Despite the reason, it was my life that you protected. For that, I feel deeply obligated."

"An obligation is a debt, Skylar," I informed her.

"I am indebted to your pack," she said casually.

I tensed, as did Josh. "Choose your words carefully," I warned.

"Should I not appreciate what you all have done?" Skylar asked, confused. "I would have died a torturous death if it weren't for your pack. Is it wrong that I feel that I owe the pack a great deal?"

I closed my eyes, shaking my head slowly. She clearly had no idea what she was offering, but ignorance was no excuse in the eyes of the law. I had no right to refuse an offer freely given. "On behalf of the pack, I accept your debt," I answered in a cool, professional voice. "Understand that at some point, you will be asked to repay it." Skylar reacted as if just realizing her words had consequences, but I didn't have the energy or the desire to explain her mistake.

Josh shook his head as well, offering Skylar a wry, forced smile. Her eyes followed him as he left the room.

"Is being indebted to the Midwest Pack a stupid thing?"

"Being indebted to anyone is never wise. But there could be far worse things. I advise you, in the future, to choose your words carefully and be cautious about whom you accumulate debts with."

"Can I retract?"

"No." *We all must pay the price for our mistakes.* "Your debt has been accepted."

CHAPTER 17

An all-consuming sense of victory filled the house as we met in Sebastian's office to finalize our plans for the extraction. "What happens once we have the Gem?" I asked Josh.

"The disenchantment spell is simple. With the Gem in my possession, success is guaranteed."

"Why should we destroy it?" Gavin asked, surprised.

Sebastian turned to Josh. "Is there a way for us to safely wield the Gem's power?"

"I can't," Josh said, troubled, "but Skylar can. She has the unique ability to draw magical energy from a source and then use it. Since she is bound to the Gem, she should be able to wield its power, but she is inexperienced. She has no training."

"So train her," Gavin said abrasively, earning a warning glare from me.

"I've offered." Josh sighed. "She doesn't want it."

"But she could be convinced," Winter stated.

"Even if Skylar accepts the training, it could be years or decades before she could control an artifact as powerful as the Gem of Levage. An artifact like that has its own consciousness. If Skylar isn't strong enough, it could wield her instead, which could prove very dangerous for all of us."

"And Skylar," I insisted. Josh nodded.

"Is there a way to test the Gem's connection with her?" Sebastian asked.

Josh considered, running a hand over the stubble on his chin. "If we want to test her ability to control the Gem, we need to put it directly into her hands. But there are risks. Once the Gem understands that I am going to disenchant it, it will do everything in its power to stop me. While it cannot use its own power directly, it can use Skylar as a surrogate."

My brother looked to me, as if anticipating my objection, but there was much to consider—if Skylar's safety could be assured. "What if the Gem takes control of her?" I asked.

"She does something like what she did in the infirmary," Winter said, "only worse."

"There must be a way to break the binding between Skylar and the Gem," I insisted.

"There is." Josh frowned as he drew an odd-colored knife, the blade wrapped in cloth, from his belt and handed it to me. "You'll have to kill her." I accepted the weapon with a scowl. Gently unfolding the cloth, I revealed a single-edge blade with an unusual lilac hue. "The blade is made from Trincet," Josh continued, finding his own words distasteful as he explained. "It's a poison known as the 'pleasant death.' The Trincet will stop her heart, while simultaneously blocking her body's natural ability to heal quickly. It's the best I can offer her."

As Beta, responsible for the security of the pack, I could not ignore the Gem's potential. If Skylar could wield the Gem's power, the pack would gain an enormous advantage over its competition. Skylar would once more become valuable to the pack. Her safety would be guaranteed for the foreseeable future. *Risk versus reward.* The gamble didn't settle with me. What should've been an easy call became an unpleasant quandary. "Is there another way to take the Gem away from her?"

I saw Josh's own struggle in his expression as he shook his head. "The bond will be broken at the moment of death. Once the blade is removed, there is a small chance she can be revived, but Skylar's death will also break her bond with Maya, and I don't know if Skylar can live without Maya."

I considered the knife and all its implications, like a rock weighing against my heart. As Ethan, my answer was "no." I would not be responsible for Skylar's death, but I was the Beta of the Midwest Pack, a position that carried an enormous amount of responsibility that superseded my own desires.

"Ethan?" Sebastian asked. He knew what this meant to me and was gracious enough to give me the horrible responsibility.

"Yes," I said, my mouth suddenly dry.

Winter stepped up to me, holding out her hand for the knife. "I can do it," she said. It took me a moment to recognize the empathy in her voice.

"No," I stated, leaving no room for doubt. If I was going to put Skylar's life at risk, I was going to take the responsibility.

"If she survives," Josh said, "she will be free of all her bindings, including me. Caleb and Ethos will be unable to find her or use their link with her."

Small consolation.

As we left Sebastian's office, Skylar joined us from the stairs, wearing a jacket and carrying a small bag of weapons. "No," I commanded, directing her back up the stairs. Of course, she refused to obey.

"Like it or not, I'm going with you."

"No."

"I'm fully capable of taking care of myself."

"It is unnecessary to risk your life." She answered me with a determined look. I was prepared to pick her up and carry her upstairs when Sebastian intervened, his tone gentle but insistent.

"Skylar, it's a simple extraction if things go as planned. However, if they don't, you in the vampires' home with the Gem is a bad combination. One we choose to avoid."

Should the Gem fall into her possession before we were prepared to deal with the consequences, we might lose control of both of them. For Josh's plan to work, for Skylar to have a chance of survival, we needed to keep the Gem and her apart until they could be united in a controlled environment.

"Dakota," I snapped at the were-bear. "Stay behind. Make sure Skylar doesn't follow."

He frowned miserably, but obeyed.

We disembarked from our vehicles several blocks away and then converged on the home of the Seethe from three directions, sneaking into positions thirty meters out. The mission was simple. If our intelligence was correct, the vamps would be out hunting; the home should be empty, but we came prepared for the worst. Winter and Gavin led the reserve team that would clean up if things went to hell. Sebastian and Steven led the scout team that would probe the house first, while I led the extraction team.

"No guards or patrols," Steven whispered over the two-way radio on my belt, connected to my ear by a wireless device.

"None here, either," Winter whispered.

I wasn't surprised. Demetrius had hidden the Gem well, and he was prone to an arrogant confidence, but we weren't taking any chances.

"Moving into position," Sebastian said. A moment later I saw him, Steven, and the rest of their team sneak up to the garage and then spread out around the house. They were our eyes and ears, and our first line of defense once I took my team inside. Sebastian went behind the house, while Steven remained closest to the front door. "All clear," Sebastian said. "Go."

I had one boot forward onto the lawn when Steven interrupted. "Hold," he hissed. I pulled back just as the front door of the house opened and two figures emerged, lighting cigarettes as they strolled onto the lawn. Humans. I knew by the smell, though, they were steeped in the stench of vampires. These were members of Demetrius's garden.

"Marko," Steven whispered, "take the tall one, on my mark."

"Copy," Marko whispered.

I waited, watching intently. A moment later, I saw Steven darting silently and low across the lawn. The shorter human chuckled and flicked the orange glow of cigarette just before Steven leapt up to pull the human down flat on the grass. The tall human barely had a moment to take in the danger before Marko, in wolf form, took the human by the throat and dragged him across the lawn into the bushes. Steven lay on top of the other one. For a moment, nothing happened, and then I saw the flash of Steven's knife as he plunged it into the human's heart. The garden was useless and pathetic—hardly a threat, but we couldn't risk them calling for help. Steven dragged the body across the grass and stashed it in the bushes beneath the front window.

"All clear," he whispered.

I gestured to Hannah beside me and then ran across the lawn at full sprint, jumping to the roof by vaulting off the two walls that formed an *L* at the doorway. Hannah did the same, following me as I climbed to the blacked-out window of the master bedroom. Hannah offered me the glass cutter, but I decided to try the window first. It opened easily. The vamps really had no sense of security, but why would they? A normal burglar was in for quite a surprise, breaking into the Seethe.

I slipped through the window. Hannah followed and took position at the open bedroom door, slowly closing it while I retrieved a flashlight from my pocket. The door creaked and we both froze. We waited, listening for any hint of trouble. For a moment, I thought I caught the scent of that peculiar non-vampire, Quell, but it receded quickly. There were too many vampire scents in the house, old and new, to be sure. We needed to hurry up and get out.

I quickly found the Bible on top of the nightstand, as Josh had described—a clever disguise—and then returned to the window. "I have it," I whispered, and then passed through the window. Hannah followed as we worked our way down the roof.

"Clear," Steven whispered, and we dropped down to the yard in front of the door and ran to our staging area, where Josh was waiting. I handed him the Bible while we waited for the others. He smiled as he ran a hand across the cover. Steven, Sebastian, and the rest of their team joined us. Winter, Gavin, and their team met us a few minutes later. Only Gavin appeared more disappointed than Winter. They wanted a fight, but not all victories required blood. We drove away in three vehicles, lights off at first, not stopping until we returned to the retreat. My curiosity was piqued by a white Mazda CX in the driveway—Joan's vehicle. She was always welcome, but it was not like her to arrive unannounced.

Once outside the SUV, Josh held up the Bible. "I need a moment to break the disguise. Find Skylar. I'll find you momentarily," he said, and then disappeared.

Inside the house, I was surprised to not find Skylar waiting impatiently in the doorway. Where was Dakota? Where was Joan? There was fear here. Sebastian smelled it as well. An uneasy feeling came over me as I caught the unexpected scent of geranium and sage.

He tensed. "What is it?"

"Owen." Where was Skylar's scent? "We need to find Skylar. Now."

At Sebastian's signal, Gavin took a handful of were-animals to search the house.

I followed Owen's scent to the kitchen, where I found Dakota gagged and hog-tied with plastic ties on the floor. He was unconscious, but alive, with no visible wound. A spent syringe lay next to him, but any injection mark on the were-bear had already healed. Each of us tensed, anticipating the worst as we continued searching for Skylar. *My fault.* None of this made sense. I had missed something that might have cost Skylar her life.

Sebastian picked up on her scent first and led us to a storage room at the back of the house. A circular stairwell led down to an old pantry that had been converted to hold an isolation cell. Skylar's scent was strongest at the top of the stairs, mixed with geranium and sage and the reek of blood. Winter, Steven, and I rushed down the stairs behind Sebastian. My worst fears seemed realized when I caught sight of a mangled, gnawed corpse near the open, empty cage. An anguished rage filled my body, followed by relief when I saw Skylar alive, cowering in a dark corner of the room. Joan, in her jaguar form, lay languidly at Skylar's feet. At a second glance, I realized the corpse was part human and part lion—Owen, caught in transition. I had been a fool not to see it. Owen had finally come for his revenge. To obtain it, he had shamefully aligned himself with Demetrius. I sneered at the coward's corpse, wishing there was something left to kill.

Seeing us, Joan let out a stifled roar and licked her lips. Sebastian nodded, and she returned to her human form. Steven rushed past me, taking off his t-shirt and handing it to her. She pulled the shirt over her head and looked down at

Owen's remains with a sad expression. "Pack betrayal," she finally stated hoarsely. "It was an error on my part to convince my Alpha to take him in."

"There is no shame in trying to save a pack member's life when possible," Sebastian stated.

Joan shook her head, looked at what she'd done again, and started up the stairs. Jaguars were solitary animals. Pack life did not come naturally to Joan. At times, she suffered for her choice. Obviously she had suspected Owen and followed him to the retreat. I had more questions for her, but now was not the time to ask. Steven followed her up the stairs. "Mom," he whispered, concerned. She rested a hand on his cheek, smiled, and then hugged him before the pair disappeared up the stairs.

Skylar rose to her feet, balancing awkwardly on what seemed an injured ankle. Before Sebastian or I could ask our questions, Josh popped into existence next to her. Surprised, she jumped, bumped into him, and nearly fell. She threw him an angry scowl as she righted herself. "Not cool, Josh!"

He grinned and held out the palm-sized Gem of Levage to her. "Peace offering."

She gingerly accepted. "How do we destroy it?" she asked, an odd expression overcoming her as she studied the Gem.

"A simple spell I can do in my sleep."

Skylar's countenance grew dark. She took in a sudden, deep breath and shifted her hips slightly, as if the tattoo on her lower back had suddenly become painful. Josh noticed as well. He turned to me with a troubled expression. We both watched as Skylar's fingers tightened around the Gem. When Josh reached for it, she brought it close to her chest and gave him a defiant look.

"Skylar, give it back to me," he ordered in a low voice.

"No! You can't destroy it!" she yelled, inching backward toward the stairs.

Josh's eyes transformed into dark pits as he muttered a spell, and then commanded the Gem, "Come to me."

Skylar squeezed the Gem to her chest. "No!" she shouted, emitting a burst of power that shook the house, bringing me, Sebastian, and Winter to our knees.

"Skylar, you cannot protect it," Josh insisted. "It needs to be returned. As long as it exists, you will always be in danger. Others will be in danger." He stepped closer, and she pushed him, shoving him into the cage. He came to his feet quickly and waved his hand in front of him, throwing her back with magical force. Skylar nearly struck the wall before catching her balance.

"It doesn't want to be destroyed," she pleaded. "We need to keep it."

"No." Josh's lips moved quickly, reciting a string of incantations as he tried to release her from her binding to the Gem. Skylar's eyes went black. A rapid string of commands in what seemed an ancient, alien language spewed from her mouth, countering Josh's magic. As they dueled, she backed away from him and started up the stairs, but I caught her on the third step. Pinning her to my chest, I dragged her back into the middle of the room. She reeked of darkness, and her skin was ice-cold. I held her while Josh chanted feverishly as he reached out to take the Gem. Skylar's fingers trembled around it.

"Skylar, please."

"No."

Resigned, he lowered his arm and gave me a remorseful look. He had exhausted his options. My heart sank as I gripped Skylar's shoulder, drew the poisoned knife, and drove it into her heart. From inches away, I watched her pupils dilate like dark moons as her eyes snapped open wide in shock. She gaped at me, the unspoken question on her lips, *How could you?* Swallowing my own horror, I wrapped my fingers around her throat and squeezed and watched the life slowly drain from her until there was nothing left but a shell. Her body tried to recover, but the poison prevented it. Skylar's face turned purple. I died inside as I watched fear and horror and accusation become acceptance. A tear streaked down her cheek. Without breaking my grip around her throat, I gently wiped away the tear with my thumb. I couldn't watch any more. Instead I turned my gaze down to the knife handle jutting from her chest, and I squeezed harder, trying to spare her as much pain as possible. I heard her spine crack, but her heart continued to fight, jumping in erratic beats for its own survival until it finally stopped altogether and she died.

I waited for what seemed an anxious eternity while Josh verified there was no pulse. A nod from him, and I withdrew the knife, sliding the offending weapon across the floor to the far wall. I directed Josh to Skylar's feet and together we picked her up and carried her to the infirmary. We placed her on a bed while Dr. Baker and his nurse, Kelly, rushed into the room. Kelly began CPR while Dr. Baker prepared the defibrillator. The knife wound was already starting to close, but that was the last gasp of her body as it ran out of energy.

Come on, Skylar. I wanted her to live. I needed her to live. Death was a part of pack life. I had certainly delivered my share, but I'd never regretted it until now. She didn't deserve to die. *I should've said "no." I should've said "no," dammit.*

"Clear," Dr. Baker commanded. Kelly raised her hands from Skylar's body. He pressed the paddles to her chest. I heard a click and then her body arched from the electricity. All eyes turned to the heart monitor, but the line remained flat. Kelly returned to administering CPR while Dr. Baker charged the defibrillator once more.

"Come on, Skylar," Josh said.

Come on. Don't leave me with this.

"Clear."

I heard the snap of the defibrillator, saw Skylar's body

arch and collapse, and then heard the slow thump of her heart even before the beep of the monitor announced that her heart was beating once more, but erratically. Relief flooded my body until I saw the concern on Josh's face. "She's not there," he explained as Dr. Baker set the defibrillator aside and went to work on Skylar's wound.

"Let Maya go," he whispered into her ear. "Let her go, Skylar. Send her away, and come back to me." He continued pleading while she received treatment. I didn't fully understand what was happening, but I knew what was at stake. I was tired of being helpless, but I left Josh alone, counting on him to bring Skylar back. "Send her away before she takes your life with her. I can force her to go, but it's better if you send her away. She has to obey you." He gave me a perplexed look and then prepared his spell.

I knelt next to Skylar and whispered so softly I wasn't sure if she could hear me, "Come back to me."

Her heart rate jumped, and then steadied, and I felt a calm return to her body. I knew by the burning curiosity in Josh's eyes that he didn't hear me, and I had no intention of explaining it to him.

"She's back," he said. "She's in her body, but Maya is still there. Skylar invited her to stay," he said, surprised.

"What now?" Sebastian asked from the door.

"We won't know if the Gem did any damage to her until she wakes up. Hopefully she's the same Skylar we know and love. For now, we wait."

Dr. Baker urged us out of the room so that he could work.

CHAPTER 18

*T*he infirmary had been cleaned of glass and debris, and the double doors restored. Much of the necessary equipment and supplies had already been replaced. Dr. Baker had insisted on backups, and the pack spared no expense when it came to its hospital. I watched from the corner of the room while Skylar lay supine on a bed, IV lines stuck in her arms. Dr. Baker stood over her while Sebastian remained close.

A great relief filled the room when Skylar turned her head slightly, moving of her own volition for the first time. I wanted to rush to her side, but the vision of her death at my hands remained fresh in my mind. Dr. Baker leaned over her as she blinked, and then opened her eyes. Confused by her surroundings, she began to pull at her IV lines. Dr. Baker gently brushed her hands aside, gave her a reassuring smile, and then disconnected the lines for her.

"Thirsty," she mumbled in a forced, rough voice. As Dr. Baker fetched a glass of water from the sink, she propped herself up to examine the brace on her ankle. When her water arrived, she greedily drained the glass, and then returned it to Dr. Baker. She returned her attention to her restricted ankle.

"You really did a number on it," Dr. Baker explained. "Two breaks. It should be healed by now." He removed the brace. Skylar tested her ankle, turning it from side to side, apparently without pain.

"How long have I been out?" she asked.

"You were clinically dead for three minutes." Dr. Baker shined a bright light in her eyes, instructing her to follow the light as he moved it. The test lasted for only a few seconds.

"Two lives down," she said with a forced smile. "Do I have seven more?"

"Not likely, you barely held on to this one. But you did much better than I anticipated," Dr. Baker stated solemnly. "You, little wolf, are simply amazing."

"Which type of amazing? The good kind or the bad?"

He chuckled, turning to Sebastian. "She's fine. I am done here. She's your problem now." He walked out of the infirmary.

For the first time, Skylar became aware of the rest of us in the room. Out of respect, I chose not to make direct eye contact until I realized she was staring at me. I met her gaze directly, suppressing my guilt. I expected to weather her fury, and I would.

"You killed me," she stated coolly, as if reading my mind. I could only stare back at her.

"He had to." Josh walked into the room. "Your bond with the Gem could not be broken. You wouldn't let us destroy it—"

"So you destroyed *me*."

"Something like that." He shrugged. "It was quite the task. I had this made especially for you." Josh handed Skylar the Trincet knife I had killed her with.

She stared at the lilac hue of the blade. "Did you know that would happen?"

"We were prepared for the worst-case scenario. It's hard to kill a were-animal in any other manner but brutally. We tried to make it as gentle as possible. We stopped your heart and prevented the osinine from reviving it so that you would die."

"If you knew that would happen, why did you give me the Gem?"

Josh's face tightened into a pensive expression. He shot a sneaky, accusatory look in my direction. "We needed to see how strong the connection was between you and the Gem," he admitted, stepping closer to Skylar. "It's good that you died," he stated, his tone quiet and serious. "All those who have been bound to you think you no longer exist. Neither Caleb nor Ethos can sense your presence. Now you are free of all bindings, including mine."

Steven quietly entered the room, relieved to see Skylar awake.

"You were dead for three minutes but out for four days," I said, harsher than intended. "Where were you? Jeremy said you were alive but in a state that you refused to leave."

"Sleep, I guess."

I had more questions, but Josh interrupted with an expectant look. His eyes shifted suggestively toward the double doors. I considered ignoring his request, but caught a look from Sebastian and reluctantly followed Steven from the infirmary. Sebastian lingered until Josh nodded once, letting us know that Skylar was herself. I felt a rush of relief wiping away four days of tension from my body. Satisfied, Sebastian backed out of the infirmary, his eyes on Skylar until he finally turned and pushed through the double doors.

I watched Josh, chatting, pull a chair up to Skylar's bed. After a moment, I reassured myself that she was herself again, and then I left them alone.

· · ·

The next day, Skylar stood between myself and Josh, the three of us facing the Gem of Levage on the table before us in the library. *Symbols of Death* lay open next to the Gem. Josh hadn't wanted Skylar present for the disenchantment. She had persistently made her case, and for once I agreed with her. How could she truly be free of the Gem without witnessing its destruction? If she was not free of the Gem, I would be there to restrain her.

Josh began the incantation. Magic radiated from him with an intensity I had never known him capable of, its quality surprisingly calm and focused. I stepped aside, turning to watch the other two intently, ready to carry Skylar from the room if she attempted to save the Gem. While Josh's heart rate remained steady, Skylar's seemed caught up in the rush of my brother's magic. Her face flushed. Her hand slowly drifted toward his until they touched.

After a moment, the chanting ceased, but Josh maintained his focus. The Gem shuddered violently for a few minutes, then slowly lost its will until its resistance was reduced to feeble thumps against the table. The room temperature dropped to nearly freezing as the Gem crystallized from the inside, icicles forming around its edges. Skylar suddenly bent over, gripping the table for support, as if overtaken by a sharp pain. My eyes shifted to the tattoo hidden by the lip of her jeans. I tensed to intervene, but Josh stopped me with a look.

"Are you okay?" he asked Skylar, splitting his attention between her and the spell as he continued the work of destroying the Gem. She held on to the table as if only the strength of her grip held her in place. She struggled to let the Gem die, I realized, but she did not take on the energy of the Gem as she had in the basement. It drew her, but it no longer possessed her.

Josh waved his hand over it and it burst into flames,

burning until all that remained of the Gem of Levage was a cloud of vapor gathering itself over *Symbols of Death*. Slowly, the book absorbed the vapor until, a few minutes later, any trace of the Gem was gone. The temperature in the room returned to normal but Skylar remained rigid, still clutching the table, her gaze fixed on the book. The pain in her expression was gone, replaced by a void. Gently, Josh pried the fingers of one hand loose from the table, and then the other. He stepped between her and the table, blocking her view of the book. She continued to stare, seemingly oblivious to his presence. He placed his hands on her hips and gently turned them both until her back was to the table. I watched anxiously as he pushed aside the hair that had fallen over her face, obscuring her eyes. Drawing Skylar's gaze to his, he slowly placed his hands on the table behind her, enclosing her.

"That was intense," she stated nonchalantly.

"Yeah, it was," Josh answered, concerned.

"Can I see the book?"

Skylar tried to turn her head but Josh cupped her chin in his palm, returning her focus to him. "What happened to you?" he asked, closing the space between them until she backed up to the table.

"It was just intense," she said, confused and flustered. "I seem more sensitive to magic. That's all."

I wasn't sure if my brother was keeping her off guard or simply being opportunistic, but my patience with his antics was wearing thin.

"Okay," he said, unconvinced. He turned to me. "Ethan, can you put the book away?"

I hesitated, glancing between the two of them. Josh was playing at something. Was she completely free of the Gem? Skylar turned to watch me as I strode to the table, picked up the book, and offered it to her.

"Put it away," Josh urged.

"You wanted her here. Don't cheat her out of this. She should be allowed to see it all—from beginning to end."

"I don't think—"

Before Josh could finish, I pressed the book toward Skylar. She snatched it from my grip and held it protectively to her chest. Her gaze flicked between Josh and me. Convinced we wouldn't snatch it back, she opened the book and flipped through the pages until she found the image of the Gem. She stared at it only for a moment, and then willfully snapped the book shut and held it out to me. Josh and I shared a surprised look. Could it be that easy for her?

As I accepted the book, Josh slid his hands behind Skylar's back to the tattoo just under the edge of her jeans.

"What are you doing?" she gasped, pulling away.

He smiled. "It's gone. The mark—it's gone."

I felt a rush of relief. She was fully free of the Gem. Josh nodded, and then left the room. I remained, waiting for Skylar, who seemed about to say something, but decided to leave instead. I followed, locking the library door behind me. There was no need to give Skylar any further temptation.

"Sky," I said, stopping her.

"-lar," she added. "Sky-lar."

Her stubbornness caught me by surprise, but it was welcome. I suppressed a smile as I moved closer to her. "You intrigue him," I admitted, staring into her eyes. "Josh likes magic. It's what he is." I stepped even closer, as if drawn to her by an unseen magnetism. I studied every inch of her, remembering the taste of her lips, the feel of her willing body pressed to mine. My tongue slid slowly across my lips, moistening them in anticipation. Skylar stared back at me, aroused and defiant, but I stopped myself. Since our embrace, I found her difficult to resist, but I needed to. "It's not what you are," I continued. "My brother can be very persuasive. He's quite talented that way. You don't have to do

259

everything he asks. If you don't want to explore magic, or anything else with him—then don't."

She smiled. "I know how to say 'no,' Ethan. I got that little education when my mother taught me the difference between boys and girls." She slowly backed away from me, and then turned toward the stairs. "Riley Fisher kissed me on the playground when I was twelve," she said over her shoulder. "He asked. I said no. But he did it anyway. I punched him in the kisser. That day, he learned that 'no means no.' Warn your brother. If I say no, and he doesn't listen to me, he's going to end up like Riley Fisher."

I laughed openly as she disappeared up the stairs.

A short time after Sebastian made his offer, I found Skylar on the back porch, staring blankly into the woods. I had the impression she had been standing there for some time. Either she held on to the fear that the vampires were lurking just beyond the trees, waiting for her, or she was contemplating Sebastian's offer. "Want to go for a run?" I asked as I emerged from behind her.

She reluctantly agreed. As I began to strip, Skylar meekly went around the side of the house to change. *A setback.* Still, she had made great progress since first arriving at the retreat. I changed and waited, sniffing around the nearest trees. After several minutes, she still hadn't returned. I padded around the house and found her crouched, naked and frustrated at her inability to transform. Had I retained any doubt that Skylar had returned to her normal self, such doubts evaporated. I grinned as I padded toward her and placed my muzzle into the crease of her neck. I waited a moment, until she began to stroke the scruff of my neck, and then I triggered her transformation.

As she changed into her wolf, I ran into the woods, circling back and taking alternate paths to confuse my scent, and then waited for her to find me. When she finally did, I howled playfully and then licked her face. She obviously hated that, turning away, so I licked her again. I gave her an encouraging smile, and then darted off into the woods for her to chase me. She kept pace, staying close despite my various tricks.

We ran through the woods for almost two hours until we were exhausted. When we neared the house, Skylar ran around the side to where her clothes waited. I transitioned in stride, picking up the trail of my clothes and dressing. When I rounded the corner of the house, I was surprised that she remained in wolf form. After exercising her wolf, I had expected her to transition easily. I knelt next to her and spoke slowly to make sure she understood. "You need to do this on your own. I won't always be around to help."

As I strode toward the door, Skylar snapped at me, just missing nipping my hand. I answered with a wry smile but decided to wait as she flopped down on her paws and attempted to change. I watched her struggle for nearly a half hour before I decided to help. Skylar growled, baring her teeth at me as I knelt before her. "It shouldn't be hard, not for you," I said, suppressing a grin. "Human form, you want it. Just relax into it, Skylar."

She glared at me for five minutes, stubbornly refusing to try again until I left her alone. She didn't return to the house until shortly before dinner, enticed by the smell of cooking food, as was my plan.

"Hungry?" I asked as she walked into the kitchen. She nodded. We ate mostly in silence, though I tried to encourage conversation. "Will you stay in your mother's house?"

She nodded. A sad expression came over her. "I'll sell it. I'm just not sure when."

Memories. After all she had been through, Skylar still remained unused to violence and loss. Perhaps that was a good thing. She wasn't meant for the cruelty of our world.

"Sebastian asked you to join our pack," I said as I took our empty plates to the sink and washed them. He had made the decision unilaterally, over my objection, and Winter's.

Skylar hesitated. "Is that what the run and dinner were all about?" she asked, suspicious and aggravated. "Are you here to influence my decision to join the pack?"

I turned to her, at first shocked, then offended. "No. I was going for a run anyway. I thought you could use a little escape from the house. Perhaps it was a poor decision on my part." I considered my next words carefully. "Pack life is all that I know. It's the way I was raised, and if it weren't, I doubt I would choose otherwise. But it's not for everyone. Not all people who join the pack are assets. Some become complications and others ... acceptable liabilities. Sebastian seems to think you would be an asset to the pack and your unique qualities an acceptable liability." I met her gaze steadily. There was no point in being dishonest. Better she understood now, without delusion. "I disagree."

"You don't want me to join this pack?" she asked, stung.

"I think the life of a lone wolf would be best suited for you."

"Why don't you want me ..." she said in a rush, and then added awkwardly, "in your pack?"

I wanted her, but the distraction of her could prove a liability for me—just as Chris had. And I didn't relish the thought that pack life would eventually leave Skylar jaded. "Do the reasons really matter?"

"I guess not." She stood up to leave.

I reached out to grasp her hand, but she quickly withdrew before I could touch her. I needed her to understand, but expressing my desire for her wouldn't help the situation. "Skylar, it's not that I dislike you. Quite the contrary, I actually find you quite tolerable. You are a chaotic mess, and it's ... endearing."

"And you're an ass," she snapped. "We're quite the pair, aren't we?"

I let the insult slide. "I will always want what is best for my pack, and you aren't good for us." *For me.*

"Message received," she answered curtly. "Thanks for the run and dinner."

"You're quite welcome," I said as she stormed out of the kitchen. After a moment's hesitation, I followed her, calling her name from the bottom of the stairs. When she didn't answer, I went up to her room. She poked her head out from the door as I approached, her expression irritated.

I wasn't sure exactly what I wanted to say. "It has been quite interesting knowing you."

"Same here," she declared through clenched teeth and then slammed her door shut.

The next morning, I remained out of sight as Steven led Skylar to the SUV and drove her home. She hadn't answered Sebastian's offer to join the pack, which precluded her from pack protection. As the pack Beta, it was my obligation not to risk the pack's safety or security to protect Skylar, but she was not safe. Demetrius wouldn't bother with her, at least not until he knew she no longer enjoyed our protection. But there were more immediate threats. She had enemies. Skylar was on Michaela's radar, now. And Gabriella would want revenge for what Skylar had done to Chase. The pack wouldn't protect her, but Josh would keep tabs on Skylar, and so would I.

PSIA information can be obtained
w.ICGtesting.com
d in the USA
HW031141110920
8625BV00001B/18